BOCA MOURNINGS

Boca Mournings

Steven M. Forman

A Tom Doherty Associates Book

New York

BOCA MOURNINGS

Edited by James Frenkel

A Forge Book
Published by Tom Doherty Associates, LLC
175 Fifth Avenue
New York, NY 10010

www.tor-forge.com

Forge® is a registered trademark of Tom Doherty Associates, LLC.

ISBN 978-0-7653-1988-3

First Edition: February 2010

Printed in the United States of America

0 9 8 7 6 5 4 3 2 1

To Barbara and Our Family

In Memory

My dear friends Phyllis Farmelant and Arthur Pickman

ACKNOWLEDGMENTS

Special thanks to my agent, Bob Diforio, and my editor, Jim Frenkel, for bringing out the best in me; to my publisher, Tom Doherty, for believing in me; to friends Burt Bines, Mike Bernstein, Howard Novie, Derek Moore, Larry Moses, Renee Leonard, Lew Ginsberg, Dr. Glenn Kessler, Stan and Sue Starr, Liz and Joey Baker and their son Danny for their contributions to the story; to the librarians at the Spanish River Library in Boca Raton who put up with me; to Rabbi Fogelman and Attorney Steven J. Brooks for their technical input . . . and to all my friends and family for their support.

Boca Mournings

Prologue

A serpentine ribbon of numbers rattled from the ticker-tape machine, slithered through thirty-two-year-old Jacob Dubin's trembling hands and descended into the snake pit of poisonous news already coiled on the floor. There was no antidote. He was dead financially and the cause of death was self-inflicted wounds.

He walked to the only window in his thirty-seventh-floor office atop the Banker's Trust Building and opened it. Without hesitation he sat on the sill, then swiveled his hips and legs around until his feet dangled five hundred feet above Wall Street. How long would it take him to fall? Ten seconds? Twenty seconds? Would he feel or hear anything when his head hit the pavement? He pressed his palms down on the windowsill and eased his buttocks slightly off the ledge. He leaned forward and closed his eyes. It had taken Jacob twenty-four years to put himself in this position but it seemed like only yesterday. He relaxed and leaned back. He hadn't changed his mind. He just wanted a minute to remember.

Jacob Dubinsky had been eight years old when he left Poland in 1905 with his parents, Aaron and Frieda. His mother's older brother, Joseph Kaplansky, had immigrated alone to New York City from Warsaw in 1899 and written his sister many times to join him. His last letter sounded desperate.

Dear Frieda,

My tailor shop does good business here, but my health is so bad I can barely work. The doctor says my lungs will only get worse and I will not be able to take care of my-self. I need your help. Your husband is a tailor and can do my business. There will be enough money to support all of us. You can live with me and when I die all I own is yours. I put money in this envelope for your trip. Please come soon.

Love,

Joseph

They got off the boat on Ellis Island in New York City, where a disinterested immigration officer shortened their family name to Du-bin and told them how to get to the east side. They located Frieda's tubercular older brother, Joseph, at the address he had given them and moved into his one-bedroom apartment above the store. Aaron did the tailoring, Frieda nursed Joseph, and Jacob was sent to school. One month after the Dubins arrived in America, Joseph died. Aaron and Frieda continued the tailoring business while Jacob suffered at the local public school. He was good with numbers but could barely speak English and was slow to learn. Impatient teachers ignored or ridiculed him and classmates taunted him. Jacob was a sensitive boy; he became self-conscious and reclusive. His only refuge was with his parents, in the tailor shop, where he learned to work but not to play.

He made no real friends but his parents were too preoccupied to notice. When he graduated high school at eighteen he spoke accented English and had learned enough about accounting to help his parents manage the business. Eventually, Dubin Tailors became successful enough for the family to rent a two-bedroom apartment above the store.

Jacob was hardworking but lacked his parents' passion for the business. He went through the motions of caring but he didn't care. He made a good appearance, always handsomely dressed in clothes he helped make. But underneath the custom clothing he was still the frightened, persecuted schoolboy from the Old Country, who felt he didn't belong in the New World.

One night, walking alone in New York City, he wandered aimlessly into a nightclub and found what he thought he had been looking for: the Roaring Twenties. His first cocktail emboldened him and the attention of beautiful women energized him. He was soon hopelessly addicted to the lifestyle and couldn't get enough. He began staying out late at night, arriving late for work, and trying hard to become someone he was not. His parents noticed the changes in Jacob but blamed it on his age and the age they were living in. He would outgrow it, they thought, but he never did.

Five hundred feet above the ground, the wind buffeted Jacob's hair, ruffled his shirt, and blew his necktie like a flag. But he sat absolutely motionless, still thinking of his parents and wondering why he hadn't listened to them. Why had he made such stupid mistakes . . . like confusing love with lust?

It happened on a booze-filled night, in the afterglow of having sex at a petting party with a woman he barely knew. She was beautiful. She was exotic. She was rich and exciting. She was everything he was not and she had made love to him with passion. He was overwhelmed. He asked her to marry him. She laughed.

Her name was Ethel Bengloff, the headstrong, incredibly spoiled daughter of Wall Street scions Abraham and Rachael Bengloff. The young woman didn't take Jacob's proposal seriously until she casually mentioned it to her elitist parents . . . who took it very seriously. They said they were mortified that their daughter would even keep company with a ragman's son and they ordered her to never see him again. Ethel reacted with typical defiance and to spite her parents she accepted Jacob's proposal. She didn't love him. She wasn't even sure she liked him. She just loved getting her way.

When Frieda and Aaron Dubin met Ethel Bengloff they urged Jacob not to marry her. They could tell immediately that Ethel and Jacob weren't in love and were only using each other to get something they thought they wanted. They were certain such a marriage couldn't last.

The wedding took place at the Algonquin Hotel in September 1920. Jacob remembered that night as the beginning of the end.

Jacob looked down from the ledge into the five-hundred-foot abyss and thought of his father-in-law: The Walrus.

To Jacob, Abraham Bengloff had the comical look of a bull walrus. He had thick skin, a plump body, a bushy mustache, and sleepy eyes. But Jacob knew that a bull walrus had the power to kill a polar bear and there was nothing comical about that. Within months of the wedding The Walrus had offered Jacob enough money to convince him to leave the "embarrassing rag business" and to join Bengloff Financial as an analyst.

"You'll never be your own man," Aaron warned his son when Jacob told him about Bengloff's offer.

"Maybe I wasn't meant to be my own man," said the frightened little boy from Poland.

Jacob did extremely well at Bengloff Financial, earning large profits for the company and the respect of his peers. But despite his success he was never fully accepted or respected by the Bengloff family. He became increasing resentful of their rejection and after only one year of marriage he wanted out. He realized he had sold himself too cheaply and that he could not buy the Bengloffs' love and respect at any price. He detested Rachael and Abraham Bengloff for their hubris and despised their daughter for her selfish indifference. Only when he made love with his wife did he enjoy being with her. But even that blessing became a curse when she became pregnant with twins.

Then there was the fire.

Late on a hot day in August of 1922, a fire at Dubin Tailors destroyed the entire building, trapping Jacob's parents in the back room. They died from smoke inhalation before the flames reached them. Their charred remains were found side by side. The fire department blamed the blaze on spontaneous combustion caused by cleaning solvents stored too close to dirty clothes. But Jacob blamed himself for not being there to protect them and he buried himself under an avalanche of guilt.

In 1923, twin boys were born and strongly resembled the Bengloffs' side of the family. Ethel didn't want to be a mother and after Jacob's parents died he was emotionally incapable of being a father. Ethel's mother assumed the responsibility of raising her grandsons. She hired two full-time nannies and supervised everything. The twins would be in the Bengloff image . . . of that there was no doubt.

Ethel and Jacob became like strangers, sharing only the same house. She was drinking heavily and eventually started seeing other men. Jacob didn't care. Other men could have her . . . but not until he was ready, not before he proved to the world that Frieda and Aaron Dubin's son was as good as anyone and that they had not died in vain. He devised a plan to beat the Bengloffs at their own game. He would secretly open an account at another Wall Street firm, analyze and trade stocks with his limited resources, eventually make enough money to establish Dubin Investment . . . and destroy Bengloff Financial. He would show them all. He put his plan in action shortly after the twins were born.

Using his gift for numbers, Jacob decided that public utility stocks were greatly undervalued and he began slowly accumulating a position in that industry. Year after year, from 1923 to 1929, Jacob Dubin amassed a fat portfolio of utility securities and watched them skyrocket in value while his personal affairs continued to plummet. He stayed out late, drank too much, and avoided his family. Ethel did the same. On those rare occasions they were together they would attack each other with the vitriolic gibberish of the very drunk. One night, the fighting turned physical. She slapped him, he slapped her. They wrestled each other to the floor in front of a roaring fireplace. Somehow their flailing and fighting led to fornicating, which they both regretted as soon as it was over. Weeks later they regretted it even more. Ethel was pregnant again.

In the 1920s, abortions were socially unacceptable for people like the Bengloffs and dangerous for anyone. Reluctantly Ethel had a third child, a girl, late in the summer of 1929. Once again the baby was relegated to the supervision of Grandma Bengloff, who hired a new nanny . . . and life went back to business as usual.

Unfortunately for Jacob, business would never be usual again. In the fall of 1929, the Massachusetts Public Utility Commission refused Edison Electric's request to split its stock. The commission also announced that there would be investigations into the highly leveraged utilities industry. Utilities declined five billion dollars in value almost overnight and Jacob was ruined. His investments and his life were now worth less than nothing.

He looked to his left at the windows of his father-in-law's enormous corner office and shook his head sadly. The market collapse would hurt the old Walrus but not destroy him as it had destroyed Jacob. What a fool he had been to think he was as good as the man in the corner office.

Jacob had no way of knowing that his secret trading account had never been a secret at all. He never imagined that the gentlemen of Wall Street would keep his father-in-law constantly informed of his private activities or that the old man would mimic Jacob's successful strategy. He couldn't fathom anyone copying the ragman's son.

He readied himself on the ledge and closed his eyes. Instead of seeing only darkness, the vision of his three-month-old daughter crossed his mind. He regretted that he would never get to know her. She was the only pure thing in his life . . . still too young to be contaminated by the Bengloffs.

"Maybe I could save her," Jacob thought . . . and then he slipped and fell.

Jacob turned his body quickly and reached for the windowsill. His fingers grasped the inside of the ledge and he held tight. He scraped the toes of his shoes wildly against the wall trying to find a foothold. His fingers grew numb and his arms ached but he kept pulling and kicking until he managed to haul his chest onto the window ledge. He leaned forward and tumbled head first into the safety of his office. He rolled onto his back and stared at the ceiling, his chest heaving. He gasped for breath. He was soaked in sweat and his body ached. After a few minutes he got up, staggered to his desk, and slumped in his chair. It was a miracle he was still alive. There must be a reason.

Inspired, he reached for pen and paper and began to write feverishly. He wrote to his wife about her selfishness and the deadly virus of greed in her family. He told her he intended to save their daughter by taking her away with him. Thoughts poured through the tip of his pen like blood from an open vein. He signed the letter with an exuberant flourish, folded it in an envelope, and put it in his shirt pocket.

Exhausted but excited, Jacob hurried to the private elevator that took him safely to the ground floor. He ran from the building onto Wall Street and breathed deeply. He was euphoric. Finally, his life had purpose.

He threw back his head, held out his arms, and looked up jubilantly—just in time to see the bulging red face of Abraham Bengloff falling from the sky at a hundred miles an hour at the end of his suicide jump. Neither Dubin nor Bengloff heard the sickening sound of their skulls exploding, nor did they see the gruesome sight of their brains, blood, and bones splattering the austere walls of Wall Street like human shrapnel.

On the same day that Abraham Bengloff jumped off a New York City skyscraper, Ferris Dewey jumped off the Atlantic City Steel Pier.

Bengloff jumped because he had lost everything. Ferris Dewey jumped because he had nothing to lose.

Bengloff jumped with the weight of the world on his shoulders. Dewey jumped with the weight of Dixie the Diving Horse between his legs.

Every summer thousands of people gathered to watch Dixie and her professional riders plunge head-first into the diving pool at the bottom of a forty-foot-high tower. But on this blustery fall afternoon the Boardwalk was deserted, the clouds were the color of slate, the wind was erratic, and the platform swayed dangerously. The little man on the tower was too drunk to notice the danger and shouted in his brogue, "I'm Ferris Dewey, and I'm the greatest fookin' horsback diver in the whole fookin' world."

Ferris Dewey was not a horseback diver. He was a stable boy, who had been shoveling shit against the tide since the day he was born in 1901. He was the descendant of Irish immigrants who had fled Ireland in 1847 during the Great Potato Famine and settled in the deadly New York slum called Five Points. Irish gangs with names like the Plug Uglies and Dead Rabbits terrorized the streets, and disease ate away the neighborhood. Sullivan Dewey, Ferris's great-grandfather, fled the Five Points to avoid being drafted by the Union Army during the Civil War. He stopped running when he reached Atlantic City, where he settled down and married a local woman. They produced more Deweys who in turn produced more Deweys, and eighty-two years later one of those Dewey descendants was standing on top of the world . . . preparing to jump off.

Ferris bravely pulled himself onto Dixie's bare back and slid off the other side, landing on his head. "Fook it," he chuckled, staggering to his feet and pulling Dixie's ear playfully.

"Hold still, old girl," he said, and kissed her nose.

Dixie snorted, raising her long face, and nudging the little drunk, nearly knocking him off the platform.

Dewey laughed. "Useta seein' me at yur otha end with me shovel, aincha dahlin?"

He pulled himself onto Dixie's back again and went halfway over the other side, held on for a moment, then fell on his head again. This time he just lay on the deck and laughed at himself. Dixie prodded him with her nose. She was born to fly and was anxious to take off.

"I'm coming sweetheart," Dewey said, struggling to his feet. "Hold your horses."

He finally managed to pull himself upright on Dixie's back.

"Ladies and gentlemen," he tipped his cap to the empty boardwalk. "Your attention, please."

He pulled his hat tightly down on his head, waved to the nonexistent crowd, grabbed Dixie by the mane, and urged her over the edge. Horse and rider descended together until Dewey let go of the mane and held out his arms like Jesus on the cross. He flew off the horse's back, did half a flip in the air, and landed awkwardly, off-target, on a cresting wave. Dixie hit the pool perfectly and survived to dive another day, but twenty-eight-year-old Ferris Dewey broke his neck and died the way he had lived . . . totally out of control. He left a wife and an infant son to survive if they could.

Chapter 1

Boca Raton—November 2005
Time and Again

BING!! A bullet slammed into my right shoulder. BANG! A second bullet slugged my left leg. BOOM! A baseball bat bludgeoned both my knees and I went down. I was an easy target kneeling motionless in the snow and another bullet punched my right shoulder knocking me over. I fell on my side.

I struggled for consciousness.

My stomach was on fire.

Get up before it's too late.

I struggled to my feet and opened my eyes. There was no blood, no wounds, and no snow. I was standing next to my bed, naked, wet with the sweat of a bad dream. I had a painful erection. I had to pee. I walked to the bathroom and stood at the toilet waiting and remembering.

I had been shot in the shoulder the first time in 1970. My left leg was hit in '76. The bat to my knees was 1982. These isolated incidents from my ancient history as a Boston cop had

melded into a single nightmare . . . except for the second shot to
the right shoulder that happened only last year in Boca Raton.
Boca? What was I doing in Boca Raton?

I had been one of Boston's most decorated policemen from
1966 to 2000, but now I was just a sixty-year-old retired cop living in Florida. I was five feet seven and weighed slightly over my
fighting weight. I was in great shape for an antique and there was
a beautiful woman in my bed. She was fifty-percent black Haitian,
fifty-percent white European, and twenty percent more than fifty
percent my age. Best of all, she was one-hundred-percent awesome.

When I retired to Boca last year I expected to live a peaceful
life as a golf-course ranger in a gated community called Boca
Heights. Things didn't work out. I quit the ranger job after a
few days because three women golfers refused their right to remain silent. Later that same afternoon I uncovered a Russian
Mafia crime ring in Boca and survived a shoot-out with them. In
less than a year I had solved a local mystery, stopped an assault
on two women, and gone to war with an army of neo-Nazis. My
exploits received a lot of attention from the press.

A local news reporter dubbed me the "Boca Knight" and
when a CNN reporter asked me, on national television, to de-
fine a Boca Knight I said, "Anyone willing to fight for everyone's
right to live in peace," which was all that came to mind.

Suddenly everyone wanted to be a Boca Knight because ev-
eryone *could* be a Boca Knight. It was easy: live and let live. Boca
Knights baseball caps and T-shirts began appearing in Palm
Beach County. I was a mini celebrity.

I didn't feel so famous standing by the toilet waiting to pee
and when I finally did it was a weak effort. I trudged back to the
bedroom and looked at the woman in my bed. She was one of
the damsels in distress I had had rescued. *Good save!*

I eased back under the covers, trying not to wake her. She
stirred in her sleep, parted her luscious lips, and groaned.

Again!

I squinted at the illuminated numbers on the bedside clock.

Again? I wondered aloud. It's two thirty in the morning.

I don't care.

We did it again.

4:15 A.M.

You're kidding me, right? I said, opening my eyes.

No, I'm serious. We have to do it again.

I felt like I was in a Nike commercial.

5:30 A.M.

That's it. I've had it, I said, sitting up in bed.

One more time.

Can't you control yourself?

No.

We did it again then slept three straight hours.

8:30 A.M.

I woke up and watched the breathtaking woman next to me taking shallow breaths while she slept. I found it hard to believe that a woman so young and gorgeous was actually with me. I kissed her beautiful brown face.

Good morning, Claudette, Mr. Johnson, my penis said in a voice only I could hear. Mr. Johnson and I have been together for as long as I can remember, although we didn't start communicating until I was about eleven. He just popped up one night in bed and introduced himself.

Hey, look at me. I can stand up.

In the beginning, our relationship was touch and go, but we eventually reached an understanding. He agreed to stop showing up at school and family gatherings, and I agreed to a more hands-on relationship when we were alone.

Mr. Johnson poked Claudette's side. *Wake up, Sleeping Beauty,* I heard him say.

Claudette couldn't hear him, of course, but she understood him perfectly. She smiled without opening her eyes and reached for him.

I gotta hand it to you, Mr. Johnson said.

"And what do we have here?" she asked in a husky morning voice.

Your breakfast sausage, said my one-eyed friend.

"Didn't you get enough last night?"

Redundant question.

"So what did you have in mind," she teased me with a grin.

How 'bout blowing revelry? Mr. Johnson suggested.

Sex with Claudette Permice was a wild, exuberant, pulverizing experience that usually ended with Mr. Johnson needing first aid. Claudette looked like Halle Berry. Once, while we were having sex, she punched my shoulder and told me to stop pretending she was Halle Berry.

"I'm not pretending you're Halle Berry," I assured her.

"Then why do you keep screaming '*Fuck me, Halle*'?"

"Sorry."

Making love and having sex with Claudette Permice were two different things, and I loved that about her.

"Man, you're good, Eddie," she said when our morning session was over. "You're a sixty-year-old wonder."

Thank you, thank you, Mr. Johnson said. He bowed and just kept going down.

"Almost sixty-one," I reminded her, "and I'm not ashamed to tell you I'm exhausted."

"No wonder," Claudette said, swinging her long, gorgeous, coffee-colored legs out of bed. "You got up to pee three times last night."

"Nice ass, Halle," I said, watching her walk to the bathroom and wanting to change the subject.

"Never mind my ass," she said.

She turned to face me with her hands on her hips.

I tried changing the subject a second time. "Great tits, Halle."

"Don't try to change the subject," she said. "You were talking in your sleep in bed and talking to yourself in the bathroom."

"I wasn't talking to myself," I said defensively.

"Oh, really? Who were you talking to?"

How could I tell her I was talking to my penis? I had shared that secret with only my beloved late wife, Patty, who responded to my revelation by saying, "All you men are alike."

But that was more than twenty years ago. Claudette Permice was nothing like Patty McGee Perlmutter. But, I decided to take a risk and share my secret.

I tried to break it to her gently. "I was talking to my penis."

"All you men are alike," she said. "I suppose the little fella has a name."

"Mr. Johnson," I said. "And watch that word 'little.'"

"And what were you and Mr. Johnson talking about?" she asked with a tired sigh. "All I heard was something about *again* and *not again.*"

"He kept waking me up to pee," I answered honestly. "I was talking to him about timing."

"I'll tell you about timing," Claudette said. "The two of you woke me up at two thirty, four fifteen, and five thirty."

"Thank you, Big Ben."

"And after all that talking you peed like a gerbil."

"Oh, so now you don't like the way I pee?"

"You used to pee like a racehorse," she explained. "Not a seahorse."

"Now you've gone too far," I said.

"When was your last physical?" she asked.

"President Carter's administration."

"Be serious."

"I am being serious. He was our thirty-ninth president."

"I want you to have a prostate exam," she insisted.

"No. And that's final."

"Today."

"Okay."

CHAPTER 2

THE FICKLE FINGER

We went to the yellow medical building on Clint Moore Road. I stopped at the directory. I was in no hurry for a prostate exam.

"What's nephrology?" I asked, reading the directory.

"Kidney problems," Claudette, a registered nurse, told me.

"What's ANP?" I asked, hoping she wouldn't notice I was stalling.

She tugged my arm. "Adult Nurse Practitioner, and stop stalling."

I dug in my heels. "What about RD?"

"Registered Dietician," she said impatiently. "C'mon. These appointments are hard to get. We're lucky he had a cancellation at three."

4:45 P.M.

"I'm gonna kill someone," I whispered. "We've been waiting two hours."

"Be patient," Claudette spoke to me like I was a child.

"Why do I have to be patient to be a patient?"

"Fill out your questionnaire," she told me.

"I did that an hour ago," I complained.

QUESTIONNAIRE/ANSWERS

Q: Are you married?
A: Why do you ask?

Q: Do you wear a hearing aid?
A: What?

Q: Are you allergic to anything?
A: Questionnaires.

Q: Are you an organ donor?
A: What organ and who's asking.

Q: Is it painful when you urinate?
A: No. It's painful when I can't.

Q: On a scale of zero to ten, how would you describe your pain?
A: The pain in my ass from waiting is a ten!

Q: Do you have a primary doctor?
A: No, but I do have a primary nurse.

I went to the men's room and when I returned I approached the stonefaced, blue-haired receptionist.

"Has anyone ever died of old age in this waiting room?" I asked.

Before the receptionist could answer Claudette was standing

next to me. "Don't pay any attention to him," she said, ushering me to my seat. "He's not well."

"And I'm not getting any better," I complained.

"Try thinking of something pleasant," Claudette said, shushing me.

I thought about strangling the doctor.

Then I asked myself, *"What am I doing here?"*

I'm the grandson of a legend: Sirota the Orphan, sole survivor of a pogrom in the Ukraine when he was two years old. Thirteen years later the fearless son of a bitch jumped on the back of a five-hundred-pound brown bear and stabbed it to death with a stolen Cossack dagger.

Then he walked from the Ukraine, across Eastern Europe, wrapped in brown bearskin, armed only with that dagger. In Hamburg, Germany, he boarded a ship bound for Boston wearing a dead man's clothes and carrying bloody documents that identified him as Hans Perlmutter. The real Hans Perlmutter, a German teenager with terminal tuberculosis, rested in peace at the bottom of Hamburg harbor, wrapped in brown bearskin.

My grandfather settled in Dorchester, Massachusetts, married a Ukrainian girl he had known in the Old Country, and had one son, Harry.

I was Harry's son but I was more the second coming of my grandfather. I was a street fighter as a kid, an undefeated Golden Gloves boxing champion as a teenager, and one of Boston's most respected policemen as an adult.

I never feared jumping on the bear's back. The bears feared me.

I married my high-school sweetheart, Patty McGee, in 1964. She died of a brain aneurysm twenty years later. I never remarried. Twenty years after Patty died, I retired.

In 2004, I moved to Boca Raton where I had now sat in a room for two hours, waiting for some inconsiderate asshole to stick his finger up mine.

"Is this fair?" I asked myself.

I went to the bathroom for the third time. When I returned, I resumed my reverie.

In the short time I had been in Boca I had gone from an obscure golf-course ranger to the legendary Boca Knight. I thought I was some-one special. After this two-hour wait, however, I was reminded that I was just another Social Security schmuck at the mercy of the system.

I went to the men's room for the fourth time and shoved the heavy bathroom door open. It banged against the wall and a short old man leaning over the sink bolted upright, startled.

"Sorry," I said.

He stared at me but said nothing. I noticed he was wearing a Boca Knights hat and had a slight head tremor. His eyes were red and glassy, but there were no tears.

"You're a Boca Knight?" I asked, pointing at his hat.

"Usetabe." He nodded, and shuffled out the door.

I followed, watching him move slowly toward the elevator. His body language, his voice, and his ten-mile stare seemed fa-miliar to me.

When I returned to the doctor's office, Claudette was agitated.

"They called your name. The doctor's waiting for you."

"Let him wait," I said.

5:15 P.M.

Tall, handsome Dr. Alan Koblentz stood behind his desk reading my questionnaire.

"Mr. Perlmutter," he smiled. "Interesting answers."

"I had plenty of time to be creative."

"I've heard a lot about you," he said. "It's an honor to meet the Boca Knight."

"You could have had the honor two hours ago," I told him.

"I've had a busy day," he explained without apology.

"Yeah, well, keeping people waiting for hours takes hours," I said.

"You've made your point."

"No, I haven't. You'll do the same thing tomorrow."

"Mr. Perlmutter," the doctor said politely, "I haven't got time for this—"

"Neither do I," I interrupted. "And neither do the people sitting out there."

"Perhaps you should see another doctor," Dr. Koblentz suggested with no remorse. He might as well have said, "Fuck you, I have plenty of patients."

"I *will* see another doctor," I said. "But before I go, I want to ask you a question."

He nodded tiredly. "What's your question?"

"Are your parents alive?" I asked.

My question surprised him. "Yes. Why?"

"How would you feel if a doctor kept them waiting for two hours?"

He blinked. I had hit a nerve, but he didn't answer.

"Let me answer for you," I said. "I bet you'd be as pissed off as I am right now."

"Did you actually wait two hours just to tell me off?" he asked.

"No. I waited the first hour for my exam. I waited the second hour to tell you off."

"Medical care doesn't run on a schedule, Mr. Perlmutter."

"Is that the answer you'd give your mother?" I challenged him.

He paused a moment. "Point well taken," he finally conceded.

He wasn't a bad guy. He was just so full of himself there wasn't room for anyone else.

"Would an apology make you feel better?" he asked.

"If you apologize to every person in the waiting room . . . yes, I'd feel better," I told him. "Maybe you would, too."

"Don't you think you're carrying this a little too far?"

"I don't know. Ask your mother?"

He either loved his mother very much or was scared shit of her. In either event, he walked to the door, opened it, and stepped into the waiting room.

"Hi, everyone," he said to the remaining patients. "I'm sorry to have kept you waiting so long. I'm willing to work as late as it takes to see all of you or I'll come in Saturday. Just tell the receptionist what you want to do."

"Did Eddie Perlmutter threaten to beat you up?" Claudette asked.

"He beat me up verbally," Dr. Koblentz admitted.

"He can do that, too," Claudette said.

The doctor closed the door.

"Now, what's your problem, besides a short temper?" he asked me.

"I'm having trouble peeing," I told him.

"How old are you?"

"Sixty."

"Have you ever had a prostate exam?"

"Maybe," I said. "What is it?"

"It's a finger inserted in your anus—"

"Yeah, I've had that done," I interrupted.

"Who was the doctor?"

"It was a nurse."

"That doesn't count."

"Damn." I cleared my throat. "Do I really need this?"

"You could have a prostate problem."

"What kind of problem?"

"Worst-case scenario, prostate cancer. We need to do blood work for that test."

Fuck!

"My guess is it's just an enlarged prostate, inhibiting your urine flow. It's very common." Dr. Koblentz pulled on a rubber glove. "Drop your pants." He extended his arm like a maitre d' showing me to a table.

"Could we have dinner first?" I asked, assuming the position.

Draped over the examining table, I had a decent view of the outside and I saw the old man from the men's room in the parking lot. A bell went off in my head as a finger went up my butt.

I flinched. "Hey!"

"Relax," Dr. Koblentz repeated. "It's just a little KY Jelly."

"It's déjà vu," I told him.

"You said you never had a digital exam before," he reminded me while poking around.

"I'm talking about that guy," I said, pointing out the window. "I remember where I saw that look."

"What guy?" Dr. Koblentz didn't back out. "What look?"

With his finger wending its way to my prostate it was hard to explain the "life is no longer worth living" look of the hopeless. So I pointed and shouted, "That guy, that look . . . and take your finger out of my ass."

I yanked his hand away and pushed off the table.

"Easy, Eddie," the doctor protested, rubbing his wrist.

"Sorry, Doc," I said as I bunny-hopped toward the door. "Call nine-one-one."

"This is not an emergency," he insisted.

"Doc, trust me," I shouted. "Call nine-one-one."

I must have looked like I was in a potato-sack race as I hopped through the waiting room, pulling up my pants.

"Eddie Perlmutter," Claudette called after me. "You come back here."

I finally got my pants up and ran to the elevator. I waited a moment then took the stairs instead, using the railings on each side of the staircase like an ancient acrobat.

The KY Jelly squished in my pants as I hobbled outside. I saw the old man getting into an old Lincoln.

"Hey," I shouted, waving my arms. "Wait."

I was about twenty yards away when he looked at me, tipped his hat, shut the door, and put something to his head. I heard the shot and saw his brains splatter on the driver's window. His head slumped against the spiderweb cracks in the glass created by the bullet's exit. The hat was still on his head but this Boca Knight was dead.

I heard a siren and saw two Boca police cars speeding into the parking lot. Dr. Koblentz apparently had followed my instructions. The first police car screeched to a halt behind me and Officer Matt McGrady jumped out. Matt was a friend of mine on the Boca Police Force. We taught boxing together at the Police Athletic League gym on Second Avenue and I had helped him adopt a child. He looked surprised to see me.

"Eddie," Matt called to me. "What's up?"

"Suicide," I told him.

"Did you see it?" He was by my side, looking at the bloody, shattered window.

"Yeah." I nodded. "I tried to stop him."

I told Matt the whole story, omitting the part about the KY Jelly.

"Any idea why?"

I looked at the medical building. "Probably a bad prognosis," I guessed.

I saw Claudette and Dr. Koblentz rushing toward us as a crowd formed around the death car. Everyone stared at the splattered window.

"What happened?" I heard a young man ask.

"Someone just blew his brains out," another youngster replied.

"Who was it?"

"Nobody," the punk decided.

Nobody's nobody, I thought.

A BOCA KNIGHT'S OBITUARY

Carl Mann, 81, a widower from Chicago, died yesterday in Boca Raton, Florida, from a self-inflicted gunshot wound to the head. Mr. Mann had been fighting pancreatic cancer for a year.

Mr. Mann was an outstanding athlete in high school, lettering in football, basketball, and baseball. He threw two no-hitters during his three-year varsity career. Upon graduating high school in 1943, Mr. Mann enlisted in the United States Army and was part of the 352nd Division that landed on Normandy Beach. He was awarded a Bronze Star for bravery and received a Purple Heart.

He enjoyed a successful fifty-year career as an executive in the life insurance business.

He was an avid golfer and a master-level bridge player.

He is survived by his wife Charlene, four children, and twelve grandchildren.

My blood-work results showed no evidence of cancer. Dr. Koblentz told me I had an enlarged prostate. I was relieved. I was still somebody, at least for a while.

Chapter 3

In Sylvia's Memory

"Go away," seventy-six-year-old Sylvia Goldman screamed hysterically from behind her closed front door. "I'll call the police."

Damn it. She's out to lunch before we're out to lunch.

I turned the doorknob. She had forgotten to lock it again. I pushed gently against her feeble resistance and entered the house. She didn't recognize me.

"Sylvia, it's Eddie," I said softly. "We're having lunch today. Remember?"

"Harold, help," she called for her husband, who had been dead five years.

"Harold isn't here, Sylvia," I said softly.

She trembled, her eyes rolled back in her head, and she fainted.

I scooped her up and carried her in my arms to the sofa.

She weighs nothing, I thought.

I put her gently on her back and placed a cushion under her

head. I sat in the chair next to her and waited for her to come back. I had become very attached to Sylvia while she became increasingly detached from reality.

When Sylvia was Sylvia, she was wonderful: smiling, alert, and a pleasure to be with. When Sylvia was not Sylvia, her eyes were like shuttered windows in a haunted house. I imagined tiny devils inside her head, hacking away at her brain with pickaxes, destroying her mind, cell by cell, day by day.

Sylvia's eyelids fluttered, and she looked up at me.

"I must have dozed off," she whispered.

I nodded, but she saw through my charade.

"I had another episode, didn't I?" Sylvia said, sitting up.

I nodded.

"Oh, Eddie," she said despondently. "What am I going to do?"

I first became aware of Sylvia Goldman less than a year ago. I saw her sneaking bagels and a pile of pink Sweet'N Low packets into her purse from the free buffet table outside the health club. She was so comically inept that I assumed everyone knew what she was doing and didn't care. But when people have too much time on their hands there is always someone eager to make un-important things important, and I was eventually approached to bust the little old lady.

"You should do something about that woman," a chubby woman in a tennis outfit reported to me one morning. She pointed to Sylvia. "She steals all the bagels."

"She doesn't take all the bagels," I replied. "She takes four a day."

"The food is supposed to be eaten here," she insisted.

"Is that a rule?"

"It's an unwritten rule."

"Can I see that in writing?"

"She's stealing."

"The food is free," I reminded her. "How can you steal free stuff?"

I defended Sylvia successfully until the day she stole the toaster off the buffet table. I could rationalize taking free food but not a kitchen appliance.

"Mrs. Goldman, I was wondering what you planned to do with that toaster," I inquired politely, following her to her car.

She looked at the toaster.

"I-I-I don't know," she said softly, and handed it to me.

I know bullshit from bewilderment. She was bewildered.

As I watched Mrs. Goldman drive away I was conflicted. Yes, she had inexplicably tried to steal a toaster but I knew she really wasn't a thief. She was confused and maybe a little senile. What was the proper response from me as a security officer to a delicate situation like this? I made a tough decision.

The next morning I went to Boca Appliances on Old Dixie to buy Sylvia Goldman a toaster. I was immediately impressed with the retro-styled Russell Hobbs 2MT model so I bought two of them . . . one for me. The model had the styling of an old Sunbeam T35 from the 1960s but had been updated with two wide slots for bagels.

In the forties and fifties, toasters were produced primarily for white-bread America. But as babies boomed the bagel business bloomed, and Russell Hobbs supplied the increasing demand with the 2MT. Now I was a proud owner of one but I had to figure out how to give Sylvia her Russell Hobbs without confusing or insulting her. I wasn't even sure if she would remember me or the incident at the clubhouse. I decided to do the considerate thing. I would trick her.

I took one of the boxed 2MT toasters to a mailing store where I had it wrapped and addressed to Boca Heights Country Club— *Sylvia Goldman—Contest Winner*, and I personally delivered it to her modest house in Boca Heights. It was eleven o'clock in the morning when I rang her bell. She opened the door with a bright smile and shining eyes but didn't recognize me.

"Sylvia Goldman?" I asked with a smile.

"That's me," she said, looking at the big box. "What is that?"

"I don't know," I lied. "It came to the main office to your attention. Did you enter a contest?"

"I get calls for contests all the time."

"Well, you're a winner."

She clapped her hands like a little girl then looked concerned. "It's so big," she said.

"Would you like me to help you open it?" I volunteered.

"Yes," she said, accepting my offer.

She let me into her house and led me to the kitchen where I put the box on a counter.

"Do I know you?" she asked, with a cute tilt of her head and a smile.

"I'm with security," I said. "My name is Eddie."

"Well, thank you, Eddie."

I loved her smile.

She must have been a beauty.

She was delighted when I took the retro-toaster out of the box.

"It's beautiful," she told me. "I don't have a toaster."

We set up the 2MT and admired the design.

"It reminds me of when I was young," I said.

"I don't remember being young," she said, slowly shaking her head.

Strange.

"Do you want to test toast a bagel?" I asked.

"I-I-I don't have a bagel," she said.

I looked around the kitchen. No bagels. I went to the refrigerator and opened the door. No bagels. Sylvia watched me.

When I opened the stand-up freezer section, a plastic bag containing four frozen bagels tumbled out and landed on my foot. Another bag of bagels followed, then another and another. I looked in the freezer. There were five shelves, stacked with plastic bags of bagels. Each bag held four bagels; a morning's haul. Some bags contained frost, a clue to their age.

"You have bagels," I said, taking one from a bag and returning the rest to the freezer.

"Of course I do," she said.

Okay.

I put half the bagel in each oversized toaster slot and tested the defrost feature. It worked. I set the bagel-toasting adjustment and within minutes we had a beautiful browned bagel. We sat at her kitchen table, ate, and talked.

I told her a little about myself, my work, and my late wife.

"I married my high-school sweetheart," I informed her.

"I think I did, too," she said, uncertainly.

Oh boy.

When I was leaving she was smiling.

"It was so nice to meet you, Eddie," she gushed. "I don't get much company."

"No family?" I asked.

"No."

"I could visit you again?"

"Promise?"

"Promise."

"I won't forget," she said, pointing an index finger at her temple.

She forgot. The next morning she took the customary four bagels and several Sweet'N Low packages from the free buffet, and I was certain she didn't recognize me. I decided to learn more about Sylvia Goldman.

Through my administrative contacts in Boca Heights I

learned that Sylvia's bills were paid promptly by her late husband's trust fund. A local lawyer named Sanford Kreiger was trustee. I contacted him.

We agreed to meet that afternoon at St. Andrews Country Club, where he lived.

The young security guard checked my ID and I checked his name tag. "Where you from, Tito?" I asked.

"Jamaica," he said with an island accent and a friendly smile. "You know how to get to the clubhouse, Mr. Perlmuttah." He handed me back my ID.

"Do you think it's my first time at a fancy club, Tito?" I asked.

"No suh," he said respectfully, and lifted the security bar automatically.

"Well, it is," I smiled. "Where's the clubhouse?"

Tito laughed and handed me printed directions.

As I rolled in, Tito called to a black gardener. "Hey, Santos. You see dat guy?"

"In dat MINI Cooper?" Santos yelled back.

"Yeah," Tito said. "Dat's a funny munh."

"Dat's a funny car." Santos had a high-pitched laugh.

I parked a distance from the clubhouse, not wanting to embarrass my host with my MINI.

Sanford Kreiger met me at the front door. He was slim and short like me, with a full head of well-groomed silver hair. I guessed he was in his early seventies. We sat in large sofa chairs in the lounge and ordered coffee.

"Why is Boca Heights investigating Sylvia Goldman?" Kreiger asked.

"Broken Heights isn't investigating her," I said. "I am."

"Why?" He raised his eyebrows dubiously.

"I'm a friend of hers."

"She never mentioned you," he told me.

"She never mentioned you, either."

He smiled and looked away. "I can't talk about personal matters," he said.

"I want to discuss her mental condition."

"I'm not a doctor," he said, "but I know a little about her Alzheimer's. Her late husband, Dr. Goldman, kept me informed. She has a disease of the brain created internally by an imbalance in her system. Basically, plaque is growing on her brain."

"Was Dr. Goldman an expert on Alzheimer's?" I asked.

"He was an expert on all forms of mental illness," the lawyer said.

"Did he treat Sylvia himself?" I asked.

"I can't discuss that with you," Kreiger said.

"How long were you his lawyer?"

"Over twenty years," he said, "but I knew Harold most of my life. We grew up in the same area in New York. He was eight years older."

"What was he like as a person?" I wanted to know.

"He was a very unique individual," Kreiger said, "and he was a genius. At one time he had a very promising, high-profile position in his field. But he dropped out of the big time without explanation and became a professor at some obscure college. I never knew why."

"Sylvia told me she and Dr. Goldman were high-school sweethearts."

"I can't talk about that," he said professionally.

"Why not?"

"Doctor's orders." He smiled. "Besides, I didn't meet Sylvia until long after they were married. Why is this information important to you?"

"I want to help her."

"Prying into her past won't help."

"The woman has no memory of her childhood," I said. "Why?"

"I can't talk about that."

"Was Dr. Goldman trying to hide something?"

"Her privacy, I assume," Kreiger told me. "He was very protective of her."

"Well, he can't protect her now," I reminded him.

"He's protecting her from you right now, isn't he?"

"Okay. I guess he is. But what if she becomes incapacitated?" I asked.

"There are provisions in his will for that."

He stood up, indicating our meeting was over.

"I'm going to continue to look into this," I promised.

"I won't try to stop you." He shrugged. "I just can't help you."

It was time for me to come through for Sylvia.

Chapter 4

The Black Hole

When Sylvia became Sylvia again she got up from the sofa. I escorted her outside.

"I like your new car," she told me for the twentieth time.

"Thank you, Sylvia," I said patiently. "We're going to the Ale House on 441, right?"

"Yes. I love the spinach dip there," she said.

She ate three chips the last time.

We chugged past the security gate and I saw a green right traffic arrow turning yellow at Yamato Road.

Make that light.

I accelerated and made a screeching right turn onto Yamato just as yellow turned red.

Yes! I congratulated myself as the front right tire of the MINI slammed into a pothole, and bounced out. The right rear tire followed.

"Shit," I exclaimed as we bounced out again.

Sylvia got whiplashed and yelped.

At Yamato I pulled onto a grassy knoll.

"Are you alright?" I asked.

"I think so," she said quietly. "What happened?"

"Pothole," I told her. "Damn thing has been there for months. I forgot. Sorry."

I got out of the MINI and checked the car. The right rear hubcap was dented but everything seemed intact.

When I got back in the car Sylvia said, "Drive carefully and watch your language." We both laughed.

At the Ale House, I watched Sylvia mishandle her spinach dip. Her first scoop resulted in a chip fracture.

I took a fresh chip, dipped it adeptly, and handed her the prize.

"I wish I could do that," she said.

"I wish I could eat that," I said, envying her while I took a bite of my tasteless veggie burger. "But I have to watch my diet."

"Why? You look good." She patted my arm.

"My doctor told me to watch what I eat," I confided in her. "My HDL is bad."

"What's HDL?"

"Cholesterol."

"Bad cholesterol."

"No, HDL is good cholesterol," I tried to explain.

"Your good cholesterol is bad?" she asked, puzzled.

"Yeah."

"Is there bad cholesterol?"

"Yeah, LDL."

"Is your LDL bad, too?"

"No. It's good. Can we talk about something else?"

"You could ask how I'm feeling."

"Okay. How are you feeling?"

"Don't ask." She shook her head.

Sylvia!

"My internist says I have fibromyalgia."

"What's that?"

"Everything hurts but nothing is wrong," she explained.

"That sounds bad."

"It's not good. And my back hurts," she went on. "I have spinal stenosis."

"What's that?"

"A narrowing of the spine," she explained. "I get numbness in my legs."

"That's not good."

"No, it's bad, and I need two new knees."

"Do your knees hurt?"

"I don't know. My legs are numb."

Stupid question.

"I have tendonitis in my rotator cuff," she continued.

"What's a rotator cuff?"

"Muscles and tendons in the shoulder," she said, pointing. "I have plantar fascia, too."

"I'm afraid to ask where that is," I said.

"It's in the foot," she said. "I'm a mess, head to toe."

"Your head looks fine," I tried.

"My hair is thinning."

"How's your hearing?"

"What?"

"Sylvia," I sighed. "Does anything feel good?"

"Yes," she said. "Being here with you."

"I wish my mother had said that to me when I was a kid," I told her.

"I don't remember my mother," Sylvia said.

"I know." I patted her hand. "You told me your husband analyzed your condition as infantile amnesia."

"My husband, Harold, was a very famous psychiatrist, you

know," she informed me for the hundredth time. She took a quick deep breath as if she had just remembered something. "Did I tell you I dreamed about the two-headed boy again last night?"

"No, you didn't mention it," I told her. "Was it the same dream as always?"

"Exactly." She nodded. "I was looking up at the two-headed boy and the wicked witch. Both the boy's heads were laughing at me and the witch was screaming."

"Any ideas this time?" I asked hopefully.

"It means nothing to me. It's just a stupid dream," she said.

"You're sure you never had that dream when your husband was alive?"

"I never dreamed at all when Harold was alive," she said. "Since he died I sometimes dream about him but mostly it's the two-headed boy and the wicked witch."

After lunch we sat in my car in front of her house.

"I loved my meal," she said cheerfully.

"I could tell." I smiled. "You ate four chips."

"And I have leftovers for tonight's dinner," she said, proudly holding up her Ale House bag.

"And breakfast and lunch tomorrow," I said.

An elderly couple hobbled slowly past the car.

"Do you know them?" I asked Sylvia.

"No, but I know what's wrong with them," she said. "He just had both hips replaced and she has osteoporosis."

Sad.

I kissed Sylvia's cheek and promised to see her soon. I watched her wave good-bye and close her front door. I felt guilty leaving her. I knew the two-headed boy and the wicked witch were only a dream away.

I checked my watch. It was two thirty on a Tuesday afternoon. The municipal offices were still open on First Avenue, twenty minutes away. I exited Boca Heights, and turned east on Yamato. In my rearview mirror I saw a VW Rabbit hop in and out of the hole. The VW's right rear hubcap popped loose and spun crazily across Yamato, nearly hitting a pedestrian panhandler before crashing into a curb and twirling to a stop at the feet of a young bicycle rider.

That pothole had to be stopped, literally.

I went for help.

"Can I help you?" a pleasant, middle-aged woman asked from the government's side of the counter at the municipal office.

"Can you fix a pothole?" I asked politely.

"No, but I'll get you someone in the Street Division who can," she said. "You're Eddie Perlmutter, aren't you?"

"Yes, I am," I said.

"I think you're great." She was smiling and pushing telephone buttons. "Hi, Ralph, this is Betty at the front desk," she said into the phone. "We have a celebrity here who wants to talk about a pothole."

She listened.

"What pothole?" she repeated his question for my benefit. "Don't you want to know which celebrity? It's Eddie Perlmutter. . . . Yeah, the Boca Knight. He's right here in front of me." She listened again. "Yeah, he is a cool guy. I agree. I'll send him right up."

"Who says I'm a cool guy?"

"Everyone," she said.

She gave me directions to Ralph's office in the Street Division.

Ralph was a big, brawny guy with a large round head and a broad red face.

"Eddie Perlmutter," he boomed, offering his hand. "What can I do for you?

"Fix a pothole," I said, watching my hand disappear into his.

"You bet," he said. "Where's the hole?"

"At the exit of Boca Heights and Yamato, heading west," I told him.

"Yup, that's a bad one, alright," Ralph said, nodding.

"You know about it?"

"Sure. But we can't touch it. Yamato is a state road and we're the city."

"Cut the shit."

"I'm serious," Ralph said. "The hole is seven inches off city property."

"Ralph," I pleaded, "that hole is dangerous."

"I agree," Ralph said. "But I can't help you. It's a state hole, like I said."

"Have you reported it to the state?" I asked, trying not to lose my temper.

"Of course, I did. Six months ago," Ralph said. "The guy at the State Department I reported it to got transferred. Then the guy who replaced him went on vacation and when he got back the paperwork was lost."

"Can we reapply?" I took a deep breath.

"Sure," Ralph said cheerfully. "But it's a lot of red tape and a lot of time."

"Why can't the state just authorize you to fix the damn hole?"

"We asked, they refused," he said. "Liability issues, they said."

Bullshit!

"With all the new products available it's only a one-man job anyway." Ralph sighed.

"What new products?"

"Rapid Road Repair, for one," he said. "We've had samples here for a year."

"Does it work?"

"Who knows? We never used it," he sighed. "My boss told me to dump it months ago."

"Do you still have it?" I asked.

"I think so." He looked embarrassed. "Look, Eddie, I must sound like a real screwup to you but we have over two hundred miles of asphalt and concrete roadways to maintain, twenty-five miles of bike paths, and three hundred and sixty miles of concrete sidewalks."

"I understand," I said, sympathizing with him. "Who's got time to throw away Rapid Road Repair?"

"Right," Ralph said, appreciating my understanding.

We're bonding.

"I'd be happy to dump those containers for you, Ralph," I volunteered.

Wink.

He hesitated for a moment, then understood.

"I can't let you do that," he said. "That's city property. But I can put the canisters out back by the Dumpsters myself . . . right now . . . like I was supposed to do months ago."

Wink.

Wink.

Rapid Road Repair consists of fifty-pound buckets of asphalt, polymer adhesives, and graded limestone. Four of them are tough to load in a MINI but it can be done.

It was Boca Midnight (10:00 P.M.) when I left my apartment to fix the hole from hell. I parked about twenty feet east of the pothole and used the MINI as a shield from westbound traffic. I kept my headlights on so I could see.

I carried the four heavy buckets of RRR, two at a time, to the rim of the little canyon and read the simple instructions. *"Sweep clean, remove base debris, yadda, yadda, yadda."* I pulled off the seal on one, pried off the lid, and emptied the claylike contents into the hole. I did this three more times until the hole was filled then stomped down the excess until it was flush with the street.

No big deal. I admired my work.

I heard screeching tires and a horn blaring. I turned and saw a speeding black Cadillac sedan in the right lane passing a slow moving car in the left lane. The Cadillac was bearing down on me. I dove off the road as the sedan whooshed by.

An instant later I heard the car crash into the empty buckets of Rapid Road Repair. I got up and watched the Caddy shimmy to a stop about a hundred yards away. A small man got out of the driver's side and looked back at me. I expected an apology or an inquiry about my health. Instead he walked to the right side of the car, he squatted down and pulled something out from under the fender. It was a Rapid Road Repair lid. He stood up.

"Asshole," he shouted, and threw the lid in my direction. It fell ninety-five yards short.

Asshole? Red spots exploded in front of my eyes and I started running toward the guy.

"Oh shit," he said, and scurried to the car.

By the time his wheels stopped spinning in place, I was close enough to see his license plate. Florida. I memorized it.

Catch you later.

I packed up what was left of my equipment and threw it in the MINI.

The worst drivers in America live in South Florida, I thought.

Chapter 5

Valentine's Day Massacres

Last spring Frank Burke, Boca's police chief, had encouraged me to get my Class C Private Detective's license.

"You're a natural at solving crimes," he said.

"I specialized in violent crimes," I said. "There isn't much of that around here."

"You're right," Burke said. "Murder in Boca is rare and rape is ninety percent below the national average."

"So is consensual sex," I pointed out.

After I finished with the Russian counterfeiters, the Aryans, and other assorted oddities several months ago I got my detective license and a gun permit. I formed Boca Knights Detective Agency and rented a small office in an executive suite; eight ten-by-fourteen offices that shared services including a receptionist. Our suite consisted of three young lawyers, one old lawyer, a CPA, a travel agent, a party planner, and me. The building was around the corner from the Boca Police Station.

My friend Jerry Small, a reporter for the *Palm Beach Community News*, gave my new agency a nice write-up in the Community Section of the Sunday paper, and since I already had minor celebrity status in the area, my phone was ringing the first morning I officially opened.

The receptionist answered all the calls for the eight companies. By eleven my first morning, she had answered ten calls for me and I had been offered ten jobs, all for the same day: February 14.

Valentine's Day for detectives is apparently like Christmas for retailers. Demand exceeds supply.

I told my fifth caller what I told the first four. "I only investigate crimes."

"It is a crime," my fifth caller insisted. "He's spending my money on that bimbo."

"That's a shame, not a crime," I said, disagreeing.

The tenth call sounded different.

"Betsy Blackstone, line one, Eddie," Olivia, the tattooed receptionist told me.

I only had one line.

"Eddie Perlmutter," I said. "How can I help you, Mrs. Blackstone?"

"I think my husband is cheating on me, and I want you to tell him to stop."

"*You* should tell him to stop," I said. "I'm a detective, not a marriage counselor."

"He won't listen to me," she said. "He'll listen to you."

"Why would he listen to me?"

"Because you're the Boca Knight," she said.

I rubbed my forehead with my fingers.

"Mrs. Blackstone," I said patiently, "that's just a nickname. There is no Boca Knight."

"Tell that to my husband," she insisted. "He said he wants to be just like you."

"I never cheated on my wife."

"Tell him that, too," she said.

"In all due respect, Mrs. Blackstone—"

"Betsy."

"In all due respect, Betsy, your husband sounds like a Boca Bullshitter to me, not a Boca Knight."

"He wasn't like this when I married him." She blew her nose. "And it's my fault."

"You're talking like a battered woman who blames herself when her husband beats her."

"My husband doesn't beat me," she defended him.

"He seems to be giving you a mental beating," I disagreed. "Look, Mrs.—Betsy, I just don't think I can help you."

"Can I tell you why I think it's my fault?" she asked.

"I'd rather you didn't," I told her.

"I've had two miscarriages," she sniffled, ignoring me. "The first one was in my thirteenth week. My doctor told me it was perfectly normal and to try again. We tried again and the exact same thing happened in the thirteenth week."

"What did your doctor say that time?"

"The same thing," she told me. "He told us to try again."

"Is this guy a rich doctor or a witch doctor?" I asked.

"His name is Dr. Ronald Cohen, and he's very popular."

"So is Ronald McDonald," I said. "Did you try again?"

"No."

"Why not?"

"My husband and I haven't had sex for over a year."

"That's none of my business," I said quickly.

"Sex has become painful for me physically and mentally," she said, ignoring me.

"You should talk to your doctor about this, not me," I told her.

"I have talked to him," she sniffed. "He said it's all mental and there's nothing wrong with me physically."

"How is your husband reacting?" I asked.

"He says he understands, but he's changed," she said. "He stays out late at night now and I'm sure there's another woman. What should I do?"

"You don't want my advice," I said. "I solve problems the way they do on the *Jerry Springer Show*. I'd break a table over his head. You need Dr. Phil."

"I only want you," she whined. "My husband trusts you."

"He doesn't even know me."

"He thinks he does," she said.

A nut job.

"What does he do for a living?" I asked out of curiosity.

"He's a manager at Mendy's Grill at Mizner Park," she said.

I know that place.

"What does he look like?"

"He's gorgeous."

"Can you be more specific?"

"He's tall with a great build and wavy black hair. He's thirty."

Lucky bastard.

"His name is Bradley," she volunteered. "Are you going to talk to him?"

"I charge fifty dollars an hour."

"How many hours do you think this will be?"

"None, if I don't take the case," I told her.

"Please take it," she pleaded.

"How long have you been married?" I asked, wondering why I cared.

"Five years."

"Newlyweds," I joked.

"No," she sighed. "When we were newlyweds, we were happy. We were high-school sweethearts. We got married one year out of college."

"I married my high-school sweetheart, too," I told her.

"I know," she said. "I read about you in the paper. She died. I'm sorry."

"Thanks. Do you have proof your husband is cheating on you?" I asked, changing gears.

"No."

"So, it's just this feeling."

"Yes."

I took her phone number and told her I would get back to her if I was interested.

Later that night I had too many concerns about Dr. Cohen's casual answers to Betsy Blackstone's serious questions.

I decided to take the case.

Chapter 6

No View at Delray Vista

Early the next morning Olivia announced, "You have a call on line one, Eddie. He says his name is Izzy Fryberg and he's president of the Delray Vista Condo Association."

I was sure there were no great views at Delray Vista, just like there was no point at Boca Point.

I waited a few seconds then picked up the phone and pressed my one line.

"Eddie Perlmutter," I said into the phone. "How can I help you, Mr. Fryberg?"

"Call me Izzy."

"Okay, Izzy. How can I help you?"

"I've got a case for you, Mr. Perlmutter."

"Call me Eddie."

"I'd rather keep this on a professional level."

"You just told me to call you Izzy," I said.

"I did?"

We settled on first names and he told me his problem.

In 1982, fifty-five-year-old Izzy Fryberg, his fifty-four-year-old wife, Emma, and eleven other couples from Chelsea, Massachusetts, bought reasonably priced condos in a new community called Delray Vista. The completion date was twelve months away.

All the buildings had two floors with six two-bedroom units per floor. The complex consisted of twenty-five buildings, three hundred units altogether. Within two years all the condos were purchased. By the time Izzy sold his small office-supply business in Chelsea, Massachusetts, Delray Vista was a bustling community of energetic retirees.

"Sounds like a great place," I interjected.

"It was," Izzy said. "Not anymore."

"What happened?"

"The community and the residents got old."

"Sounds like you need doctors and repairmen."

Izzy assured me that he needed a detective.

"What would I be doing?" I asked.

"Watching an elevator," Izzy told me.

Before I could decline, Izzy offered to pay me if I would meet him at the condo.

Why not?

We met an hour later in front of 550 Buena Vista Boulevard in Delray Vista.

As I suspected, the views were no big deal.

The condo complex was past mature and so was Izzy. He was fire-plug wide, with thin white hair and broad shoulders. He stuck out his chin when he talked as if he was daring me to hit him.

"You're shorter than I thought you'd be," he said, looking up at me.

"I'm shorter than *I* thought I'd be." I used an old line.

We walked to the building and looked at the elevator.

"You won't believe the trouble this thing has caused," he said sadly.

Izzy told me that during the final building stage of the community many years ago, the developer went bankrupt. Elevator shafts had been put in all the buildings but no actual elevators were installed. The bank took over the project from the builder and offered the owners discounts if they would accept their buildings without elevators. The condo association at 550 voted unanimously to accept the discount.

"Hey, we were young," Izzy explained. "We weren't worried about climbing one flight of stairs."

"And then the years flew by." I nodded my understanding.

"Like a fart in a windstorm," Izzy said. "And the stairs became a pain, literally. So, a few years ago we had a meeting to vote on installing a working elevator in the existing shaft at a cost of thirty thousand."

"Let me guess," I interrupted. "Everyone on the top floor voted *for* and everyone on the first floor voted *against*."

"One apartment on the second floor voted against."

"Why?"

"They just said we didn't need it," Izzy said. "Rather than fight about it, five of the families on the second floor voted to pay six thousand apiece for the elevator provided the nonpaying residents signed an agreement not to use it. It was an insurance issue mostly."

"So the first-floor people signed the agreement and used the elevator anyway," I guessed.

"You're good," Izzy said. "We have a card room on the second floor and no one from the first floor walked up the stairs after the elevator was installed. When we reminded them of our agreement, we got a registered letter from a lawyer saying the agreement was nonbinding because the building bylaws were never changed."

"Legally they're probably right," I said.

"We're not talking about legalities," Izzy said. "We're talking principle. They broke their word to old friends. The paying members got so pissed off they had a lock installed on the elevator. No key, no ride."

"That had to cause problems," I said.

"Within two weeks the lock had been so badly mangled the keys wouldn't work," Izzy said. "We had to disconnect the system to get the elevator operating again. Now we're trying to get a temporary restraining order against those bastards from using the elevator until the matter is settled in court."

"That sounds like a good interim solution," I said.

"Yeah, except now no one will use the elevator. It's suddenly become dangerous." Izzy folded his arms across his chest.

"What happened?"

"The damn thing has stopped in between floors, with people inside, at least seven times during the last two weeks. It always starts up again but everyone is afraid so no one rides."

"How long does it stop?"

"It varies," Izzy said. "One time it was stuck for over a half hour. The guy in the lift started to hyperventilate. He almost died."

"What does the elevator company say?"

"They swear nothing is wrong with their equipment. They checked it out three times."

"You think it's sabotage."

"You tell me," Izzy said. "That's the job."

"I'm not an elevator operator," I told him.

"I don't want you to operate the elevator," Izzy said. "I want you to find out if someone else is operating the elevator."

"I dunno. It's not my thing," I said. "Can I poke around before I decide?"

"Do we have to pay for a poke?" he asked.

"I'll give you a free poke," I told him. "Have you got a ladder?"

Izzy walked to a door marked MAINTAINENCE and opened it with a key from his bulky chain. He took out a six-step ladder and gave it to me.

"What else is in there?" I asked.

"Telephone stuff, tools, and the circuit breakers."

I checked the room and saw nothing unusual.

Izzy followed me to the elevator.

I pressed the button and the door slid open. The inside of the elevator did not appear haunted. On the ceiling I saw the outline of a removable panel. I positioned the ladder, climbed up five steps, reached up, and dislodged the panel.

"The elevator boys already looked there," Izzy called up to me.

I poked my head through the opening in the ceiling and saw a standard pulley system that appeared clean and functional.

I replaced the panel and stepped down the ladder. I pressed the button for the second floor. The elevator door slid closed and the unit went up uneventfully.

No problem.

I pressed the first-floor button and descended smoothly. I took four round-trips.

Izzy was waiting for me on the first floor.

"See anything?" he asked me.

"The second floor," I told him.

We walked toward my car.

A nice-looking older couple was approaching from the opposite direction, holding hands. I was envious. I never got to grow old with my wife.

The woman smiled at me and waved when they got closer.

"You're the Boca Knight, aren't you?" she asked in a sweet, small voice.

"Yes, I am," I said.

"We were at your rally last spring in Palm Beach," her husband said. "We're better people because of you."

"That's very nice of you to say," I told them.

They nodded before turning to Izzy, who stood silently next to me.

"Fuck you, Fryberg," the sweet old woman said.

Her husband gave Izzy the finger.

They walked away.

"I'll take the case," I said.

Chapter 7

Unacceptable Outcomes

When I was young I saw the world in black and white, and raged in red. I never saw shades of gray, which got me put on probation my second year on the force.

During my first mandatory probation meeting with Dr. Glenn Kessler, a Boston Police Department psychiatrist, he asked me, "Are you angry often?"

"I'm never angry," I growled like a pit bull.

"You're not taking this interview very seriously, are you?" Kessler smiled patiently.

"I'm here, aren't I?"

"You have to be here or you'll be suspended from the force," he said pleasantly. "So why don't we try to make the most of it?"

"Okay." I shrugged.

"So, what makes you angry?"

"Stupid questions." I smiled this time.

He returned my smile. "What else?"

"Injustice," I said seriously. "I don't think anything pisses me off more than injustice."

"You're in good company," Kessler said. "Martin Luther King, Jr. said, '*An injustice anywhere is a threat to justice every-where.*'"

"Then some asshole shot him in the head," I said. "The ulti-mate injustice."

"Actually he was shot in the throat," said Dr. Kessler.

"I don't care if he was shot in the ass. It was an injustice," I said.

"Do you feel you have to strike out against every injustice?"

"Only if I'm within striking distance."

"Did you ever try counting to ten?"

"I only got to five."

"When you get angry and lose control, do you ever think of your own safety?" he asked.

"I don't think of anything," I said honestly. "That's why I'm on probation."

When I told Dr. Kessler I actually saw red spots when I got angry and couldn't remember my outbursts afterward, he diag-nosed me with compulsive explosive disorder—uncontrollable rage. He suggested I try to think of the consequences before I acted impulsively.

I promised him I would try but I didn't keep my promise until I got much older, moved to Boca, and began to see shades of gray.

According to the Sixth Amendment, everyone has the right to a speedy trial. Randolph Buford, the Aryan Army punk who had attacked Claudette and her grandmother, Queen, last spring wasn't getting one. Under normal circumstances I would have considered this an injustice, but in Buford's case I really didn't care. As far as I was concerned, the Buford family was getting what it deserved, except maybe for their mentally challenged daughter, Eva.

They had moved to Boca Heights from South Carolina, in the winter of 2003. Their mission was to infiltrate and assimilate the Jewish community on behalf of Aryan Army, a white suprem-acist organization that had some long-range, evil plan. They managed to blend in for a while until Randolph, the Bufords' teenage son, told a neighbor that Hitler hadn't killed enough Jews. Outraged neighbors wrote letters to Mr. and Mrs. Buford demanding an apology from their son. Forrest Buford, Ran-dolph's father, wrote letters back saying he agreed with his boy about the number of Jews killed by Hitler.

When irate members of Boca Heights wrote letters to the newspaper editor, the elder Buford wrote long anti-Semitic, venomous letters in response.

I wrote a few letters myself . . . on Buford's house. FUCK YOU, NAZIS was my primary message.

I used a bright Israeli blue for the block letters, which I bookended in between two Stars of David. It was just my simple way of telling the Bufords, *There's a Jew out here crazier than you.*

I also started following Randolph Buford around town look-ing for an excuse to bust him . . . physically or legally. It didn't take long. One night I witnessed Randolph and two friends at-tacking an old woman and her granddaughter, Claudette Per-mice, in the parking lot of the Boca Mall. Randolph was in heat, tearing at my future girlfriend's clothes, when I kicked him in the nuts to cool him off. I put his friends in the hospital and him in jail. That's when the shit hit the fan and Aryan Army marched on Palm Beach County to "Free Randolph Buford."

Free Randolph Buford, my ass!

Randolph's first trial delay was his own fault. At his arraign-ment he attacked Judge Avery Jacobs when the Jewish jurist set bail at two hundred and fifty thousand dollars.

"Are you kidding me?" the Nazi youth screamed at the judge.

"Why don't you make it two hundred and fifty million, you Jew bastard?" Randolph's father, Forrest, bellowed.

"You can appeal the amount." Judge Jacobs banged his gavel. "Get these people out of my court."

Randolph moved fast for a chunky Nazi. He sprang toward the judge, trying to sidestep two burly black police officers who eventually wrestled him to the floor.

"Get off me, niggers!" Randolph shouted, introducing himself to the guards.

Forrest Buford then did a belly flop onto the pile of three struggling men. Fists were swinging, and epithets were ringing.

Order in the court, I mused, watching the Bufords dig their own graves.

A gunshot rang out. Randolph screamed and the room went silent. The guards got up from the floor as did Forrest Buford. Randolph Buford stayed down. He had a smoking gun in his hand.

One of the officers stepped on the kid's wrist and disarmed him.

"He grabbed my gun and shot himself in the foot," one of the cops said to the judge, looking embarrassed.

"He certainly did," the judge agreed.

"Your Honor," Assistant DA Barry Daniels shouted. "These men are in contempt."

"These men are beyond contempt," the judge disagreed, rendering his judgment.

Randolph Buford exited the courtroom on a stretcher, his father in cuffs.

Two weeks later the Appellate Court upheld the high bail.

Aryan Army's lawyers filed a second appeal while their client sat in a jail cell, his injured foot confined to a walking cast. It didn't take long for sympathetic bigots to start picketing outside the jail demanding Buford's bail be reduced. I wanted to wade into the protesters and reduce their status to rubble but I actually gave the situation a second thought and counted to ten once. Dr. Kessler would have been proud of me but I wasn't so proud of myself. I was thinking too much.

I must be getting old.

I considered three possible outcomes to the Buford situation but each of them was unacceptable to me.

Possible Outcome One: Buford is found innocent by the same jury that acquitted OJ.

Possible Outcome Two: Buford is found guilty, goes to jail a Hun Hero, and comes out worse.

Possible Outcome Three (developed by yours truly): I totally fuck Buford up with the Aryan Army by spreading a rumor that Buford is cooperating with authorities in exchange for a lighter sentence. Under my contrived scenario, Aryan Army believes the rumor without substantiation (*"What luck for the rulers that men don't think."—Adolf Hitler*) and withdraws Aryan Army lawyers from the case. Buford then goes to jail and dies after a brief honeymoon in the jailhouse shower.

Although I hated the little Nazi I didn't want to be responsible for his death so I modified Outcome Three a little, developing a plan I could live with . . . and maybe Buford could live with, too. I set it in motion.

I invited my newspaper reporter friend, Jerry Small, to lunch where I asked him one simple question:

"Is there any truth to the rumor that Buford is testifying against Aryan Army in exchange for a lighter sentence?"

Jerry choked on his chicken soup. "Where did you hear that?"

"I didn't hear anything," I said. "I was just asking a question."

"C'mon, Eddie, tell me."

"There's nothing to tell," I said.

"Is there a story here?" he asked.

"How should I know?" I answered a question with a question.

Jerry took my answer as a "yes" and started looking for a story. He called the DA's office and got no comment, which he also took as an affirmative answer. He contacted the police departments in West Palm and Boca and took their denials as affirmation of his suspicions.

His next column opened with a question: "Is there any truth to the rumor that Randolph Buford is cooperating with authorities against Aryan Army in exchange for a lighter sentence?"

Jerry offered no answers and no evidence. He just asked the question and the rumor spread like an oil spill.

I was certain that Aryan Army hadn't forgiven the Bufords for the catastrophe at the Boca Knights rally last spring. I knew they wouldn't hesitate to turn on the Bufords if given a reason . . . so I gave them a reason—a whiff of "betrayal." Within days the Aryan Army lawyers withdrew their defense of Buford, citing a conflict of interest. Their actual conflict was that Randolph Buford wanted to keep breathing and talking while Aryan Army wanted him to stop.

Buford insisted that he was not cooperating with the police but the only person who believed him was me. Soon he was receiving anonymous death threats.

Excellent.

Within a week I received a phone call from Chief Frank Burke of the Boca Police, telling me to be at his office the next morning at eleven.

I arrived at the station early.

"How's Boca's finest sergeant?" I asked Billy Simms at the front desk.

"What do you need, Eddie?" Simms asked without smiling.

"Can you find the owner of this car for me?" I asked, handing him a note.

Simms read my note and shook his head. "No can do."

"Thanks, Billy." I walked through the station saying hello to everyone and feeling at home. By eleven o'clock I had worked my way to Frank Burke's office. He sat behind his desk.

"What's up, Chief?" I asked cheerfully.

He looked up at me tiredly.

"The Bufords will tell you," Frank said as he got up. "They're in the conference room. Mrs. Buford asked for this meeting. She's a very distressed mother."

I knew Randolph had a mother. I just never gave her any thought.

"What's her problem besides living with Hitler and Eichmann?"

"Threats to her son's life seem to be bothering her," he said. "Someone, I'm not saying who, spread a rumor that Randolph Buford was cooperating with the prosecution against Aryan Army. His parents think you're the source."

"Why would I do that?"

"You tell me," Burke said.

Frank and I were friends but my methods were a lot different than his.

"I have nothing to tell you except I think you should put the little storm trooper in isolation until his trial . . . for his own protection," I said.

"He *is* in isolation," Frank told me.

"Then this is an *isolated* incident," I said. Frank didn't laugh so I moved on. "What do Mr. and Mrs. Hitler want from me?"

"They want a retraction of the rumor," Frank informed me.

"Napoleon said, 'Never interrupt your enemy when he is making a mistake.'"

Frank wasn't amused. "Do you often quote Napoleon?"

"No, he gives me a complex."

Frank shook his head. "Will you talk to them?"

"Sure, I'll ask them what they're doing for Passover. Do they have a lawyer with them?" I asked, wondering if I needed one.

"No, a public defender was just appointed to replace the Army guys," Frank said. "The PD gave the Bufords permission to meet with you as long as legal matters were not discussed."

When I entered the conference room I was confronted with the scowling, brooding, flat hard face of Forrest Buford. He was sitting at the long, rectangular conference table next to his blond wife. She didn't look malevolent. She actually looked human. I could tell she had been crying. She may have raised a vulture in a vacuum, but at this moment she looked as vulnerable as her husband looked vicious. I had to remind myself that she was the mother of a menace and the missus of a monster.

"What can I do for you Nazis?" I asked.

Buford started to get up from his seat but his wife grabbed his shoulder. My eyes locked on his. He wanted me dead. I wanted him dead. This meeting should have been held at a funeral home. As we stared at each other I thought of the words written by an Auschwitz survivor: *The head takes the longest to burn; two blue flames flicker from the eyeholes . . . the entire process lasts twenty minutes—and a human being, a world, has been turned into ashes.*

I sat down across from them, and Frank Burke sat at the head of the table.

Mrs. Buford broke the silence in a soft, shaky voice.

"Mr. Perlmutter," she said, "you've put our son's life in danger, and I am asking you to publicly renounce your false rumor."

I felt nothing and said nothing. I was thinking of burning skulls.

"I know you don't like us or our politics—"

"I hate you and your politics," I interrupted. "But I am not threatening your son's life. Aryan Army is. Talk to them."

"They refuse our calls," she told me. "And they've told us to move out of the house they rented for us. You have to tell them the truth."

"Aryan Army doesn't care about the truth," I said.

"They believe your lie," she said, her voice quivering.

"They believe what they want to believe," I told her.

She looked down at her hands. Tears were in her eyes. I resisted feeling sorry for her. She married the shit. She slept with him. "Mr. Perlmutter, please—"

"Martha," Buford snarled, "you said your piece. Enough."

He got up from his chair and I got up from mine. We glared at each other.

"Can't we just talk?" Martha Buford pleaded. "My son's life is at stake."

"Blame your psychotic husband and his friends," I told her.

I had no one to blame but myself for what happened next. I should have known not to take my eyes off an uncaged wild animal. Buford lunged across the conference table and his thick fingers were around my throat in an instant. His thumbs pressed into my windpipe and I knew I was in serious trouble. I saw Frank Burke go after Buford, but I couldn't wait. I reached for the full pitcher of water on the table, grabbed it by the handle, and crashed it down on top of Buford's head. The pitcher shattered and Buford crashed face-first onto the table. Glass and water flew through the air, and blood began to seep from the gash on Buford's head. Mrs. Buford screamed.

Burke grabbed my wrist and held out his other hand. "Gimme that damned pitcher," he growled.

I handed him the handle. "I'm sorry, Frank," I said calmly. "Did you want some water?"

Chapter 8

Emotions and Motions

Forrest Buford was taken to the Boca Community Hospital in the backseat of a police car. I waved good-bye and gave him the finger.

"Nasty cut," I said to Burke as we returned to the conference room.

"At least ten stitches," the chief said, looking at the mess.

"Twenty," I predicted.

"Why the water pitcher, Eddie?" Frank was upset with me. "You could have killed him. What were you thinking?"

"I wasn't thinking, Frank," I said, rubbing my neck and sitting down. "The oxygen to my brain was shut off. So, I guess this means the meeting is over."

"Mrs. Buford is still here. She's in the ladies' room washing the blood off her hands."

"Nazis do that a lot," I said.

The door opened, and a small, mousy-looking, middle-aged woman entered carrying a mop and bucket. She had two outstanding features: two large, protruding breasts and four large, protruding teeth. I noticed the teeth first while Mr. Johnson took the low road as usual.

The woman was followed by a janitor in a gray uniform, who carried a push broom and a dustpan. The woman was dressed in blue slacks and a neat blue-striped shirt buttoned to the collar. Her hair was pulled back in a tight bun, accentuating her black-rimmed glasses, perched on her pointy nose. She smiled at me and I thought of a chipmunk.

"I see we had a little accident here," she said diplomatically.

"No, this was deliberate," I said honestly.

She looked uncertainly at me then pointed.

"You're him, aren't you?"

"Who?"

"The Knight guy?"

"Do you like the Knight guy?"

"I love him," she gushed.

"I'm him." I held out my hand and she took it.

Frank Burke rolled his eyes.

"Joy Feely, meet Eddie Perlmutter," Frank made the introductions. "Joy does our computer upgrades and maintenance."

"You don't look like a cop," I said, thinking she looked more like a ferret with a great body.

Joy and I shook hands. "I'm not a cop," she said. "I have my own business but the police department gives me a lot of work."

"Well, your job description doesn't include cleaning up broken glass," Frank told her.

"I don't mind helping Fred," Joy said, referring to the janitor.

"You're overworked already," Frank said.

"This cleanup won't take much time," she told us.

The intercom rang, and Frank picked up the phone.

"Mrs. Buford is in my office, Eddie," he said. "She wants to meet with you again."

"But I almost killed her husband just now."

"Maybe she wants to thank you," Frank said, taking a shot.

We left Joy Feely and Fred to clean up my mess.

Mrs. Buford sat in Frank's office, her hands folded in her lap. She looked sad and embarrassed. Frank went to sit behind his desk. I remained standing.

"Mrs. Buford," I said, "I had no choice but to defend myself."

"I understand," she said softly. "Can we talk about my son?"

"What about him?" I said, sitting down.

"He's only nineteen years old," she began. "He's just a boy."

"In the eyes of the law he's a man and in my eyes he's a bad man," I said.

"He needs help."

"He needs a muzzle."

"I need help," she pleaded.

"Believe it or not, I *am* trying to help," I said.

"How? By getting my son killed?"

"No, by narrowing his options," I said. "Mrs. Buford, I didn't start a rumor. I asked one man one question and human nature did the rest. Aryan Army believed a false rumor because they wanted to believe it."

"That doesn't make any sense," she said. "He's one of them."

"Not anymore," I said. "He shot off his mouth last year and there's no room in Aryan Army for a loose cannon."

"You put him in this position." She needed someone to blame.

"You're as much to blame as anyone."

"I'm not responsible for this," she insisted angrily.

"You're his mother," I told her. "You helped make him a danger to society."

"I did not," she said. "It was Forrest. I couldn't stop him, he's uncontrollable."

"I just controlled him by hitting him over the head with a water pitcher."

"I couldn't do that," she said.

"No, but you could have gone for help," I said without sympathy.

She started to cry softly.

I looked at Frank.

What do you want from me?

"Maybe that's enough for now," Frank suggested.

"No, we have to keep talking," she insisted. "Mr. Perlmutter, you said you were trying to help. What did you mean?"

"Yeah, what *did* you mean?" Frank leaned forward in his chair.

"It's difficult to explain," I said.

"Give it a try," Frank told me, and Mrs. Buford nodded. "This I gotta hear."

I talked nonstop for about twenty minutes, thinking how proud of me Dr. Kessler would have been. I explained my idea and how everyone could win. When I was done, they were both looking at me like I was insane.

"Where did you come up with your harebrained ideas?" Frank Burke asked.

"It's a gift," I answered.

"My husband would never agree to this," Mrs. Buford said.

"Your husband doesn't have to agree with anything. Randolph is an adult," I reminded her. "He can make his own decisions."

"What makes you think Randolph will agree with something like this?" she asked.

"It's his best option," I answered.

Mrs. Buford stared at me for a moment. "This is crazy."

"But it's not impossible," I told her.

"How long would he be away?"

"I figure we can get him eighteen months," I said.

"That's a pretty light sentence," Frank speculated.

"It's not a sentence," I explained. "It's a pretrial diversion. It's more like an agreement."

"Do you think he'll be safe?" she asked.

"Safer than jail," I said.

"Can you really get this done?" She looked at me hopefully.

"I honestly don't know," I answered. "A lot of people need to agree but I think it's worth a try."

They sat in silence for a few minutes considering my plan.

Mrs. Buford surprised me with a quick answer. "If you can get this done, do it."

"Mrs. Buford, I strongly advise you to think this over," Frank interrupted. "This is highly unusual."

"I understand, Chief Burke," Mrs. Buford said, "but my son's options are limited now, thanks to Mr. Perlmutter, and I have to get Randolph out of harm's way as soon as I can."

"He'll still be in harm's way," I said.

"Yes, but with a better chance of surviving doing it your way," she decided. "I accept your offer."

"It's not an offer," I emphasized. "It's just an idea."

"I understand," she said, getting up from her chair. "And I don't know whether to hate you or thank you for it."

"You don't seem like a hater to me, Mrs. Buford," I said.

"I'm not," she replied.

"Why did you marry one?" I said.

"Forrest wasn't always like this. We grew up together in South Carolina," she said. "He was a typical kid from South Carolina."

"When did he decide to become Adolph Hitler?"

"It was a gradual thing," she said reflectively. "Forrest had some major setbacks in his life and after enough of them he felt like a loser. He started drinking heavily and hanging out with other losers in town and they'd sit around a bar, get drunk, and figure out who to blame for their failures."

"How did your husband fail?"

She sighed. "He lost the tobacco farm that had been in his family for three generations."

"What happened?"

"It had something to do with the savings and loan scandal in the eighties." She shrugged. "I don't know much except it was bad. We lost everything."

"I know a little," I said. "A lot of people lost everything but most of them didn't become Nazis."

"I'm explaining him not defending him," she said. "Things got out of control after we lost the farm. We moved to Lancaster where Forrest found some odd jobs. But then he got laid off and got real angry. He found another bunch of losers in Lancaster who drank all night and blamed the Jews and blacks for everything."

"Why Jews and blacks?" I asked an old question.

"I don't know," she said. "If you don't want to admit you're a loser I guess you blame someone different."

"Sure, why not?" I said. "Then one thing leads to another."

"You got it," she sighed. "Eventually Forrest and his buddies got organized. They started raising money from other folks in the area who felt the same as them."

"Did they find many?" I asked.

"They found plenty," she said, raising her eyebrows expressively. "They raised a small fortune and a small army."

"What were you doing while this was going on?" Frank asked.

"I had all I could do to put food on the table," she said. "And my daughter Eva needs a lot of attention."

"If money was such a problem how could you afford to move to a fancy house in Boca Raton?" I asked.

She shrugged. "Forrest said it was Aryan Army money and Aryan Army business."

"What were you supposed to do?"

"He just told us to blend in and wait," she said.

"The wait's over," I told her.

Chapter 9

When Eddie Met Louie

I looked for Sergeant Billy Simms when the meeting was over. He wasn't at his desk but I saw a pad of paper on his blotter with big bold letters:

LOUIS DEWEY—1453 GLADES ROAD APT 101—BOCA

For me?

I committed the message to memory and left the notepad untouched.

Dewey lived in an apartment building on Glades Road near the entrance to the Florida Turnpike. It was a two-story brick building with all the charm of a tollbooth. There was no lobby so there was direct access to every apartment from the outside. Each apartment door had a number on it and 101 was easy to find. A dented black Cadillac sedan was parked nearby and the plate matched.

I got out of my car and approached the black sedan. I braced myself against the driver's side and began rocking the big boat until the alarm went off. The sedan's lights flashed, and the horn started to blast in rhythm. I walked to a shadowy corner of the lot and waited. The door to apartment 101 opened and Louis Dewey appeared. He was a little guy like me, and I estimated he was in his fifties. He had an Elvis hairdo from the 1950s and buck teeth for all ages. He reminded me of Joy Feely, the woman at the police station.

Dewey's hair was neatly combed but he wore a bathrobe and slippers as if he had just got out of bed. I wondered if this was the way he dressed for work.

"*Motherfucker.*" I read Dewey's lips and watched him walk toward the shrieking, flashing Cadillac. He had a set of keys in his hands. While he fiddled with the car lock, I stepped out of the shadows and approached him from behind. He turned and saw me.

"Fuckin' car," he said by way of explanation as he silenced the alarm with the key.

"Yeah, that fuckin' car almost ran me over the other night," I said to him.

His face went from frustrated to frightened, to feral . . . fast.

"I don't know what you're talking about," he said as he dodged his way around me and shuffled in his slippers toward his apartment.

I pursued him and grabbed him by his shoulder. "You almost ran me over."

"You got the wrong guy," he said, trying to pull his shoulder free.

"No, I don't. How did you get that damage to your right fender?" I challenged him.

"Somebody hit my car in a parking lot." He continued

struggling toward his apartment. He opened his apartment door and I followed him inside like a two-man conga line.

"Get out of my apartment," he shouted.

I looked around the living room. There was computer paraphernalia everywhere. Paper was spewing out of a printer. Stacks of computer paper were on tables and the floor. Computer lights were flashing, and the machines were whirring. It looked like rush hour at a Chuck E. Cheese arcade.

"Get out," Dewey said, and he made an effort to shove me toward the door.

I put my right leg behind his left leg and eased him to the floor like a folding lawn chair.

"Take a seat," I said to him.

"You're trespassing," he said.

"Call the police." I offered him my cell phone. "I have them on speed dial."

When Dewey didn't reach for my phone I knew I had stumbled onto something serious. Sometimes you have to be a genius to catch a thief, and sometimes you just get lucky. Today was my lucky day.

I picked up one stack of papers and thumbed through it. Each page had a long list of names and a corresponding column of numbers. I was able to distinguish three categories of numbers: one was telephone numbers, another was Social Security numbers, and the third looked to be credit-card numbers. From what little I knew about computers, I figured that Louis Dewey was a cyberthief.

"You're stealing identities," I said, proud of my limited computer knowledge.

"No, I'm not," he said, standing up. "I'm just a hacker."

"You can tell your story to the police," I said as I picked up another ream of paper and ran my index finger over the long list of names. I saw a couple I recognized from Boca Heights.

THUMP!

I felt a jolt in my chest.

THUMP! THUMP!

My throat ached. Dewey's face suddenly looked like a wavy television picture. His lips were moving, but I couldn't hear any words.

THUMP! THUMP! THUMP!

First, I felt dizzy and I know I staggered. Then I felt a sharp blow to my forehead. Then I felt nothing.

I jolted awake in pain and saw several, unclear faces above me. I heard garbled voices in the distance. I felt lightning pass through my body and I gasped. There was no more pain. I figured I had died.

Chapter 10

Heartbroken

I was lying on my back, looking up at a pure white sky.

I'm dead, I thought until I saw an air-conditioning vent and realized I was looking at a ceiling.

The coffee-colored face of an angel looked down at me and I knew I was alive.

"Hi, Halle," I croaked softly.

"He's fine," she said turning away. "No more brain damage than usual."

A man's face appeared above me.

"Eddie Perlmutter," he said, "we have to stop meeting like this."

"Okay," I said. "Tell me who you are so I can stop meeting you."

"I'm Dr. Farmelant," he said. "I treated your shoulder wound last year."

"Nothing personal, Doc," I said, "but you seem to be a fuckin' jinx."

He turned to Claudette. "You're right. He seems perfectly normal."

I put a hand to my forehead and felt bandages. "What happened?" I asked.

"You passed out in Mr. Dewey's apartment," the doctor explained. "He said you had just arrived for your computer lesson when you collapsed and hit your head on a table. He called nine-one-one and probably saved your life."

I remembered the events vaguely. I also remembered that I had uncovered Dewey's computer-crime operation. Why would he help me? I had seen enough to put him in jail.

"What happened to Dewey?" I asked the doctor.

"He's in the waiting room."

"You're kidding."

"You can thank him personally after we talk about your medical condition," the doctor assured me.

"I had a heart attack, right?" I guessed, forgetting Dewey for the moment.

"You had a heart event known as SVT."

"What the f-u-c-k is S-V-T?" I asked, confused.

"Supraventricular tachycardia," he explained.

"I have no idea what you just said."

"I'll make it simple," Dr. Farmelant said. "The heart is a muscle with four chambers. The upper chambers are known as the atria and the lower chambers are known as ventricles."

"You call that simple?"

"Sorry." The doctor smiled. "How about . . . the heart is a blood pump for the body?"

"Said like a true simpleton," I told him.

Dr. Farmelant laughed and turned to Claudette. "Is he always like this?"

"Worse," she said without hesitation.

"Okay." The doctor sighed and continued. "We're all born with a natural pacemaker that controls the rhythm of the heart. The pacemaker sends electrical impulses through the heart regularly to make it beat normally but if the impulses are interrupted—"

"You fall and hit your head," I interrupted.

"Not necessarily," the doctor said.

"I did."

"Your heart was racing at two hundred and fifty beats a minute when the medics got to you," Dr. Farmelant explained. "Normal is a hundred and fifty or less."

"Did I set a world's record?"

"No," he said. "But you could have died if you weren't in such good shape."

"Good shape?" I laughed. "My prostate's the size of a bocce ball and my heart just qualified for NASCAR."

"You're in good shape for your age," he said.

"Does anything improve with age?"

"Wine."

"What made my heart slow down?"

"First we injected you with a medicine called Adenosine," he said. "But it didn't work."

"So?"

"We used the defibrillators."

"The paddles," I said in disbelief. I imaged myself flopping on the floor like a haddock. "I thought the paddles started your heart."

"The paddles are used to start or stop the heart with an electrical impulse a thousand times stronger than our own natural pacemakers."

"It sounds like getting hit by lightning," I said. "Do I have heart damage?"

"No, but I think you should have an ablation," the doctor said.

"I'm not pregnant."

"Ablation," he said slowly, "not abortion. It's a very effective procedure. Catheters are inserted into veins in the upper groin—" Dr. Farmelant began.

"I don't like things stuck in my groin," I interrupted him.

Me, neither, Mr. Johnson agreed.

"It's painless," he promised. "Doctors advance the catheters to your heart with a fluoroscope and can record the electrical signals. If they can locate the exact spot where the SVT originates they can coagulate the tissue with radio waves."

"AM or FM?" I asked.

"Eddie, stop joking," Claudette reprimanded me.

"Okay," I said. "Could I die from this procedure? Is that serious enough?"

"Nobody has died yet," the doctor said. "However, the ablation may not work. In order to find the abnormalities the doctor has to be able to induce your rapid heartbeat while he's got you on the table. If he can't find the abnormalities, he can't fix them."

"Why wouldn't he be able to find them?"

"Good question," the doctor said. "Picture yourself in a totally dark room. You can't see a thing and you're trying to locate a glass of water. If you find the glass, it will be easy to drink. The trick is to find the glass."

I actually understood the explanation. "What are my options?"

"We can try medicine like beta-blockers," he said. "But some men lose their sex drive from that kind of medication."

"Forget the blockers," Claudette decided immediately. "He's having the ablation."

Mr. Johnson seconded the motion.

I nodded in agreement.

"Okay, good," Dr. Farmelant said. "I'll get you Jeremy Rothstein. He's known as the rhythm doctor."

"I don't want to learn to dance," I said.

"He's the best," the doctor assured me.

"Only the best for my groin," I agreed.

Thank you, Mr. Johnson said.

"Can I see Dewey now?"

"Of course," Dr. Farmelant said, and made his exit.

"I'm glad you're trying to learn new tricks, you old dog," Claudette said when we were alone.

"What are you talking about?"

"Taking computer lessons," she explained. "I was surprised to hear that."

So was I.

Lou Dewey appeared at the door. "How you doin'?" he asked self-consciously.

"Claudette," I said, squeezing her hand, "could you leave us alone?"

"Of course," Claudette said.

She patted Dewey on his narrow shoulder on the way out.

"Thank you," she told the little man.

Dewey just nodded and studied the floor. Claudette closed the door behind her.

"Thanks for saving my life . . . asshole," I said.

"You're welcome."

"Why did you try to run me over the other night and come to my rescue today?" I asked him.

"You were standing in the middle of a busy street in the dark," he defended himself.

"I was by the side of the road," I told him.

"It was pitch-black for chrissakes." He held out his hands palms up and shrugged. "What were you doing there?"

"Fixing a pothole," I told him.

"Oh, pardon me," Dewey said sarcastically. "I should have known. Everyone in Boca fixes potholes in the dark."

"Yeah, just like everyone in Boca passes on the right like a maniac," I retaliated.

"As a matter of fact they do," he said.

I tried not to smile but failed. "So why did you save my life?" I asked him. "You knew I was going to bust you."

"I couldn't let Superman die," he said seriously.

"I'm not Superman."

"Compared to me you are."

"Superman fights evil," I said. "That would make us enemies."

"I'm not evil," Dewey said. "I'm bad."

"What's the difference?"

"An evil guy would have let you die," he explained.

"Okay, so you're just a plain, ordinary bad guy."

"That's right," he nodded. "It's in my DNA."

"Bullshit," I told him.

"No no . . . it's true," he insisted. "Look at you for instance. I read about your grandfather in the newspaper. He killed a thousand-pound polar bear with his bare hands and saved an entire country. He was a fearless hero . . . you have his genes . . . therefore you're a fearless hero . . . ergo, Superman."

"He killed a five-hundred-pound brown bear with a knife and he only saved one girl who happened to become my grandmother."

"He was still a hero," Dewey said, dismissing my clarification.

"Yes, he was," I agreed.

"Well, my grandfather was a drunk and a stable hand for Dixie the Diving Horse in Atlantic City," Dewey told me. "He actually shoveled shit against the tide for years. Then one day he jumped off the Steel Pier high-diving platform, riding on Dixie's back. He broke his neck on a wave."

"Why did he do that?" I asked.

"He wanted people to notice him," Dewey said.

"Did they?"

"No," Lou Dewey said. "The only Dewey in my family who ever got noticed in Atlantic City was my younger brother, Stewart."

"What did he do?" I asked.

"He stepped on a land mine in Vietnam and came home in a box," Lou told me. "Now there's a PFC Stewart Dewey Memorial Park in Atlantic City."

"So the city noticed him," I said.

"Not really," Lou disagreed. "What the city noticed was the money I donated for the construction of the playground and the annual maintenance."

"You must have thought a lot of your brother," I told him.

"My brother was a schmuck," Dewey said. "He didn't have to go to Vietnam. He didn't even have to go in the army. I could have fixed it with my connections."

"Political connections?"

"Better." Lou waved his hand dismissively. "I had wiseguy connections at the 500 Club."

"Skinny D'Amato's place?"

"You know Skinny?"

"I know *about* Skinny and his club," I clarified. "It was pretty famous. Lots of wiseguys hung out there."

"The best," Lou said proudly. "They could fix anything."

"So what happened with your brother?"

"My father took Stewart drinking on the kid's eighteenth birthday," Dewey told me. "There was a marine recruiting office near one of the bars, and they both went in and tried to enlist. My father was rejected, of course, but my brother was welcomed with open arms."

"Did your father feel guilty?" I asked.

"He didn't even remember doing it," Lou said. "Life was just a big blur to him. My mother, too."

"Wait a minute." A thought flashed through my mind. "You said your brother's name was Stewart?"

He nodded.

"Louie and Stewie Dewey?" I said in disbelief. "Your parents named their sons Louie and Stewie . . . Dewey?"

"Drunks will do shit like that if no one stops them," he said.

I shook my head. "Amazing. So why did you come to Boca Raton?" I asked.

"For the weather," he answered.

"I'd say you came here to commit computer fraud—"

"Don't I have the right to remain silent?"

"Nothing you say will be used against you," I said.

"Do I have the Boca Knight's word on that?"

"I swear," I pledged, holding up my right hand.

He nodded.

"I chose Boca because of a lesson I learned forty years ago scamming people on the Boardwalk," he began. "I grew up while Atlantic City was falling down. I was fourteen in 1964 when the Democratic National Convention was held there."

"Lyndon Johnson, right?"

"Right—big ears, ugly wife." He dismissed history with a shrug. "Anyway, all the old big hotels, the Breakers, the Chelsea, and the Traymore were gone. The Boardwalk had become a low-class place loaded with shell games, schlock souvenirs, bingo parlors, and pitchmen. While the city was falling apart I was just getting my act together. I conned tourists. I fixed businessmen up with hookers. I ran errands for the wiseguys. I was the king of three-card monte."

"I know the game," I said. "Try to pick the jack out of three cards shuffled on the table."

"Right." Dewey sat forward in his chair. "I was the best there was. I used local kids as my shills. You know what a shill is?"

"An assistant you pretend is winning to lure in the real marks," I said. "And when the marks put their money down, they lose. Right?"

"Right." Dewey smiled.

"So what's the lesson you learned?"

"I'm getting there," Dewey said. "One day I hired this nice, quiet kid from the neighborhood to be my shill. His name was Stan Starr, and he looked innocent enough to be a Jewish altar boy. His father, Joe, was a local bar owner and a tough guy. Anyway, Stan does a great job as my shill and we take some poor schmuck for everything he's got. Well, this mark gets really pissed and follows Stan after the game. Stan's clueless he's being followed so he leads the mark right to me. The guy sees me pay Stan off under the boardwalk. Then he follows Stan home and tells Joe Starr the whole story. Joe gets furious. He smacks the shit out of Stan and makes him give the guy his money back. An hour later, Joe Starr has me against a storefront on the Boardwalk. He tells me if I ever use his son in a con again he'll knock all my buck teeth out. He says Stan is gonna be a dentist and maybe he'll fix my teeth someday if I don't get them knocked out first. I'm scared shitless so I just nod. But then Joe says something that makes me laugh and he almost punches my lungs out."

"What did he say?"

"He says his son is gonna marry Suzy Sherby, the butcher's daughter."

"What's so funny about that?"

"The butcher's daughter was prime meat, man," Dewey said. "She wasn't going to marry a wimp like Stanley."

"And you told his father that?"

"I couldn't help myself," Dewey said. "Joe gets pissed and punches me so hard in the stomach he could have scratched my back with his knuckles. I collapse on the Boardwalk and start to turn blue. Joe squats down next to me and tells me this was just a warning and if I wanted to grow up without more brain damage than I was born with then . . . I had to promise not to use his son again."

"So what's the lesson?"

"Here it is," Dewey said. "Later that week I tell the story to Johnny Peepers, this big fat wiseguy at the 500 Club, and he wised me up. He told me never to screw with anyone who has a strong support system like Stan had with Joe. And he also told me never to take a sucker for all he's got because a man with nothing to lose is dangerous. Now, before I pick a mark I check the sucker's support system."

"And you figured the old folks in Boca don't have strong support systems."

Dewey nodded. "Old farts everywhere don't have strong support systems," he said.

"What about their kids?" I asked.

"Most kids have problems of their own," he said. "Besides, everything you need to know about anyone is on the Internet. You just have to know where to look. I can tell who has successful, supportive kids and friends and I can tell who's on their own."

"Don't you feel bad stealing from the elderly?" I asked. "You must have some compassion."

"I never steal enough from any one person to really hurt them," he explained. "Is that compassion?"

"Sounds more like caution to me," I decided.

"So I guess I'm cautiously compassionate," he said. "The truth is I really don't want to hurt anyone badly. It's more like a game to me. I keep score with money."

"You don't seem to spend a lot of money," I observed. "You live in a small apartment and drive an old Cadillac."

"I buy what I need, not what I want."

"Are you married?"

"Who would marry me?"

"Do you have a girlfriend?"

"I have a favorite hooker," he said.

"If you don't spend the money you steal, why do you steal it?"

"For the love of the game," he smiled.

"Seriously, why not quit while you're ahead? Retire."

"Why don't you?" He laughed. "You couldn't retire any more than I could. We both like the action. You're high power. I'm high tech."

"Speaking of high tech, how did you learn so much about computers at your age?"

"I got into the industry early," Lou said. "In 1983 I saw *Time* magazine chose the computer as the Man of the Year. Imagine that. The 1982 Man of the Year was a fuckin' machine. Then in '84, Skinny D'Amato died and I put two and two together. Skinny's world was the past and the computer was the future. I wanted to be part of the future so I started taking courses in 1984 when IBM came out with their first personal computer. I learned everything there was to learn, and by the late eighties the whole world was computerizing. Since I had connections in the gambling business I helped computerize casinos from Atlantic City to Las Vegas. It was fun and I made a bundle. But after a while everyone was doing it and the profit potential went down. It got tough to make a living legitimately so I found other ways."

"You found computer crime and then I found you," I summarized.

"You trying to say that crime doesn't pay," he said, laughing. "In all due respect to the Boca Knight . . . I wouldn't call tracking me down your finest hour as a cop. You were filling a pothole in the dark and I almost ran you over. The odds of that happening are about as high as getting struck by lightning in a fallout shelter."

He laughed and so did I. He was a funny little ferret. He was also a human contradiction and I wondered what to do with him. Twenty years ago I would have taken him directly to jail even if he had saved my life. Now I was confused.

"Go home, Louie," I said impulsively.

"You're kidding, right?" he asked in surprise.

"I need time to think," I snapped at him, irritated by my indecision. "And if you disappear I'll track you down."

"I believe you," he said. "But if I was going to take off . . . I'd be gone already."

"Why didn't you run?"

"I'm not sure," he said, looking me in the eye. "Why aren't you turning me over to the cops right now?"

"I don't know."

"Maybe it's an age thing," Lou speculated. "Maybe we're not who we used to be."

"Get out of here, Louie," I said impatiently.

"I'm outta here," the little man said, and he scurried out the door.

I put my hands behind my head on the pillow and stared up at the ceiling, wondering what was happening to me.

I closed my eyes for what seemed like a minute, and when I woke up I was on an operating table.

Chapter 11

How Do You Mend a Broken Heart?

A heart ablation is an out-of-body experience inside your body.

"There's your heart," Dr. Jeremy Rothstein said while we both looked at a television monitor above our heads. "And there's the fluoroscope on its way to the area."

"This is so cooool," I said under the influence of intravenous Valium.

"Now I'm going to try to make your heart race."

THUD-THUD-THUD!

Whoa!

"That was easy," Dr. Rothstein said encouragingly. "That's great. Now say good night, Eddie."

"Good night, Eddie." I closed my eyes for what seemed like a second.

"Welcome back," I heard the doctor saying through a fog. "You've been gone for quite a while," he told me.

"Do I have rhythm now?"

"Hopefully. Let's see."

Suddenly my heart was racing again.

"I think one of us just failed the test," I said.

"Apparently we have more work to do," Dr. Rothstein said. "See you shortly."

"Don't call me Shorty," I said.

When I woke up I felt like I was floating.

"I think we got it all this time," the doctor said, fiddling with his toys. "Feel anything?"

"Just the slow beating of my heart," I said.

After two more unsuccessful attempts to make my heart race, Dr. Rothstein let up on the accelerator.

"You've got rhythm," he announced. "You can resume normal activity tomorrow."

"That's great," I said. "Can I have more Valium?"

I drifted off to sleep again.

I was awakened by the sound of a foghorn and the smell of low tide.

"That's wonderful, Sorrell," I heard a woman's voice say.

That stinks, I thought.

"Bobbie, this gas is killing me," unseen Sorrell said.

Me too.

I assumed Bobbie was his wife, his mother, his daughter, or his sister because no one else would stay in that room.

"Sorrell Maltzman," Bobbie said. "The doctor told you that passing gas down below is good for you."

It's not good for me, I decided

"My ass is killing me," he said, then started playing the tuba.

I put a pillow over my head and tried to suffocate myself.

A nurse came to take my vital signs.

"Mr. Perlmutter, please remove the pillow from your face."

"I will not," I said through the pillow.

She sniffed the air and covered her nose with her hand.

"Whew," was all she needed to say.

She went to the bathroom, returned with a can of air freshener, and sprayed my area. I removed the pillow from my face.

"God bless you, Lourdes," I said to the Hispanic nurse, reading her name tag.

She removed her hand from her face. "Mr. Maltzman had an abdominal hernia repaired this morning," she said. "He's filled with gas."

"Not as much as he was a minute ago," I said, waving at the air.

She checked my vitals and prepared to go.

"Can you leave the can?" I begged her.

"It's the least I can do." Lourdes rolled her eyes sympathetically.

"By the way, what's this heavy weight on my groin?" I pointed.

Yeah, I'm squashed down here, Mr. Johnson complained.

"It's a sandbag to keep you immobile while you heal," she said. "You have to keep it on for about six hours."

I'll suffocate, Mr. Johnson worried.

I'll air you out, I promised.

How about inviting that nice Jewish divorcee over to lighten my load? he suggested.

You know she's not too happy with me right now, I said, referring to Alicia Fine, the fabulous woman I dated last year who stopped seeing me when she couldn't change me. *The only way we can see her is if we stop seeing Claudette and I stop being me.*

Just lie to her, Mr. Johnson said, trying the same penis logic on me he had used for years.

Before I could answer, Sorrell farted again.

"Wonderful, dear." Bobbie clapped her hands at the trombone solo.

"Thank you, Tommy Dorsey," I moaned loud enough for them to hear.

"Hey, sorry," Sorrell called through the curtain. "I'm full of gas."

"No shit."

"No, just gas. I feel terrible."

"So do I."

"What are you in for?"

"Nothing that deserves the gas chamber," I told him. "I had a heart procedure."

"How'd it go?"

"Good . . . until now," I said. "I think I'm having a heart attack."

Bobbie opened the curtain a little. "Would you two like to talk face-to-face?"

We agreed, and she pulled back the curtain. Sorrell looked to be in his late sixties, bald, and pleasant looking. His wife was much more pleasant looking and she had hair.

"You look familiar," Bobbie said to me.

"He's the Boca Knight," Sorrell said as he pointed and farted.

I sprayed.

The three of us laughed.

I couldn't describe the Maltzmans from Detroit as a breath of fresh air but they were good company for a man with his Johnson stuck in a sand dune.

I made the mistake of explaining my heart ablation to them, which opened the floodgates for a senior-citizen symposium of sickness.

"In 1999, I had abdominal surgery for colon cancer," he told me. "The surgery was a success but resulted in a hernia. I just had it fixed."

Sorrell did a really good impression of a frog exploding.

"You should have that fixed, too." I laughed.

Sorrell laughed but Bobbie didn't. "Why do guys think passing gas is so funny?" she scolded us. "You're like little boys."

She was right. Guys do think farts are funny. I've never known a girl to tell another girl to "pull my finger" and then fart when her finger is pulled. Guys do it all the time. Guys can talk while they burp, too, and think that's hilarious. It's a guy thing.

"Some friends of ours have more serious medical problems than me," Sorrell said.

"That's true." Bobbie nodded. "Homer Berger just lost his leg to diabetes."

"Penny Dobson has lung cancer," Sorrell added.

"Abe Dorfman can't remember a thing," Bobbie recalled.

"Who's Abe Dorfman?" Sorrell asked.

Bobbie moved on. "Bob Livermore got dengue fever in Africa. Carly Camfour's face looks like it melted after her stroke."

"It looked that way before the stroke," Sorrell said.

"Selma Drake looks like Michael Jackson since her nose job," Bobbie commented.

"Joan Sloan's tummy tuck got infected," Sorrell said.

"She's suing her doctor for malpractice," Bobbie informed us.

"Look out below." Sorrell sounded the alarm just before he bombed us.

"I'm going to the air-raid shelter," I said, and laughed.

Sorrell laughed.

Bobbie left the room muttering something about "big babies."

Later, a nurse woke me to take my vital signs.

"Your blood pressure is a little high," she said.

"You just woke me from a dead sleep and scared the shit out of me," I told her.

The Maltzmans were gone and the air was clear. I took a deep breath. I watched television and went back to sleep in the early evening. When I woke up in the morning I knew what I had to do about Lou Dewey.

Chapter 12

Settling Accounts

Claudette picked me up at the hospital and drove me to my apartment. She made me some chicken soup, fed me, and went to work.

I placed a call to the Atlantic City Parks Department and confirmed the existence of the PFC Stewart Dewey Memorial Park. A donation of twenty thousand dollars came in every January from Louis Dewey, his brother, to pay the park's taxes and maintenance.

I was relieved to learn he told me the truth. I phoned him.

"I'm coming over," I said when he answered.

"Why?"

"Rehabilitation or incarceration."

"I've heard rehabilitation isn't your specialty."

"Things change," I told him.

I went to Lou's apartment and explained my proposition.

• • •

"You want me to return all the money I've conned since I've been in Florida?" Lou stammered.

"Every dime."

"I think saving your life is going to prove too expensive for me."

"Look, you saved me but now I have to live with myself," I said. "Besides, you don't even spend the money you steal."

"That's up to me, isn't it?" he said defensively.

"Not anymore," I told him.

"If I refuse?"

"I'll visit you on weekends."

He stared at me incredulously. "You're serious?" he said.

"Well, maybe not every weekend," I hedged.

The little guy shook his head ruefully. He sighed with resignation and swept a stack of papers off the one chair in the room. He sat down and started pressing buttons on the computer. His fingers flew across the keyboard and lists appeared on the screen. He looked up at me. "You're making me nervous," he told me. "Why don't you go rescue someone? I'll return the money."

"Are you telling me to trust you?"

"Yes," Dewey said. "As strange as that may seem."

"Okay," I said, surprising myself.

"You will?" Dewey sounded astounded.

"You didn't lie to me about your brother's memorial park," I said.

"You checked my story?"

"Yes," I told him. "That's why I'm giving you a second chance."

"Well, as long as we're being totally honest with each other," he said, "I want you to know I intend to keep at least a hundred and fifty grand for myself. I earned that money honestly before I got to Boca."

"Okay," I said, accepting his explanation without asking for proof.

What the hell is the matter with me?

I went to my office and checked my messages. Betsy Blackstone had called three times in two days. Izzy Fryberg had called twice. I had four new calls from women wanting me to follow their husbands on Valentine's Day.

I decided to deal with Betsy Blackstone first. I called my urologist, Dr. Alan Koblentz.

"Eddie, how are you?" he asked.

"I'm still peeing like a full-grown gerbil," I told him.

"When you get down to a baby gerbil, call me," he said. "So, what can I do for you today?"

"I want to talk to you about pregnancy."

"You should talk to your gynecologist," he joked.

"I have a hypothetical question," I said.

"Okay, I'll give you a hypothetical answer."

I told him about Betsy Blackstone without using her name. "If this woman was your patient, what advice would you give her?"

"I probably would have sent her to a specialist after the first miscarriage," he said.

"You wouldn't just tell her to try again after two miscarriages, would you?" I asked for verification.

"Certainly not," he said, and then lowered his voice. "Can we talk off the record?"

"Of course. Not a word to anyone," I promised. "You have my word."

"Is Dr. Ronald Cohen involved?"

"How did you know?"

"There's been a lot of speculation about his competence for the past few years," Koblentz said quietly. "I don't like to talk about other doctors but I've heard things."

"I'm told he's very popular," I said.

"He is . . . and he's delivered thousands of healthy babies," Koblentz told me. "But there's definitely been some talk the past few years."

"Any advice?"

"Tell your client to see a specialist."

"Can you help?"

"I'm not a specialist."

"Can you give me a name?"

"The best I know is Albert Dunn," he said.

"Can you get my friend an appointment?"

"I know him well enough to ask for a favor."

"Your mother would be proud of you, Doc," I said.

"Speaking of my mother, she wants to meet you," he told me.

"Tell her to come to my office at three, and I'll see her at five."

Dr. Koblentz didn't respond immediately but then he laughed.

I called Izzy Fryberg and left a message on his answering machine, telling him I was working on his case and would get back to him in a day or two. I slouched back in my chair exhausted, and started to doze.

"Call on line one, Eddie." Olivia's voice jolted me awake.

"Olivia, I only have one line," I said, looking at my watch. It was nearly five.

"Cool," she said. "His name is Howard Larkey, and he talks funny."

I picked up the phone and identified myself. "Eddie Perlmutter."

"Hi Eddie, this is Howard Larkey."

His voice wasn't funny, but it was different.

"What can I do for you, Mr. Larkey?"

"Oh, you're one of those men who get right to the point. I like that." His inflection was vaguely familiar, but I couldn't place it. "First, let me tell you that I'm calling from Wilton Manors, where I live."

"Should that mean something to me?"

"Not necessarily," he said. "How about the word 'gayborhood'?"

"I can guess," I said, finally identifying his speech pattern.

Tell him we're not interested, Mr. Johnson said nervously.

"I'm a gay man—"

"I'm not," I interrupted.

"I assumed that," he said. "But would you have a problem working for a gay man on a gay issue in a gay community?"

"I never thought about it," I said honestly.

"Have you had any experience with gay people?" Howard asked.

Tell him to go fuck himself, Mr. Johnson urged.

"Professionally, yes," I answered him.

"Of course, professionally," he said. "I imagine you saw some gay-bashing when you were with the police in Boston."

"Yes."

"Did you do any yourself?"

"No," I said, irritated.

"What was your reaction to the gay-bashing you witnessed?"

"I had two reactions," I told him. "I saw a gay man beaten senseless for hitting on a teenage boy in a men's room at South Station. I didn't feel bad about that."

"And the other time?"

"I saw an attack on a gay couple in South Boston just because they were in the wrong place at the wrong time. I didn't like that."

"Both good answers, Mr. Knight," he said. "My partner Derek and I would like to hire you for a job."

"What job, Mr. Larkey?"

"Call me Howard," he said.

"If you'll stop calling me Mr. Knight."

"Okay, Eddie," he said. "We'd like you to investigate the disappearance of two friends of ours who vanished from Wilton Manors several weeks ago. We suspect foul play."

"Have you called the police?" I asked.

"We can't call the police."

"Why?"

"I can't talk about it on the phone," he said. "We have to meet."

"Let me ask a few questions first," I insisted. "Is it possible your friends just went away on an extended vacation?"

"They travel a lot but they always coordinate with us," Howard said.

"And this time they didn't coordinate?"

"Correct," Howard said. "And after not seeing or hearing from them for this amount of time I stopped by their house. I let myself in with the key they gave me for house-sitting. I found two airline receipts for two one-way trips to Frankfurt, Germany."

"Case closed," I said. "Your friends left town without saying good-bye."

"They would never do that," he insisted.

"Did you check with the airline to confirm they took the flight?"

"Yes," Howard sighed. "I was a flight attendant in my youth and I used all my connections to get this very confidential information. The flight attendant on their flight said Mr. and Mrs. Dietrich got on the plane in wheelchairs accompanied by a traveling companion."

"Wait a minute," I said. "You just said, 'Mr. and Mrs.' Are you telling me this is not a gay couple?"

"Of course, it's a gay couple," Howard said.

"But you said it was a man and a woman."

"No, I said it was a husband and wife."

"I don't think I want to get involved," I said, exasperated with his double-talk. "It's not my type of case if it's even a case. I think your friends just took off without telling you."

"What if I told you I was positive they would never do that?"

"I'd say you don't know them as well as you think you do . . . and I still don't want the case."

"What if I told you Eileen is a very active seventy-six-year-old and has never been in a wheelchair? Neither has John."

"I'd say maybe they got hurt . . . and no thank you."

"Okay," he said. "What if I told you they are very private people and would never hire a travel companion?"

"I'd say they decided they needed help," I told him. "And then I'd say thank you for calling . . . and hang up."

There was a silence on the line before Howard asked his next question.

"What would you say if I told you Eileen has a pair of testicles?"

"Figuratively or literally?" I asked.

"Literally."

"I would say . . . I'll take the case," I said.

"You're hired."

"When do you want me to start?"

"As soon as you can put on your little suit of armor and get here."

"How do I get to Wilton Manors?" I asked.

"Just close your eyes, click your heels three times, and say *'There's no place like home.'*"

"Cut the shit."

"Alright, do you have GPS?"

"I don't even have power windows," I told him.

He told me to follow the yellow brick road, giggled . . . then gave me detailed directions to his gayborhood.

Chapter 13

Boys in the Gayborhood

Wilton Manors is south of Boca Raton and northwest of Fort Lauderdale. I followed Howard Larkey's instructions and arrived at his modest ranch house on NW 23rd Street late afternoon.

A handsome, white-haired man in his sixties opened the door. He was in khaki shorts and a loose-fitting flowered shirt. He wore flip-flops. He was round but not fat.

"Howard?" I asked.

"Hardly," the man said, with a feminine hand gesture. "I'm Derek Benjamin."

"I'm Howard." A human block of granite appeared behind Derek.

Howard Larkey wasn't as tall as he was massive. He had a full head of white hair cut short and combed forward, like a Roman senator. His soft facial features were incongruous with his hard body and bull neck.

Howard eased past Derek and held out his hand. His grip was firm.

"I can see I'm not what you expected," Howard said, smiling.

"No one expects King Kong," Derek said, retreating into the house. I followed.

We sat at a circular table in a dining area. A small, white poodle skittered to a stop at my feet and started humping my leg.

"Beau, you slut," Howard scolded the dog, pulling him away.

The dog trotted to the kitchen where Derek was making coffee.

"He humps everyone, the little tramp," Howard said. "So, where should we begin?"

"I think we should start at the testicles," I said.

"I'd like that." Derek chuckled and poked my shoulder with his index finger as he joined us at the table.

I recoiled like I'd been Tasered.

"I'm sorry," Derek said immediately. "I was just joking."

I felt like a homophobic idiot.

"Eddie, relax," Howard intervened. "We don't want to seduce you. We want to hire you."

"I'm sorry," I apologized. "I guess I'm a little uncomfortable."

"Well, dear boy, you're perfectly safe with us guys," Howard reassured me. "We're gay men but we're monogamous. I guess you need to get to know us a little better."

"Good idea," I said. I folded my arms across my chest, leaned back in my chair, and said, "I'm listening."

"Derek, tell the nice man all about yourself." Howard held his hand out, palm up, as if he were introducing a guest speaker. "And try to keep it short."

Derek told me he was born in Palestine in 1939. His mother was a German-Jewish refugee from Berlin. His father was an

English army officer. In 1940, Derek's father was recalled to England during the Battle of Britain, and his family went with him. In 1945, when the Second World War was over, his parents divorced, and Derek returned to the Promised Land with his mother. They settled in Tel Aviv in 1948, when Derek was nine years old. The British were giving up control of Palestine at that time and the Arab-Israeli conflict began.

"A great value was placed on the toughness of children in those days," Derek said. "All the boys played soldier, except me."

"What did you do?" I asked.

"I played jump rope with the girls." He smiled. "But I was still able to contribute to the war effort. The boys learned to fight by beating me up and the girls practiced first aid by bandaging me."

Derek said he and his mother emigrated to America in 1957, after she married a German count who only seemed interested in counting her money. They in turn counted him out after a few years, and Derek left home with his mother's blessing and lived an openly gay lifestyle.

"So, your mother was supportive," I said.

"Totally," Derek said.

Howard and Derek met on a plane in 1984. Derek was a passenger and Howard was a flight attendant. They had nothing in common and had been together since.

Howard told me he hadn't come out of a great life. He said he knew he was gay when he was twelve years old and tried to keep it a secret.

"As a teenager I skulked around New York piers, truck stops on the Jersey Turnpike, and under the West Side Highway. It was rather tawdry and dangerous for a scrawny weakling like me. It wasn't unusual for me to have sex with some conflicted truck driver and then have him kick the shit out of me to prove to himself he wasn't gay."

Howard said he took up bodybuilding and the art of self-defense when "I decided no one was going to whip my ass . . . unless, of course, I was in the mood."

I laughed.

"Are you still interested?" Howard asked hopefully.

"I charge fifty bucks an hour," I told them, nodding my head.

"I used to charge ten for the whole night," Howard said. "Or pay ten dollars if necessary."

"Tell me about Eileen's testicles," I said.

"You have a one-track mind for a heterosexual man." Howard stood up. "First I want to show you Wilton Manors. I think it will make it easier for you to understand everything."

We left Derek at home and drove to downtown Wilton Manors in Howard's four-door Cadillac.

"Why didn't Derek come?" I asked.

"He's a homebody," Howard told me. "He loves to read and to listen to music. Occasionally he'll play the piano. He's quite good. Me, I'm still a flirt but I'm monogamous."

We rode in silence for a while until Howard turned onto a busy street.

"This is Wilton Drive," he told me. "It's the epicenter of Wilton Manors."

Wilton Drive seemed like any other small, downtown area to me except ninety-nine percent of the people on the street were men, walking arm in arm, hand in hand.

"This town has twelve thousand residents and around sixty percent are gay people. Twenty years ago, Victoria Park in Fort Lauderdale was the number one gayborhood. Now it's Wilton Manors."

"Technically, what's a gayborhood?"

"Loosely defined," Howard said, with a flick of his wrist, "a gayborhood is a neighborhood that's over forty percent gay.

Anyway, when George's Alibi opened in 1997, a lot of the gay community relocated here."

"What's George's Alibi?"

Howard turned into the parking lot of a small shopping center and pointed to a restaurant with a sidewalk café. "That's George's Alibi. A guy named George, naturally, converted a boarded-up bank into an openly gay nightspot, and the rest is history." Howard eased the Cadillac into a parking space and opened his car door.

"Are we going inside?" I asked, apprehensively.

"Don't worry, sweetheart, I'll protect you."

We stood in the parking lot and looked around.

"Check out the shops," Howard said.

I read the signs: HUMPEE'S PIZZA. MAIN STREET GYM. GAY MART. JAVA BOYS.

"Welcome to ground zero," Howard told me.

"What are Underoos?" I asked, reading a sign in the window of the We're Everywhere clothing store.

"Underoos is a brand name. Ginch-Gonch is another big name in gay underwear. They have different styles with names like Pocket Rockets and Weiner Eaters."

"How subtle," I said as we entered George's Alibi.

The place was jammed with men: short, tall, fat, thin, young, old, good-looking, and homely. I checked the time. It was not quite seven.

"George's has three shifts every night," Howard said. "From four to nine it's the cocktail crowd, ages forty to sixty. The younger ones you see here at this hour are usually hustlers or tourists."

"Are the tourists gay?"

"It's an eclectic group," Howard said. "The gay tourists are cruising. The straight tourists are curious. From nine to twelve you see the in crowd: attractive, single, young professionals looking to meet someone. From twelve to four in the morning you get all the sluts looking to get laid. I come here almost every night around now to shoot pool and to have a few drinks. I know a lot of the people here."

To prove his point Howard said hello to several men on his way to the pool tables in the back of the room. He was invited to play.

"Will you be alright if I shoot some pool?"

"Sure," I said, unsurely. I saw an empty seat at the crowded bar and sat down.

I looked at the men at the bar. They looked at me. Mr. Johnson looked away. Some of the men stared brazenly, some furtively, but when I didn't make eye contact they quickly lost interest.

The body language of the older men at the bar was loud and clear. They understood they now had to pay for what came free and easy in days gone by too fast. Their well-worn faces could no longer be cleaned and pressed enough to hide the wrinkles and age spots. Complicated comb-overs couldn't cover hairless heads of fools who only fooled themselves. Their "use by" date had expired and their futures were less comforting than the memories of their pasts.

"Can I buy you a drink?" someone asked from behind.

I turned slowly and saw a smiling man wearing eye shadow, face powder, and a touch of lipstick. Under the makeup he appeared to be my age.

"I'm not gay," I told him.

"Of course not," he said. "My name's Gill."

"I'm serious, Gill," I said. "I'm not gay."

"None of us here are." He laughed.

"Gill, one more time," I said, starting to stand. A red spot popped before my eyes and Gill must have seen it, too.

He stepped back and held up his hands in a passive gesture.

"No offense," he said, "but you do know this is a gay bar, don't you?"

"Yes, I know." I sat down again and took a deep breath. "I'm here with a friend."

"Is your friend gay?" Gill asked hopefully.

"Yes, but he's married," I said.

"Oh, you mean he's still in the closet." Gill sounded disappointed.

"No, he's not," I said, defending Howard's gayness. "He's married to a man."

"Does your friend happen to be Howard Larkey?"

"How did you know?" I asked, surprised.

"Well, first of all, I see him shooting pool over there"—he pointed to the tables—"and second of all, Howard and Derek refer to themselves as married. It's too bad the state of Florida doesn't agree."

"I don't understand."

"The state of Florida doesn't recognize same sex marriages," Gill said.

"Apparently that doesn't bother Howard and Derek."

"Oh, it bothers them," Gill said, rolling his eyes. "Without legal status, gay couples lose about one thousand federal and state benefits—like parenting, jointly owned property, annuities, pensions, wrongful death benefits. Would you like to hear more?"

I shrugged to let Gill know I didn't care one way or the other.

"Did you ever hear of the Defense of Marriage Act?"

I shook my head.

"It's an act of Congress that bars federal recognition of same sex marriages and allows states to make their own decisions," he explained. "In other words, Uncle Sam won't let Uncle Max marry Uncle Judd because a marriage isn't a marriage unless there's a penis and a vagina involved. Tits are optional."

I felt fingers on my back.

Oh jeez, Mr. Johnson reacted.

I saw Gill's hands in front of me, so it wasn't him.

"I see you've met the local gay lawyer," Howard said, patting my back now.

I sighed, and Howard sensed my relief.

"Did you almost punch me just now?" he asked, removing his hand.

"You can't sneak up on me like that," I said, unhappy.

"Especially not in a gay bar," he added, and he slapped his palm on his forehead. "*Duh*, what was I thinking? Sorry." He turned to Gill. "He's not gay, you know."

"That's the first thing he told me." Gill made a sad face. "How disappointing."

"Do you know who he is?" Howard said.

I knew Howard was about to introduce the Boca Knight to the gayborhood, so I grabbed his shoulder and squeezed a random nerve ending.

Howard winced and got the hint.

"We have to go," I said, getting off my bar stool and pulling Howard with me.

"Who are you?" Gill wanted to know.

"Nobody," I told him.

"We're all somebody," Gill said, waving a fond farewell.

When we were outside I reprimanded Howard while he rubbed his shoulder.

"Don't tell anyone who I am," I said. "Our business is confidential."

"You're right, you're right," he scolded himself, still rubbing his shoulder. "That hurt."

"Good."

We walked the streets of Wilton Manors.

"The New Moon is for lesbians," Howard said, pointing at a sign over a door.

We didn't go inside.

We stopped in front of a real-estate office and I read some ads.

"What does LGBT mean?" I asked Howard, pointing at a sign in the window.

"Lesbian, Gay, Bisexual, and Transgender," he explained. "That's an ad for affordable housing for seniors of one of those persuasions."

"I never thought about those kinds of seniors." I shrugged.

"Everyone gets old," Howard said. "And you don't outgrow your condition."

We walked on.

"Hi, Sanford. Hi, Dirk." Howard waved to a couple passing us, going in the opposite direction. They waved back and looked me up and down.

"Are you cheating on Derek, Howard?" Sanford asked.

"Moi?" Howard pointed to himself. "Never!"

They shared a laugh. I walked ahead of Howard.

"Are you embarrassed?" Howard asked, jogging to catch me.

"They probably think I'm gay now," I said.

"You wanted to be anonymous."

"Yeah, but I didn't want to be gay," I grumbled.

"Neither did I," Howard said. "I wasn't like I was asked to fill out a multiple-choice form—"

"Enough," I said, holding up a hand.

He held up both hands. "Okay, okay."

We continued walking. We visited a gay strip club called The Boardwalk and a sports bar named Sidelines.

"What's the hottest pickup place in town?"

"The Publix Supermarket at Five Corners," he said. "Don't ask me why."

I didn't.

We finished our tour at Tropics, a mellow place. The crowd

was older and the music slower. People were either having dinner in a quiet restaurant atmosphere on one side of the place or milling around the bar area across the room. Howard and I took a quiet table near the bar.

"Eileen and John came here a lot," Howard told me. "Everyone knew them."

"Not everyone knew about Eileen's scrotum, I assume," I said.

"Correct. I think Derek and I were the only ones they trusted with their secret."

"So, for appearance's sake, they were a nice, elderly, heterosexual married couple, retired in Wilton Manors," I said.

Howard nodded.

"What about their backgrounds?"

"John was a Baptist, oddly enough," Howard said, "and Eileen was a wandering Jew. They lived together in New York City first; Ames, Iowa, second; San Francisco next; and now, here."

"Have you talked to anyone else about your missing-person theory?"

"Sure. I brought it up one night here at the bar," Howard said. "One of the bartenders said he overheard the Dietrichs talking about taking a trip to Europe. That made me less worried. Then a few days later, postcards started arriving at the bar from all over Europe. I'd know John and Eileen's handwriting anywhere and the cards were definitely written by them."

"Is that the bartender who overheard them?" I pointed to a medium-sized blond man behind the bar.

Howard nodded.

"He looks familiar," I said.

"I doubt it. He's only been in Wilton Manors a few months. His name is Edik Davidavitch, Russian."

"Is he gay?"

"No," Howard said. "And he lives with the most dreadful

woman. A Miss U Da Worst contestant if there ever was one. Her name is Irene Kostanski and she's a waitress here. I'll point her out to you before we leave. Both of them said they heard the Dietrichs discussing a European trip."

"Would the Dietrichs confide in them?"

"People tend to talk to their bartenders," Howard pointed out. "They could have said something in passing, I guess."

"Did anyone else hear Eileen and John talk about a trip besides those two?" I asked.

"Not that I know of," he said. "Why do you ask?"

"Why would two people who happen to live together be the only two people in this place to hear about the Dietrichs' trip?"

"Coincidence?"

"Maybe," I said. "Do you know Edik and Irene well?"

"Not really," Howard said, stroking his chin. "Let's see . . . They said they met in New York City right after Edik came over from Russia. She said something about coming from a town in western Massachusetts." He scratched his head. "Chica-something."

"Chicopee?" I guessed. "There's a large Polish population there."

"Could be." Howard shrugged. "They said they met at a restaurant where Edik was working as a bartender. She came looking for a job. They've been together ever since."

"Did you check out their story?"

"Why would I?" Howard asked.

I watched Edik for a while. He was a little slow preparing drinks and referred to the order slips repeatedly, indicating to me that he had a limited memory.

Not too smart, I put in his file.

He strutted behind the bar and seemed to be trying too hard to be macho.

Hiding something?

After a half hour of observing him I got up and headed for the door. Howard followed me. When we passed the dining area, Howard pointed out Irene Kostanski. She had short brown hair streaked with purple. She had square shoulders and big hands. I guessed she was in her late thirties.

"She doesn't look like much," I observed.

"She looks like a dyke to me," Howard commented bluntly.

"That would be an insult to all dykes," I said. "Let's get out of here."

Howard drove me back to his house and parked in the driveway.

"Okay," I said, as he shut off the engine. "It's time to tell me more about Eileen Dietrich's testicles. How long has he been in panties?"

"Over thirty years."

"How did you find out the missus was a mister?" I asked.

"They confided in us," he said. "They said they needed a support system."

I remembered Lou Dewey talking about a support system.

"Tell me the whole story," I said, slouching down in my seat.

"You're going to find this hard to believe," he said, shaking his head.

"Try me."

Howard told me the whole story and he was right. It was hard to believe.

Chapter 14

Boys and Girls Together

It was a little after 11 P.M. when I got onto I-95 North. I drove slowly but my mind was racing to process the bizarre story of Eileen and Johnny Dietrich . . . as told to me by Howard Larkey.

Eileen Dietrich was actually born Elliot Davidson in 1930. He was a cute kid with such delicate facial features that some people said he was too pretty to be a boy. By the time Elliot was nine years old, he knew he was different. He liked to dress in his mother's clothes and wear makeup. He liked to play with dolls. He was sexually aroused by the sight of naked boys in the shower after gym class at school. When he was a teenager, Elliot dated girls and enjoyed kissing them but he knew he would prefer kissing boys. Elliot realized he was gay but never acted on his tendencies and graduated high school still a virgin . . . and still in the closet.

When Elliot Davidson met Johnny Dietrich of Flushing, New York, during their freshman year at City College they immediately became lovers. They kept their relationship secret at school but when they graduated in June 1951, Elliot and Johnny barged out of the closet.

Bad timing.

The fifties were not good years for gay pride. Their parents disowned them, their few heterosexual associations became strained, and they became outcasts in the straight world. They moved to Greenwich Village where their lifestyle was accepted within the borders of Broadway, the Hudson River, Houston Street, and Fourteenth Street.

John became an interior decorator and did well enough to support the two of them. Elliot could afford to dabble in unmarketable poetry and unpopular politics. He frequented the same smoky coffeehouses on MacDougal Street that acclaimed poet Allen Ginsberg had. Unfortunately, none of Ginsberg's talent rubbed off on Elliot but some of his politics did. Ginsberg talked openly about communism and the establishment of a counterculture in America and Elliot listened. In 1951, when Julius and Ethel Rosenberg went on trial for spying on behalf of the Russians, Elliot joined the legions of protesters who insisted the husband and wife were innocent. When the United States was at war in Korea in the early fifties Elliot was among the first war protesters in the east. He protested the cause, the war, and the unfair selective service draft. Elliot protested everything that he believed needed protesting until J. Edgar Hoover's FBI agents came knocking on his door and threatened him.

"J. Edgar Hoover is concerned about you," a very serious agent told Elliot.

"I'm concerned about him, too," Elliot said. "I hear he's a homosexual."

"Then maybe you've also heard he has the power to harass political dissenters and amass secret files using illegal methods," the agent said with a mean smile.

"Which would explain why you're here." Elliot pointed at the agent.

"Correct. Do you realize you never registered for the draft?" the agent droned.

"I do. Uncle Sam doesn't want me," Elliot said.

"Maybe he does now," the agent said, and never stopped smiling.

"Isn't the army concerned about gay people being susceptible to blackmail from foreign powers?"

"We are concerned about the Lavender Scare but that doesn't mean we don't want you."

"I feel better already," Elliot said.

"Did you know that you're on a list of twelve thousand names of disloyal Americans?" the agent told him.

"Who else is on the list?" Elliot asked.

"I ask the questions," the agent said. "Did you know I can arrest you right now?"

"On what charge?"

"The draft for starters," he said. "Then we can move up to sedition . . . like the Rosenbergs. My guess is that those two will get the electric chair."

"Are you trying to intimidate me?" Elliot put his hands on his hips, defiantly.

"Absolutely."

"It's working."

In 1953, the Rosenbergs were found guilty and were executed in the electric chair.

That same year Johnny bought Elliot a small coffee shop in the village named What Now where Elliot could make a few bucks, smoke marijuana, and dispense political advice without getting directly involved. From 1964 to 1969, several rising stars and thousands of fallen angels passed through the doors of What Now. They filled Elliot's register with cash and one another's

heads with ideas. Elliot wasn't a guru but he was considered a
knowledgeable guy who could be trusted. He was one of them . . .
just an older version. Antiwar activists talked openly in his presence and listened to his advice. By 1969, Johnny had become the
"go-to" decorator in the Village and Elliot was the "go to hell"
dissenter.

Stop the war. Start gay rights.

The Stonewall Inn's three-day gay liberation protests were
partially planned in Elliot's place with his input. Peace signs and
gay rights signs appeared in his windows and on the walls of
What Now. Elliot didn't attend the Stonewall event, preferring
to keep a low profile, but federal agents took notice of his involvement anyway and made his old records new again. The FBI
started taking pictures and filming the comings and goings at
What Now and on March 6, 1969, they got a lensful.

Two young women were photographed rushing into the
What Now coffee shop. Moments later the camera caught them
running out the door with Elliot. The agents followed the trio
several blocks to an apartment house in the Village. Elliot and
the two women went into the building. The FBI was now taking
movies and photographs of the building. Within an hour, Elliot
and the two young women came out of the building looking
upset and arguing with each other. One of the girls waved her
arms wildly in the air, shouting in anger, then she started to cry
and slumped against Elliot. He put his arm around her shoulder.
The three of them walked directly toward the camera and were
perfectly framed in the scene of the third-floor apartment exploding. The blast blew out the windows, showering the street
with glass. Flames shot from the empty panes like a dragon's
breath. The cameras kept rolling and captured the clear image
of Elliot and the two girls running away. There were no pictures
of the three young bomb-makers killed by the explosion inside

the building. An innocent bystander also died when a piece of flying glass cut her throat.

In the few hours it took federal agents to get a legal search warrant for What Now and the apartment the decorator and the dissident shared . . . they had vanished. When FBI agents knocked on the door to the apartment no one answered, but Fiona Brown, a thirty-five-year-old angry black lesbian opened her door at the other end of the hall.

At this point in the story Howard did a great job of re-creating the exchange between an FBI agent and the black lesbian . . . as told to him by Elliot and John.

"Whatchu want?" Fiona said she said.

"We're with the FBI."

"Whatchu want, G-man?" Fiona said.

"We're looking for Elliot Davidson. We have a search warrant."

"Shove them warrants up J. Edgar's ass. I hear he likes that."

"I'm prepared to use force," the agent said.

"I hear he likes that, too," Fiona swears she said to the G-man.

"Who are you?" the agent asked.

"I'm da queen of denial," Fiona solemnly swore she said.

"What's your name?"

"Fiona," Fiona said.

"Do you know where these guys went?" the agent asked.

"Elliot could be anywhere," Fiona said she said. *"Johnny said he was movin' to Iowa to get married."*

"We heard they were a gay couple." The agent smiled as if he had caught her.

"Elliot is gay as a clown," Fiona said. *"But Johnny goes either way."*

"Are you sure?"

"I fucked him myself."

"Was Dietrich an agitator?" the agent asked.

"*No, he was a decorator,*" Fiona said.

"*Are you sure he went to Iowa?*"

"*I'm sure it begins with an I.*"

Fiona told Elliot that one of the agents lost his patience and broke down the door to their apartment. They proceeded to search it thoroughly. Fiona said she watched from the broken doorway.

"*Your friends left all their stuff,*" one agent remarked.

"*They tole me they didn't want nothin' no more. Said I could have everything. Furniture, too,*" Fiona said she said.

"*You'll let us know if your friends contact you,*" the agent said before he departed, handing her his card.

"*Just 'cause I fucked one of them don't make them my friends,*" Fiona said she said.

"The truth was, Elliot and John had been Fiona's friends for years," Howard told me.

He said that Elliot and Johnny had phoned Fiona a few hours after the explosion. They told her about Elliot's involvement and prior record with the FBI. Fiona told them that news of the explosion was already on television and that three bomb-makers and an innocent bystander had been killed. Pictures of Elliot and his two female friends were being shown regularly on the air. They made a decision during that phone call that Elliot Davidson had to vanish.

It was Fiona's idea to disguise Elliot as a woman and to get him as far away from the Village as possible.

"*It ain't enough for you to just put on a dress and stuff a bra,*" Fiona insisted. "*You gotta establish a new identity with papers and shit.*"

"*How do we get forged papers?*" John asked.

"*I ain't talking about forged nothin',*" Fiona announced. "*I'm talking the real thing. A real name. A real Social Security number. The works.*"

"How do we do that?"

Fiona was a cleaning woman at the New York City Women's House of Detention in the Village.

"They're planning on tearing down the jail in a couple of years," *Fiona told them. "They're already moving a lot of old records into a warehouse in the Village. I'm cleaning the warehouse, too. I can get any file I want. No one knows who the fuck is in those old convict files anymore, released or deceased."*

Fiona stole the identity of Eileen Haley, a dead hooker buried in a numbered grave on Harts Island in Long Island Sound.

Eileen Haley, born in 1929 and died in 1968, was reborn in 1969 in the body of Elliot Davidson. The newly resurrected Eileen married John Dietrich in a private civil ceremony in Ames, Iowa, and the FBI agents, following up on Fiona's lead, verified the paperwork. All the necessary legal documents were in order and Eileen and John were pronounced man and wife in accordance with the laws of the state of Iowa.

They lived peacefully in the Hawkeye state for five years until J. Edgar Hoover died in 1972, Nixon resigned in 1974, and the Vietnam war ended in 1975. America became a kinder, gentler place, emboldening the Dietrichs to move away from the country's heartland.

They moved to San Francisco's Castro District and lived there in peace for a few years. Elliot was Eileen most of the time but on a whim he would be Elliot, John's old buddy. No one knew their secret and they had fun with it.

In 1978, however, gay political activist Harvey Milk and San Francisco mayor George Moscone were shot to death by a homophobic political loser named Dan White. Claiming temporary insanity caused by consuming too much junk food (the Twinkie Defense), White was sentenced to only five years. The decision ignited the Castro District and the neighborhood was engulfed in the emotional flames of gay riots. Federal and local policemen rushed to the scene to put out the blaze, and the area became too hot for John and Elliot. They ran again, first to the gay community in Fort Lauderdale, and then to Wilton Manors, where they were welcomed as part of the heterosexual sixty percent in the gayborhood.

I noticed the Palmetto Road exit and thought of Betsy Blackstone's case. Impulsively I turned off I-95 North and drove the few minutes to Mizner Park.

I took a seat at the bar in Mendy's Grill and asked the boyish bartender, whose name tag read GIANNI, if the manager was in. He pointed to a tall, handsome young man who appeared to be in his early thirties.

"That's one of them," Gianni said. "His name's Bradley. You want to talk to him?"

"No. I was just curious," I told him.

I spent the next hour sipping an old favorite from the North End called a Godfather—Amaretto and Scotch—and watching Bradley Blackstone in action. He was all business, smiling, shaking hands, and patting backs.

"Hey, Bradley," the bartender said—I was afraid he was going to blow my cover—"didn't your shift end already?"

"I decided to stay late," Bradley answered and moved on without pausing.

"He's gotta be crazy to stay late," Gianni winked at me like we were old buddies. "His wife is a knockout. I'd be home on time for her."

"Maybe he has someone on the side," I poked around.

"Bradley? Never," the bartender scoffed. "He's as straight as they come. And he has plenty of chances. Women love him. Half the waitresses have tried to hook up with him but he couldn't care less."

I left the bar about a half hour later and sat in my MINI,

waiting for Bradley to come out. Eventually he exited the front door, got into a silver Lexus SC430 parked at the valet stand, and put down the hard-top convertible. He eased away from the curb and I chugged after him at a safe distance.

He exited Mizner Park and turned south. He lived north. When we reached A1A he turned right into a parking lot in front of a small business mall named One Ocean Boulevard. The lot was empty at this early morning hour. I continued south and turned onto a side street. I saw Bradley in my rearview mirror walking across A1A toward the ocean

He's meeting someone, Mr. Johnson said.

You're a cynic, I disagreed.

I'm a penis.

I trotted quietly across A1A. I saw Bradley's silhouette against the dim light of the moon. He was standing under a gazebo near a sign that read SOUTH BEACH PAVILION.

I hid in the bushes by the side of the road. I could hear the waves but couldn't see the ocean. I watched as Bradley paced and looked repeatedly at his watch.

She's late, Mr. Johnson said.

Give him a chance, you little prick.

I had to admit that it did look like Bradley was waiting for someone.

I hate this job, I said to Mr. Johnson.

I think it's kinda kinky, he replied.

Bradley Blackstone removed a cell phone from his pocket, poked it with one finger then held it to his ear. Whoever he called was on speed dial. I moved closer.

"Did I wake you, Kitten?" I heard him ask.

Kitten! I told you we're talking pussy here, Mr. Johnson crowed.

Shut up, you idiot.

"It's nice to hear your voice, too," Bradley said, responding to words I couldn't hear.

Pause.

"I worked late again tonight so I wouldn't have to face Betsy," he responded. "She doesn't wait up for me anymore."

Pause.

"It *is* a mess," he agreed. "But I'm not ready to confront her. She's very vulnerable right now."

Pause.

"I know it has to be done," he said. "I'll talk to her."

Pause.

"You're yawning," he noted. "Go to sleep."

Pause.

"No, it's alright. I haven't got anything more to say. I just wanted to hear your voice."

Pause.

"I love you, too, Kitten," he said. "Good night."

He snapped the phone shut and stared out at the ocean.

Told you! Mr. Johnson rubbed it in.

I had heard enough. I moved silently from my hiding place and made my way back to the MINI.

As I drove away I hit the steering wheel with my open palm. "Damn it," I said. "I hate when this happens."

Chapter 15

Joy Feely and Louie Dewey

The phone rang and startled me from a sound sleep. I looked at my watch. It was nine thirty in the morning.

"Are you still in bed?" Lou Dewey asked.

"I had a late night."

"Doing what?

"Cruising gay bars."

He's gonna think you're serious, Mr. Johnson warned me.

"Whatever turns you on," Lou said. "I just wanted to let you know I returned all the money and nearly died of an anxiety attack. I have about a hundred and fifty grand to my name now and no visible means of support. Thank you very much."

"You're welcome. I'll call you right back," I said.

I called Frank Burke at Boca Police Headquarters and I asked for Joy Feely's number.

"Why?" he asked. "You interested in her?"

"No," I told him. "I know someone who needs a job and might be perfect for her."

"She definitely could use some help," Frank assured me, and gave me her number.

Joy answered her office phone herself when I called. She seemed delighted to hear from me. I made an appointment with her for noon at her office without telling her the reason. I called Dewey, gave him Joy's office address, and told him to meet me there at ten after twelve. I refused to explain why.

I went to my office, dreading the call I had to make to Betsy Blackstone. Finally I dialed her number.

"Hi, Eddie," she said, sniffling. "Have you found anything yet?"

"Maybe," I hedged.

"Tell me, tell me," she said nervously. "He's seeing someone else, isn't he?"

"Calm down," I said. "I didn't actually see him with another woman."

"It's not a man, is it?"

"I don't think so," I said, not so sure of myself after spending a night in Wilton Manors. "Does the name Kitten mean anything to you?"

"Sure, that's what he calls his kid sister, Katherine," she said.

I dropped the phone on my desk.

His kid sister, for chrissakes. HIS KID SISTER! He was talking to his kid sister on the phone last night.

Frankly I'm disappointed, Mr. Johnson said.

Jerk!

I picked up the phone.

"Sorry, I lost my grip," I said.

"What about his sister?" she asked.

"I heard him talking to her on the phone last night."

"He talks to her all the time," she told me. "They're very close."

"Betsy, I'm convinced your husband is not cheating on you," I decided.

"He didn't come home until after two in the morning last night," she said sadly.

"I know," I said. "I followed him. He wasn't with another woman."

"Where was he?"

"He drove to the beach and called his sister," I told her.

"We had a favorite place at the beach at night."

"Near Palmetto?"

"Yes, under a gazebo."

"That's where he was," I said.

"Why would he go there without me?"

"Maybe he goes there to think about you," I tried.

"Maybe he goes there to avoid me," she sniffled.

"That, too," I agreed.

"What should I do?"

"I think you should see a doctor," I told her.

"What kind of doctor? A psychiatrist?"

"An obstetrician," I specified. "I pulled some strings and got you an appointment with a specialist in problem pregnancies."

"I told you I had an obstetrician."

"You also told me you had two miscarriages," I said. "You need a second opinion."

"I like Dr. Cohen."

"This isn't a personality contest," I reminded her. "Write this down and don't argue with me." I gave her the information.

Next, I went to Joy Feely's office on Federal.

The sign on her door read:

JOY FEELY—COMPUTER SPECIALIST

Her office was like Louie Dewey's living room: computers everywhere, printers, screens, blinking lights. Joy looked up from the papers on her desk, smiled, and waved.

"Hi, Eddie," she said, touching her hair and giving me her toothy grin. "To what do I owe the pleasure?"

"I heard you need help and I may have the perfect man for you," I said.

She seemed a little disappointed but recovered quickly.

"I do need someone really good but I can't afford really good."

"This guy will come reasonably," I assured her. "His name is Lou Dewey and he's a computer fraud."

She blinked several times but to her credit, she didn't ask me to leave.

"I can't hire a felon," she said. "I do a lot of work for the police."

"He's not a felon," I assured her.

"You just said he was a computer fraud."

"He's actually never been convicted," I offered a defense.

"Then how do you know he's a fraud?" she asked.

"I caught him in the act," I said.

"Did you turn him in to the police?"

Before I could answer her logical question, there was a knock on the door.

"That would be him," I said.

"You invited him here?" She didn't sound happy.

I nodded.

"Come in," I said, knowing she was too surprised to say anything.

The door opened and Lou Dewey entered, wearing black slacks and a black shirt with a widespread collar. He looked like a bucktoothed, homely, little Elvis.

"Well, here I am," Lou announced.

He looked at Joy.

She looked at him.

They stared at each other.

It must have been like looking in a mirror for them.

Joy seemed short of breath and Lou was breathless altogether.

I cleared my throat loudly to get their attention.

"Lou Dewey, meet Joy Feely," I said. "Lou's a computer genius, Joy."

They nodded numbly at each other.

"Say hello to Joy, Lou," I prompted him. "Joy . . . Lou."

They nodded again. Lou cleared his throat. Joy fidgeted with the top button of her blouse.

"I'll leave you two alone to talk business." I went to the door. Neither of them moved.

I exited the office and was halfway down the hall when I heard a crash from Joy's office.

Oh shit, I thought. I ran back to the office and opened the door.

Lou Dewey was lying on top of Joy Feely, who was flat on her back on her desk. Their lips were locked. At first I thought Dewey had attacked her but I saw Joy's arms around him, pulling him toward her. This was as spontaneous and consensual as it gets.

"Everything okay?" I said politely.

Lou looked back at me over his shoulder and got off Joy in a hurry.

"Oh shit," he said, stumbling away from the desk. He looked at me, then at Joy. "Oh shit," he repeated, then ran out the door.

Joy got up slowly. Her glasses were crooked on her face, and her light lipstick was smudged. Her prim hair was disheveled.

"Are you alright?" I went to her side and put a comforting arm on her shoulder.

She swallowed hard and made a futile gesture to fix her hair. "I'm fine," she said, smoothing her blouse. "Is he gone?"

"Yes," I assured her. "Don't worry."

"Where did he go?"

"I don't know for sure," I said.

"Can you find him?" she asked.

"Probably. Do you intend to press charges?" I asked.

"No, I intend to hire him," she said, adjusting her glasses.

Louie Dewey was pacing nervously in his apartment when I let myself in.

"I don't know what got into me, Eddie," he blurted the moment he saw me. "I've never done anything like that before. Is she gonna press charges?"

"She wants to offer you a job," I told him.

"After what I did?"

"*Because* of what you did, I think."

"I couldn't control myself," he pleaded with me.

"I think she feels the same," I said.

"I'll go right over," Lou said, and he was gone.

I was too hyper to go home so I called Chief Frank Burke and invited myself over for a cup of coffee. I needed the company of cops to make me feel normal again.

We sat in his office, drinking bad coffee. Our relationship had become personal as well as professional.

"Any progress with Buford?" he asked about the neo-Nazi.

"I'm just waiting," I said. "I've done all I can."

"I'm glad I'm not involved. Too much red tape." He sighed. "So, any murder cases yet, detective?"

"No. I may have to kill someone myself," I told him. "I do have four cases though."

"I've got about four hundred." Frank pointed to a stack of

folders. He picked a folder randomly. "Here's one for you. Two guys in their mid eighties got in a fistfight outside a theater."

"About what?"

"There was a long line and one guy accuses the other guy of cutting in front of him. They start shoving each other. One guy throws a punch, the other guy falls, hits his head, and dies."

"Manslaughter?" I guessed at the charge.

"The guy who threw the punch is claiming self-defense."

"What do you think?"

"I think one of them should have gone bowling instead," Frank said.

We reviewed more folders.

A husband-and-wife team embezzled more than six hundred thousand dollars from their homeowner's association and gambled it away at the Hard Rock Casino. There were plenty of witnesses but the couple pleaded innocent anyway.

Next case:

"An eighty-four-year-old woman was pulling in to a parking space in front of the Department of Motor Vehicles in Delray. She stepped on the gas instead of the brake and drove her 1998 Mercury Marquis through the registry window into the lobby. She was there to get her license renewed."

"Did she get a new license?"

"She got a five-year extension."

"You're kidding."

"Of course I'm kidding."

Next case:

"A plastic surgeon in Boca was busted for having no medical license. He had the best prices in town and was very popular. His patients are protesting his arrest."

Next:

"You're gonna love this one." Frank smiled. "A guy filed a

report a few weeks ago saying a hundred and five dollars was missing from his bank account. His bank insists he made an on-line withdrawal and they have the paperwork to prove the trans-action took place."

Oh really?

"Why is he bothering the police?" I cleared my throat ner-vously. "Isn't this the bank's problem?"

"The customer claimed Internet fraud," Frank read from the folder. "He's convinced someone hacked into his account and stole his money."

"Is that possible?" I asked feeling light-headed.

"Sure it's possible," Frank said. "But the victim had about seven hundred thousand dollars more in that same account . . . and none of it was touched. What cyberthief would go to the trouble of hacking into a bank account, steal one hundred and five dollars, and leave six hundred ninety-nine thousand, eight hundred and ninety-five?"

I know one.

"But, here's the kicker," Frank said, laughing. "The guy called this morning and told us the hundred and five bucks was back in his account. He figured it must have just been some computer error after all."

"That's a relief." I sighed.

"Yeah, except we had to go through all the motions before the guy called us back. We talked to the bank and the customer. We even talked to Joy Feely to see if she could track anything down for us. Before she could get started the alleged victim called us with the good news. It was all for nothing."

I got up from the chair.

"Where you going?" Frank asked.

"I just got a headache." I told him the truth. "I gotta go home to lie down."

I was driving to my apartment for a much needed nap when

a red Mustang coupe swooped behind my MINI, inches from my bumper. The Mustang's engine roared and the horn blared. In my rearview mirror I could see the young male driver making frantic arm motions, demanding I get out of his way.

I hate tailgaters.

I sent him a "get off my ass" message by stepping on my brakes hard and risking a rear-end collision. The Mustang never slowed down. It veered into the right lane, accelerated, zoomed past me, and then swerved in front of me. The driver gave me a single-digit salute.

I replied in kind.

Weavers piss me off.

These hyperactive idiots are incessantly weaving in and out of traffic in a one-man race to the next red light. Weaving is like a dog chasing its tail: can't win/can't stop.

The Mustang got dangerously close to the rear bumper of a worn-out sedan and honked his horn. Without waiting for the old car to move into the right lane the Mustang swerved right and accelerated to pass. Unfortunately, the old sedan was also moving right to allow the Mustang to pass on the left. The two cars arrived in the right lane at the same place at the same time. They collided side by side and careened off Yamato Road just west of the Broken Sound entrance. Both cars came to rest on the wide grass area on the north side of the street. I eased in behind them.

I got out of my car and began walking toward them. I saw the Mustang driver jump out of his car with a look of rage on his face. He was tall, well built, and young. A much smaller man with a dark complexion slowly got out of his dented sedan.

The Mustang maniac, after checking the damage to his car, charged the smaller guy and started throwing punches, screaming obscenities. The little guy covered his head with his arms and looked terrified.

I stepped in between them, shoving the bigger man backward.

"What do you want, squirt?" Mustang Man shouted.

He reached for me.

"Take a bow," I said, kneeing him in the balls just hard enough to make him bend forward to my height. I pushed down on the back of his head, forcing him to his knees. He was stunned but not seriously hurt . . . yet.

I turned to the terrified smaller man. His eyes were darting from side to side looking for an escape route.

"Are you alright?" I asked, gently placing my hands on his shoulders.

He looked confused, and I got the feeling he didn't understand English. His eyes looked behind me with alarm and I sensed Mustang Man was approaching. I did a half turn and glared at him over my shoulder. He thought twice.

"Why are you defending him?" he wanted to know. "That little bastard almost killed me."

"The accident was your fault," I told him. "You were tailgating, speeding, and weaving in and out of traffic. You did the same thing to me, you dipshit."

He glanced at my MINI Cooper. "You were driving too slow," he said, remembering my MINI. "All you old farts drive too slow."

"Have you timed all of us?" I asked him.

"I'll bet that little foreigner doesn't even have a license or insurance," the young man pointed. "He's probably an illegal alien."

I turned to the frightened little man.

"*Antilegal?*" I asked with my limited Spanish vocabulary.

His eyes opened wide and he ran away from me and out onto Yamato Road.

"Stop," I called after him, but he didn't look back.

I watched him run east, then dart south across the wide

street where a four-door Chrysler was running a red light. The poor little guy didn't have a chance. The Chrysler knocked him down, ran over him, and dragged him for several yards before spitting him out on the side of the road. The big car rolled to a stop on the grass not far from where I stood with Mustang Man.

"Holy shit," the weaver said, standing next to me now. "Did you see that?"

"Did you see it?" I shoved him away with a hand to his chest. "You caused it."

"What did I do?" he shouted.

I ran toward the bloody body on the ground. Cars were stopping and people were gathering. I knelt next to the broken man and saw he was still breathing. His eyes were open but un-focused. His lips moved, and I put my ear close to his lips so I could hear him.

"Papan," he groaned. "Papan."

His eyes closed and he died.

I knew Papan was a girl's name. Was he saying good-bye to his wife or his daughter? Whoever she was, Papan would soon be in Boca, mourning.

I got up from my knees, went to the Chrysler, and opened the driver's door. A dazed old man was behind the wheel, lean-ing against the seat back. His eyes were glassy and his forehead was bloody. A woman sat next to him. There was blood on her forehead as well. An older couple in the backseat appeared to be unhurt but seemed too stunned to speak.

"What happened?" The driver turned slowly toward me.

I guessed he was in his late eighties, maybe even ninety.

"You hit a pedestrian," I told him.

"Is he okay?" the dazed driver asked.

"He's dead," I said softly.

"Oh my God," the woman next to him cried. "You went through that red light."

"I did?" the old man asked, confused. "I didn't see a red light."

A police car and an ambulance arrived.

"What happened?" the cop asked me.

"People who shouldn't be behind the wheel of a car were in the wrong place at the wrong time," I told him.

"That happens a lot around here," the cop said.

Chapter 16

Izzy's Elevator

Later that afternoon when I told Claudette about the tragic car accident on Yamato she was visibly shaken. When I told her about Lou Dewey's past she couldn't have cared less. "He saved your life," she said. "That's all I need to know."

Point well taken.

When I told her about Lou and Joy she said, "That's so cute."

Cute is not the word I would have used.

"Do they really look exactly alike or are you exaggerating?" she asked.

"Both," I said.

"Was it love at first sight?"

"It was lust at first sight," I told her.

"When I was your nurse at the hospital did you lust for me at first sight?" Claudette batted her eyelashes at me.

"No."

"Why not?"

"Mr. Johnson had a tube in his eye if you remember," I said. "I'd just been shot and lust was low on my list. In fact, I was listless."

"I'm a little disappointed." She stuck out her lower lip and pouted.

I love the way she pouts, so sexy, Mr. Johnson said, and I had to agree.

"I just started a new list," I told her. "And I put you first on it. Let's pretend I'm Lou Dewey and you're Joy Feely."

I grabbed her in my arms.

"Okay." She laughed and stuck her top teeth over her lower lip.

"That's mean," I said as I did the same. We tried to kiss and our teeth collided.

"How do they do it?" she said, touching her lower lip, checking for blood.

"Very carefully," I said. "Let's practice."

Lou Dewey called the next morning.

"Lou, what's up?" I asked.

"That's an appropriate question," he said.

"Pace yourself," I advised.

"Eddie, meeting this woman is the greatest thing that ever happened to me," he said.

"Ohhh, Louie, that's so sweet," I heard Joy Feely gush in the background.

"Not now." I heard him struggling. "I have to talk to Eddie. Joy, stop it. I said stop it. I'm sorry, Eddie, I'll have to call you back."

CLICK!

He was breathless when he called forty minutes later. "This woman won't give me a break," he said.

"Will she give you a job?"

"I never asked."

"Now would be a good time," I suggested.

"Joy, will you give me a job?" he asked her.

Her reply was muffled.

"I mean a real job," he stipulated. "You know, where I work for you and you pay me."

Another muffled response.

"She said yes."

"Good. Now that you're gainfully employed, I have a job for you. I'll pick you up at your apartment in an hour and tell you about it then," I said.

"I work for Joy. Doesn't she have to approve?"

"You handle Joy," I said.

"My pleasure," he replied.

Just before he hung up I heard Joy giggle hysterically. It sounded like he was handling her just fine.

Lou Dewey and I were at Delray Vista at 10:30 that same morning. We stood outside Izzy Fryberg's building, drinking coffee. I glanced at Lou. "You look tired," I told him.

"I am. I've got friction burns—"

"Spare me," I interrupted him. "Let's get down to business."

"Okay, I'll summarize what you told me," Lou said. "A group of good friends from the Boston area bought apartments in this building about thirty years ago."

Lou did an excellent job of recapping the entire history of Delray Vista, Building 550, including the close personal relationships that had totally disintegrated.

"You got the whole story," I told him.

"So what do you want from me?"

"I want you to figure out what's causing the elevator to malfunction."

"Maybe it's mechanical."

"No," I said. "The elevator company checked for that. The motor's fine. The cable is fine. I think it's a computer thing."

"A computer thing?" he said sarcastically. "When did you get so high tech?"

"I think someone planted something somewhere smart-ass."

"Could you be more specific, Sherlock?"

"Check the shaft," I told him.

"Why?"

"Because no one has looked there yet and because it will be a pain in your ass to check."

"That's very nice of you," he said.

"Don't make fun of the boss."

Lou pressed the elevator button and the door opened. He got in, rode the elevator to the second floor, and came down the staircase.

"I pushed the emergency stop button," he told me. "Theoretically the elevator will not come down and crush my ass while I'm in the shaft."

He pried open the first-floor elevator door and looked up the vertical tunnel.

"To find something high tech I'm going to need something low tech," he told me.

"Like what?"

"A ladder," he said.

I called Izzy Fryberg who told me he was having a "Knish and Grits" special at the Bagel Bush. He invited us to join him, but I declined and asked him to hurry back. Izzy was there in ten minutes with remnants of grits on his upper lip. I introduced him to Lou Dewey.

"Louie Dewey?" Izzy Fryberg smirked. "What kind of name is that?"

"You think Izzy Fryberg is such a great name?" Lou asked.

Izzy opened the maintenance room with one of his many passkeys and found an aluminum ladder.

Lou carried the ladder into the shaft, opened it, steadied it, and peered up the vertical tunnel.

"How sure are you that the elevator won't come down while you're in there and crush your skinny ass?" I asked.

"I'm not sure at all," he said, and he started climbing.

When he was halfway up the ladder Izzy nudged me.

"Who is this guy?"

"Someone I'd trust with my life," I told him.

"His mother should have gotten braces for his teeth when he was a kid."

"Women love him, teeth and all," I said.

"Go figure," Izzy said.

We stood outside the elevator shaft and waited.

"Aw fuck," Lou shouted.

"What?" I asked, startled.

"I got grease on my shirt, son of a bitch," he complained. "Hey, what's this?"

"What?"

"I'll let you know."

A moment later we heard Lou descending the aluminum ladder. He stepped out of the shaft and handed me a little box with an antenna.

"What is that?" Izzy asked.

"*That* is an electromagnet with a radio-triggering device. It's not high tech but it's effective. It was well hidden in the shaft," he said.

"How's it work?" Izzy asked.

"This is not my specialty," Dewey said. "But I think when this device is triggered, a magnetic field starts a current in the leads of the solenoid actuator relay—"

"Which means?" I interrupted.

"The elevator stops," Louie said, "or starts."

"Where do you get a device like this?" I asked.

"An electronic store," he said like an impatient professor.

"What triggers the magnetic field?"

"Another device with the same ID code can trigger it," Lou loved teaching us. "Or a properly programmed computer would do the trick."

"Is it complicated?" I asked while Izzy just stood there shaking his head sadly.

"No, it's not complicated," Lou said, "but whoever installed it is very clever."

"Why do you say that?" I asked.

"Well, he could have installed a computer device like a Linksys Wireless-N router."

"Easy boy." I reminded Lou that I was a computer caveman.

"Basically he could have used parts from the disassembled circuit board of a router and rewired the elevator control panel. That would have given him better control of the device."

"So why didn't he?" I asked.

"He must have figured a repair crew would notice anything different in their wiring or in their motor. But he was betting no one would think of the shaft. He was right until you came along. You're brilliant."

"Izzy, can you give me a list of tenants in this building?" I asked.

"Sure," he said. "Why?"

"I want to check who might know enough about remote devices to install one."

"You think it was done by someone who lives here?" Izzy looked sad.

"Who else would bother?" I asked him.

He nodded and walked away slowly.

Lou looked at me curiously. "How did you know we'd find a device?"

"I didn't know," I said.

"You were fairly certain," Lou persisted.

I thought for a moment. "You ever watch a guy crack a safe?" I asked.

"Only in the movies, of course," Lou said defensively.

"Well, you know how the safecracker puts his ear to the dial and listens to the tumblers falling into place?"

Louie nodded. "Like the guy who can solve the Rubik's Cube in twenty-six moves."

"I couldn't solve that thing in twenty-six years," I said. "But for me solving a crime is just a matter of making the right moves and listening to things fall into place."

"That's how I am with computers," Dewey said.

"We make a good team," I said.

"Are we a team?" Louie Dewey asked.

I thought that over for a moment then made a decision. "Sure, we're a team. Why not?"

We gave each other a high five, which was a low five to most people.

Izzy came back with the list and gave it to me. I handed it to my new teammate.

CHAPTER 17

INSIDE BETSY BLACKSTONE

I answered my cell phone while driving to my office from Delray Vista.

"I have a retroverted, septate uterus," a woman said.

"And I have a talking penis," I replied, and disconnected the call.

I hate wrong numbers.

The phone rang again.

"Eddie, don't hang up. It's Betsy Blackstone."

"Sorry, Betsy. I thought it was a crank call."

"Did you say something about a penis?" she asked.

"Of course not. How was Dr. Dunn?"

"He was great. I have a retroverted, septate uterus," she repeated.

"Is that bad?"

"I want to tell you in person," she said.

"I suppose we should meet at least once before we talk about your uterus," I agreed.

We met at Bagel Kingdom on Clint Moore Road. Betsy Blackstone looked like an ex–prom queen/head cheerleader rolled into one perky package. She was blond, with an athletically lean, tall body, and I had to look up to make eye contact.

"I thought you'd be bigger," she said with a radiant smile.

"I thought so, too."

Old joke.

She laughed and we sat in a booth across from each other.

"Tell me about your uterus," I said to Betsy as a heavyset waitress arrived at the table.

"Excuse me?" the waitress scowled.

Betsy Blackstone put her hand over her mouth and giggled.

"I was talking to her," I explained to the waitress.

"Are you two perverts or something?"

"Do we look like perverts?" I asked her.

"You never know," she said.

We ordered coffee.

"Anything kinky here and I'm calling the cops," the waitress said, pouring.

I nodded.

"That was so funny," Betsy said after the waitress backed away.

"Timing is everything." I smiled.

We both sipped our coffee.

"Now tell me about your uterus," I whispered.

"Okay," she whispered back.

The waitress looked at us suspiciously.

"It's tipped," she said.

"I thought you said it was retroverted," I replied.

"That's what retroverted means," she told me. "A normal

uterus is vertical or tilted slightly forward, pointing toward the abdomen. My uterus is pointed the other way."

"What's it pointing at?" I asked.

I noticed the waitress approaching with a coffeepot.

"My anus," Betsy said.

The waitress did an about-face.

"Sorry for being so graphic," Betsy apologized, giggling again.

"That's okay," I assured her. "What's septate mean?"

"It means my uterus is divided into two sections. A normal uterus isn't," she explained. "If the fetus settles in only one side and doesn't get enough nutrition it can die." Betsy took a deep breath. "According to Dr. Dunn, I was probably born with the septate uterus, but it didn't tip until after I got pregnant."

"How could he know that?"

"Because I told him that having sex was never painful before my first pregnancy," she explained.

"So you're telling me a tipped uterus can cause pain during sex?"

"Yes. Wait, I took some notes." She removed a piece of paper from her purse and scanned it quickly. "Here it is. It's called collision dyspareunia."

"It sounds like an auto shop in Italy," I said.

"It *is* like a car wreck I guess. A retroverted uterus can cause ovaries and fallopian tubes to tilt backward," she said. "Do you understand what I'm saying?"

"Vaguely." I cleared my throat.

"When these female parts tilt backward they become a target."

"A target for what?" I asked.

The waitress was approaching with her coffeepot.

"A penis," Betsy said.

The waitress rolled her eyes and did a quick one-eighty turn.

"I don't understand."

"A penis can actually butt into a tilted uterus and cause pain," she explained.

I never knew that, Mr. Johnson said.

Would that have stopped you? I asked him.

No. But I never knew that.

"So, Dr. Cohen's diagnosis was wrong," I said to her.

"Yes, Dr. Cohen was wrong." Her eyes got watery. "Dr. Dunn said the ligaments around my uterus had slipped and that I had developed fibroids." She referred to her paper again. "There's this thing called endometriosis, which has something to do with lesions on the uterus and—"

I held up my hand. "Stop. That's enough details. Can we just say that both your miscarriages were caused by your female problems?"

"Yes," she said firmly. "A septated uterus is more likely to cause a miscarriage than a tipped uterus, but they can both do damage."

I leaned back and tapped my fingers on the table.

"Did you have any warning signs during your first pregnancy that you were going to miscarry?" I asked, leaning forward again.

"Bleeding from the vagina," she told me.

"Don't you two ever stop?" the waitress said. She filled our coffee cups and hurried away.

"Did you tell Dr. Cohen about the bleeding?" I asked, shaking my head at the waitress's back.

"Of course," she said. "He examined me right away and told me the baby had died." She removed a tissue from her handbag and blew her nose.

"What did he tell you to do?"

"He said it would be best if I miscarried naturally." She closed her eyes, remembering. "He told me to take walks and exercise. If I didn't miscarry naturally he said he would induce me."

She was close to tears so I waited before asking the next question.

"What happened?"

"He had to induce me the first time," she said. "The second miscarriage happened naturally in the twelfth week."

"What does Dr. Dunn recommend?" I asked.

"He said he can fix everything with minor surgery," she told me.

"That's great," I said. "I'm happy for you."

She smiled a thousand-watt smile and patted my hands resting on the table. "The Boca Knight rescues a damsel in distress again."

"That's what Boca Knights do, Betsy," I told her, already thinking of how I might save other damsels from the distress of Dr. Ronald Cohen.

We got out of the booth, and Betsy gave me a long, hard hug. "Thank you for making me feel like a woman again," she said.

"Get a room," the surly waitress snapped, and slapped our bill on the table.

Chapter 18

It's Later Than You Think

The following week Betsy's uterus was vertical again and remodeled from a duplex to a single womb. Dr. Dunn assured her it was safe to get pregnant after recuperating. When Betsy phoned me she was delirious from the good news and painkillers. She said her husband knew nothing about my involvement with Dr. Dunn. She told him it was her idea to go to a specialist. Bradley was thrilled but immediately became suspicious of Dr. Cohen.

"He thinks Dr. Cohen is responsible for my miscarriages," she said, sniffling.

"Don't let him think that way," I said, thinking that way. "Dr. Cohen has delivered thousands of healthy babies."

"That's what I told Bradley." She sniffed. "He could tell he was upsetting me so he dropped it."

"Good man. You should drop it, too, and think about the future," I said. "Don't worry about Dr. Cohen."

Let me worry about him.

Shortly after I talked to Betsy Blackstone, I got a call from Lou Dewey.

"I now know everything about the condo owners in Izzy Fryberg's building."

"Any suspects?" I asked.

"Not really. We have ex-businessmen, dentists, a flushed-out plumber, a former teacher . . . but no high-tech computer professional qualified to install a remote-control device in an elevator shaft. In fact, I don't think anyone in that building is qualified to climb a ladder."

"Let me think about it," I said, and hung up.

I put my hands behind my head and leaned back in my desk chair. If no one in the building installed the remote-control device who else would bother? I had a thought and called Lou. "What do most senior citizens have in common, Lou?" I asked.

"Flatulence?"

"Besides that."

"Memory loss," he tried again.

"Children," I helped him. "Most retired people have grown children. Maybe one of their kids is qualified. Can you find information about their kids?"

"I can find anything except Jimmy Hoffa," Lou bragged.

"He's in Giants stadium," I said.

"Prove it," Lou said. "Anyway, let me get back to you about the kids. Oh, by the way, do you know a guy named Seymour Tanzer from Boca Heights?"

"Sure," I said. "He's a retired lawyer from Scarsdale, New York. Why?"

"I just read in a police bulletin that he had a heart attack on the golf course and was rushed to the hospital."

"Is he alright?"

"The police report just said he was in intensive care," Lou told me.

"How do you get police reports?" I asked.

"You don't want to know," Lou Dewey said.

I arrived at Seymour Tanzer's hospital room just as several people were leaving. One departing visitor was the totally awesome Alicia Fine, my former lover, who had stopped seeing me when she realized I was never going to change. I missed her, but I knew that coveting someone and converting for someone have nothing in common.

We looked at each other for a tender moment, saying nothing. There was no denying the physical chemistry that still existed between us.

"Hello, Eddie," she said, with a hint of sadness in her voice. I couldn't tell if she thought she was looking at a lost opportunity or at someone who had lost an opportunity.

I noticed the people with her had moved away and were walking toward the elevators.

"How have you been?" I asked, clearing my throat like a bashful schoolboy.

"I'm seeing someone," she said quietly.

I responded with a smile but feeling a sense of loss. "He's a lucky guy," I said. "You're a wonderful person."

"Not wonderful enough for you," she said ruefully.

"That's not the whole story," I said. "I wasn't your idea of the perfect man, either."

"You could be frightening at times," she agreed.

"That's who I am," I said without regret.

"Yes, I know," she told me, sighing. "Are you still seeing that woman?"

"Yes," I told her. "Claudette."

"She's probably more your type," Alicia said without malice.

"I think I'm more her type," I said. "She doesn't want to change me."

"Maybe you don't scare her," Alicia looked into my eyes.

"Actually, she scares me sometimes." I smiled back.

"I do miss you, Eddie," she said fondly.

"I miss you, too, Alicia," I told her.

I held out my arms, offering a hug, and she stepped toward me. Her body melted into mine, and I held her tightly, loving the feel and smell of her. Mr. Johnson made an unexpected appearance against her thigh. He always managed to spoil a tender moment.

"Thanks for the compliment." She smiled, looking down. "We never had a problem there."

"No, that was a wonderful thing," I agreed.

"It's just not everything," she said.

I nodded. "No, it's not."

Yes it is, Mr. Johnson disagreed.

We said good-bye and I watched her walk away.

Can't we work something out? Mr. Johnson whined and squirmed.

What do you want me to do? I asked.

Tell her you've changed. Tell her you're not seeing anyone else.

You mean . . . lie to her?

Absolutely, Mr. Johnson said.

Have you no sense of decency?

Of course not, I'm a penis.

When I entered his room Seymour Tanzer was flat on his back in the hospital bed, staring at the ceiling.

"Who's there?" he croaked.

"St. Peter," I said.

"You've got the wrong room, Pete," Seymour managed as I

walked to the foot of his bed. "Hey, it's the Boca Knight," he said, sounding pleased to see me.

"How are you, Seymour?" I asked.

"I'm dying," he said.

"People survive heart attacks all the time and live to a ripe old age."

"I *am* a ripe old age, Eddie," Seymour said.

"You'll be alright," I encouraged him. "You're a tough old bird."

"The pterodactyl was a tough old bird and look what happened to him." He laughed and so did I.

"Remember that day at the cemetery when we faced down those Nazis bastards?" Seymour asked.

"Of course I do," I said, remembering how several senior citizen superheroes had come to my aid when I needed them. "You were very brave that day, Seymour."

"I almost shit my pants," he admitted, and laughed until he started to cough.

"Do you want me to get a doctor?" I asked nervously.

He waved me off and continued coughing. Finally he stopped and gasped for air.

"What do your doctors say?" I asked.

"I need a heart transplant," he said, "but I'd never survive the surgery."

"So what are your options?"

"I can die now or die later."

"How long do they give you?" I asked.

"A couple of months, a year at most," he told me.

"Doctors have been wrong before," I tried.

"They've been right before, too," he said. "It's okay. I can live with dying. I just regret wasting so much time worrying about life instead of enjoying it."

I've heard a lot of regrets from people who know their number's up.

"What did you worry about?" I asked.

"Everything," he said. "When I was a kid I worried about other kids and pleasing my parents. In grade school I worried about high school. In high school I worried about college, pimples, girls, and my body. In college I worried about law school. In law school I worried about passing the bar. Then I worried about getting a job, and when I eventually started my own practice, I worried about surviving in business."

"That's a lot of worry for one man," I said.

"Wait, I'm not done yet," Seymour told me. "I worried about the woman I married. I worried that I didn't love her enough and then I worried that she didn't love me. I worried about having children instead of enjoying them."

"No time to stop and smell the roses," I said, using the old cliché.

"I thought about it but then I worried about the thorns and the fuckin' bees," Seymour said. "I did try golf."

"Did you enjoy it?"

"I hated it," he said. "I only enjoyed winning but it made me worry about losing."

"You have to lighten up, Seymour," I told him. "Enjoy the moment."

"I've been thinking about that," Seymour said. "I promised myself that starting tomorrow I'm going to try to enjoy the process instead of worrying about the outcome. I'm going to make the most of whatever time I have left."

"That sounds like a good plan to me," I said.

"Yeah, that's what I'll do," he said. "I'm going to change."

Seymour Tanzer smiled at me, closed his weary eyes, and an hour after I left his room he died.

Chapter 19

A Shot in the Dark

"We have a winner in the elevator FX category," Lou Dewey announced when I answered my phone the morning after Seymour Tanzer died.

"And the winner is . . ." I played his silly game.

"Noah Paretsky."

"Who?"

"Child prodigy Paretsky; a graduate of Chelsea High at sixteen years old, an MIT special honors student who graduated in '64 and was recruited by the National Aeronautics and Space Administration in Houston, Texas."

"NASA? As in *Houston-we-have-a-problem* NASA?"

"As in *man-on-the-moon* NASA," Lou confirmed.

"From the moon to a two-story elevator in Delray Beach?"

"It sounds like a crash landing to me," Lou agreed. "He worked for NASA for over twenty years then became an inventor."

"What kind of inventor?"

"The dangerous kind," Lou said. "In the early nineties he invented Baby Big Teeth, a moon-faced girl doll with baby teeth that could be pulled out one at a time and a big tooth would grow in the empty spot."

"Is this a joke?"

"No, it's quite serious," Lou answered. "Bancroft Toys sold millions of these things until kids started swallowing the baby teeth. It became an epidemic. Children were coughing up plastic doll teeth all over America. Fortunately there were no fatalities but the recall put the manufacturer out of business."

"What happened to Noah Paretsky?"

"He continued inventing dangerous things," Lou said. "His next creation was an electrified window screen that zapped flies."

"Shocking," I surmised.

"You bet your ass it was," Lou said. "One installer almost lost his fingers and one guy short-circuited his pacemaker."

"Both inventions had basic conceptual flaws," I noted.

"To say the least," Lou said. "But failure didn't discourage our boy. Next he invented The Velvet Glove, a undulating, five-fingered simulated hand for a stimulating massage."

"Sounds like a good thing for stiff joints," I said.

"That it was," Lou said. "Unfortunately, the primary users of The Velvet Glove were adolescent boys who only had one stiff joint in mind. Gloves with outrageous stains on them were returned across the country. Another loser."

"This sounds like a guy definitely capable of manipulating an elevator," I concluded. "What's his connection to Delray Vista?"

"He's the fifty-five-year-old unmarried son of Bennett and Bertha Paretsky, who own a condo on the second floor of Izzy Fryberg's vertically challenged building."

"The second floor? Why would Noah Paretsky sabotage his parents' elevator?"

"He didn't," Dewey said. "The Paretskys were the only second-floor residents who voted against the elevator and refuse to use it. They said it was divisive."

"He's our man," I concluded. "Nice going."

"He lives in his own condo on the beach near the Deerfield Hilton," Dewey told me. "I have a map of the location plus a sat-ellite view of the building. Are we going to contact the police?"

"Not just yet." I thought for a moment. "Maybe he's into something else illegal we don't know about. Follow him for a couple of days. See how he spends his time."

"Okay," Lou said enthusiastically.

"Nice job, Lou."

"Thanks, Eddie," Lou said softly. "That means a lot coming from you."

Later that afternoon I drove to Wilton Manors to do additional research in the gayborhood. I went directly to Tropics, the Dietrichs' favorite hangout to take a closer look at Edik Davida-vitch, the bartender. He was one of only two people who said they heard the Dietrichs talking about an overseas trip, and there was just something about him . . .

Why not check him out?

The bar was busy at five thirty in the afternoon. I sat on a stool and smiled at two young men seated next to me.

"Looking for a date?" One of them batted his eyelashes at me. He was wearing eye shadow and lipstick, and appeared to be a third my age.

I looked the kid up and down like I was considering his offer. "You're a little too old for me," I declined with a forced smile.

Don't get me involved with this cocksucker, Mr. Johnson warned me.

The male hooker smiled. "If you change your mind, super-boy, my name is Sammy. Short for Samantha."

"My name is Eddie," I told him. "Short for my age."

Both male hookers laughed.

"He's so cute," Sammy told his friend. I was flattered.

Stop it, Mr. Johnson warned.

Edik Davidavitch approached me.

"What can I get you?" he asked professionally.

"I'll have a Coors," I said.

"I see you here before," Edik said, pouring my beer.

"I was here once before with a friend," I told him.

"You were with Howard Larkey."

"You're very observant," I complimented him.

"I remember every face, every name, and every drink," he said, pointing at his temple.

You're full of shit, I thought, remembering his fumbling behind the bar.

"Where are you from?" I asked.

"Russia," he said. "I have been five years in this country but cannot lose accent."

"You speak English better than I speak Russian," I told him, trying to be friendly.

"Thank you," he said, looking around the bar. "Excuse me; I must take care of customers." He moved away and my eyes followed him in the mirror behind the bar.

There was something about him that gnawed at my subconscious like a name you can't remember even though you're sure you know it. I saw ugly Irene Kostanski approach the bar and give him a drink order. I watched them exchange affectionate glances before she exited the bar.

Edik returned to my end of the bar eventually.

"You look familiar," he said to me. "Are you famous?"

This guy intrigued me so I decided to blow my own cover. "I've been in the papers a few times."

"Maybe I've seen your picture." He pointed a finger at me.

"My name is Eddie Perlmutter," I told him and looked for a reaction. I got one.

"The Boca Knight guy?" Edik asked, surprised.

I nodded.

"Is Boca Knight gay?" he asked, still surprised.

Oh for chrissakes, Mr. Johnson groaned.

"No, the Boca Knight is not gay," I said.

"Then why you come to gay bar with gay friend and come back again?"

I decided it was time to bait this guy.

"I'm a detective," I said. "Howard hired me to find two missing friends."

Edik laughed, but his face didn't. "The Dietrichs, right?" He shook his head. "Dietrichs went to Europe. They talk about trip several times, right here at this bar. Howard and Derek worry for nothing."

"You and your girlfriend seem to be the only ones who heard about the trip."

"No, were several others." Edik wiped the bar nervously.

"Who?"

"I can't remember now," he said, and I could tell I was making him uncomfortable. He fidgeted a moment then excused himself. "I must go to men's room."

He's lying, I told myself, smiling. *He's gonna call someone.* I just knew it.

I waited a few minutes and when Edik didn't return I went to the men's room. No Edik.

Who is he calling, I wondered as I hurried back to the bar.

Edik returned a few minutes after me. He seemed more agitated now.

Perlmutter, you've done it again, I congratulated myself.

I paid my bill and said good-bye. Outside, my cell phone rang. It was Claudette.

"Where are you?" she wanted to know.

"I'm in Wilton Manors. I just left a gay bar."

"I'm not enough for you?"

"I'm working on a case."

"A case of what?"

"You're homophobic," I told her.

"Wanna hurry home and hump *Halle the Homophobic Half-Haitian?*"

"Can I tie you up and pretend I'm your Papa Doc?"

"Do you have rope?"

"I don't leave home without it," I told her.

As I walked to my car, I saw several same-sex couples displaying uninhibited affection on Wilton Drive; kissing, holding hands, grabbing ass, and walking arm in arm. I was more at ease now then I was the first time I had been in the gayborhood. I had pretty much accepted the fact that sexual preference isn't a multiple-choice exam.

> Q. Which do you find more titillating? Toying with tits or with testicles?
>
> Q. Do you prefer playing patsy with a pussy or a penis?
>
> Q. Do you prefer lips between a mustache and goatee or between a pair of thighs?

Mr. Johnson didn't agree with my new liberal attitude nor did most men.

Guys who are sexually aroused by the thought of women making love to women often find the thought of two men *balling* . . . appalling. The same men, who think a man's tongue in a woman's privates is awesome, think a man's tongue in his buddy's crotch is awful.

You gotta love those cavemen.

A few steps from my MINI in the back of the parking lot, I heard a gunshot and felt my forehead sizzle from left to right. I dove for the ground and touched my forehead.

Blood. Fuck.

A bullet had grazed me.

I was coherent enough to roll away from the sound of the gunshot. When I banged into a car door an alarm went off. Another shot rang out and glass shattered above my head.

Nervous shooter, lousy shot.

"Hey, what's going on over there?" a man shouted from around the corner.

"I heard shots," a woman replied.

I heard footsteps.

I peeked over the car hood in time to see the shooter running away into the night.

I struggled to my feet and was suddenly surrounded by people.

Sammy, short for Samantha, the tart from Tropics, was the first face I saw.

"Short Eddie," he said, concerned. "What happened to your forehead, dear boy? You're bleeding."

"I walked into a curb." I grimaced and slumped against the little hooker.

Sammy produced a tissue and dabbed my forehead. "Nasty scrape."

"Get your hands off him," a vaguely familiar voice said.

A painted face appeared inches from my own.

"Hi, Gill," I said to Howard's gay friend from George's Alibi who told me we were all somebody.

"You remembered." Gill was pleased.

"I saw him first," Sammy said, pouting.

"He's not gay, you twit," Gill defended me.

"He's the Boca Knight," a voice from the crowd said.

Another voice joined in. "The Boca Knight is gay? I knew it. I just knew it."

Oh shit, Mr. Johnson went into his shell.

Now Gill was wiping my wound with a pink handkerchief.

"Are you really the Boca Knight?" Gill asked, seemingly impressed.

I nodded.

"Why would anyone want to shoot the Boca Knight?" Gill asked. "You're for human rights and peace, right?"

"I'll beat the shit out of anyone who says I'm not," I told him.

This got a good laugh from the assembled gays, lesbians, heterosexuals, and undecideds.

"Do you have any idea who shot you?" Sammy asked.

I shook my head despite my strong suspicions. "I have a lot of enemies."

"Well, sweetheart," Sammy said sincerely, "you have a lot of friends, too."

My new buddies wanted to take me to the hospital for a checkup but I told them I was okay. Gill insisted on driving me home in my MINI while Sammy followed in a carful of gayborhood guys.

Gill told Claudette what happened and she listened intently.

After he left, Claudette bandaged my head and got into bed with me.

"I almost lost you tonight," she said emotionally, her head on my shoulder.

"How do you think I feel," I said. "*I* almost lost me tonight."

"It's not funny, Eddie. A half inch to the left, and you'd be dead. Do you know who did it?"

"Edik the bartender, I think," I said. "Or he knows who did. I think he's involved with the Dietrichs' disappearance."

"Do you think the Dietrichs are still alive?"

"Based on tonight I'd say it doesn't look good for them," I told her.

Chapter 20

The Beginning of the End

I woke up the next morning with a ripping headache and a roaring hard-on.

"You're kidding," Claudette said, staring at Mr. Johnson's headstand.

"Just ignore him and he'll go away."

"No way," she said. It was two against one and I didn't have a chance.

I must have looked pathetic afterward because Claudette seemed to be feeling guilty.

"I shouldn't have bothered you, huh?" she apologized, looking away.

I couldn't respond. I fell into a sex-induced mini-coma. When I woke hours later Claudette was sitting next to me looking concerned.

"I was worried. You don't look so good," she said, putting it mildly.

"I was shot last night and sexually molested this morning. How would you look?"

"You probably have a concussion." She looked carefully at my forehead. "Let's get you an MRI."

"Okay, I'll call my doctor," I said.

"You don't have a doctor," she informed me.

"Dr. Koblentz."

"He's a urologist."

"Close enough," I said, reaching for the phone.

Dr. Koblentz's receptionist put me right through to him. *No waiting.*

"Eddie, how are you feeling?" he asked cheerfully.

"Not so good," I said, and told him the whole story.

"Unless your head is up your ass I'm not the right doctor," he said. "You need a neurologist."

"I figured you could refer me to one," I explained.

"I can but I'll have to make a few calls," he told me. "Can you get to my building right away?"

I assured him I could.

"Go to the MRI lab on the first floor," he told me. "I'll make an appointment for you right now. After the exam they'll send the results to my office and I'll have a neurologist friend of mine read them as soon as possible."

"Thanks, Doc," I said. "I'll be on my way in a few minutes."

"Eddie, wait a second," the doctor said. "I've been checking your records on the computer while we're talking and I see you're scheduled for a colonoscopy in three days."

"Why are you always sticking something up my ass?"

"Just doing my job," he told me. "We scheduled this weeks ago."

"What do you insert for this pleasure?"

"A thin, flexible instrument attached to a camera—"

"You are *not* sticking a camera up my ass," I told him. "A transistor radio . . . maybe."

"Actually I'm going to postpone the colonoscopy," he decided. "We have to make sure you don't have any brain damage."

"Some people would say my ass would be the best place to look for brain damage," I told him.

Claudette drove me to the lab where I had the scan then returned home to rest.

"I have good news and bad news," Dr. Koblentz said when he phoned me later that afternoon. "The good news is the MRI confirmed that there is a brain in your head and it's not damaged."

"The bad news?"

"We can go forward with your colonoscopy," he told me.

"I hope my ass does as well as my head," I said.

We made plans for my impending colonoscopy, and two days before the exam Dr. Koblentz began preparing me.

"We have to clean out your system," Dr. Koblentz said over the phone.

"Is there a tool for that, too?" I asked.

"Do you have a fax machine?" he asked.

"You are not sticking a fax machine up my ass."

"I want to fax you instructions," he said.

"Oh, okay . . . You can do that," I said.

Claudette had a fax machine at home. Dr. Koblentz sent the instructions.

I glanced at the list.

Don't eat this . . . don't eat that . . . swallow this . . . yadda, yadda, yadda . . . then take a flying shit for yourself.

Claudette got me the recommended bowel blaster at the drugstore. She handed it to me in the morning like it was a time bomb.

"I can come home early if you need me," she offered.

"No problem. I'll be fine."

"I'll be home by six."

"I should be real horny by then."

I slept most of the morning, watched some television in the afternoon, and swallowed the first ounce and a half of Phospho-Soda at four.

This tastes like shit, I thought, getting into the spirit.

Claudette arrived home shortly after my first eruption.

"Eddie, are you alright?" she asked through the bathroom door.

I groaned. "I think I just passed my ears through my ass."

A half hour later I got the urge to breathe through my nose again. I wearily shuffled from the bathroom to the living room and smiled self-consciously at Claudette.

"Do you think I'm sexy?" I asked.

"At this moment . . . or ever?"

Before I could think of anything clever to say I got the feeling that all my internal organs were about to drop out of my body onto the floor. I did an abrupt about-face, imitated the sound of a steamship leaving port, and called "Bon Voyage," over my shoulder.

At eight o'clock I took the other ounce and a half of drain cleaner and prayed there was nothing left in me. My prayers went unanswered. I read every magazine in the house and I was starting Claudette's copy of *Palm Beach Woman* when I remembered I hadn't talked to Lou Dewey in a while. I had turned off my cell phone early in the day so as not to be disturbed but about the only thing that hadn't disturbed me was my cell phone.

"Claudette, could you bring me my cell phone?" I called to her.

"I am not coming into that room," she said. "I'll leave it at the door."

I was reminded of a scene from *Ben Hur*, a classic movie where guards lowered food into the Valley of the Lepers but would never enter.

I retrieved the phone and returned to the throne.

"Hi, Lou," I said weakly when he answered.

"Eddie, where you been?" he asked. "I've been calling your apartment and your cell phone every hour on the hour."

"Sorry, pal," I said. "But I've been out of commission."

I issued two short blasts and one long.

"That sounded like an SOS signal," Lou commented.

"Rusty pipe," I lied. "You know I went to Wilton Manors the other night."

"Yeah, on that missing gay guys case," he said.

"I must have made some real progress because someone took a shot at me."

"No shit."

"I wish that was true," I said, feeling my stomach churn. I told him the story and gave him my theory.

"Do you want me to research the bartender?"

"Not yet. Actually I want you to do something for me on Izzy Fryberg's case."

"That case is closed," Lou reminded me. "Just turn in the rocket scientist."

"I have a different idea," I said, and explained what I was thinking.

"What happened to the heartless cop from Boston I heard about?" Lou asked.

"It's like you said in the hospital." I laughed. "I think it's an age thing. Look what I did with you."

"Yeah, but I saved your life," he reminded me.

"Years ago I would have busted you anyway. I'm changing."

I erupted again.

"That pipe sounds like a pain in the ass," Lou Dewey commented.

"It is," I said. "Gotta go."

I loved my colonoscopy. A cute gastroenterologist named Dr. Veronica Bannister prescribed a dreamy anesthesia for me and I got to the point where I didn't care what they stuck where.

I was lying on my side watching a flexible tube on a small TV screen snake its way through an intestinal maze.

"That's your colon," Dr. Bannister said.

"*Fabulous*," I said, thinking of my ablation and how much I liked anesthesia.

I woke up in the recovery room still groggy.

The vivacious Veronica was at my side.

"You have a perfect colon," she told me cheerfully.

"Thanks," I slurred. "You, too."

CHAPTER 21

YULETIDE AT LOW TIDE

Christmas vacation in Boca can best be described as "more fun than a barrel of monkeys"—without the fun. The monkeys in Boca's barrel are northern children and grandchildren who descend on South Florida, demanding the best and expecting the worst.

For fourteen chaotic days South Florida resembles the deck of the *Titanic* during its final moments.

Women and children first . . . so get the hell out of my way, Grandma and Grandpa.

The inane poolside conversations of three generations that I heard in Boca go something like this:

GRANDPARENTS TALKING ABOUT THEIR
GRANDCHILDREN TO PEOPLE WHO DON'T CARE:
(Grandchild's Age Range: one minute to twelve years)

"I'm not saying this because he/she is mine but my grandchild is (fill in the blank)

(1) amazingly intelligent."
(2) unbelievably clever."
(3) extremely talented."
(4) incredibly athletic."
(5) absolutely adorable."

GRANDPARENTS TALKING ABOUT THEIR
GRANDCHILDREN TO ANYONE WHO WILL LISTEN:
(Grandchild's Age Range: thirteen to eighteen years)

"When did he/she get so fresh?"

"That's some body my granddaughter has."

"Those kids keep fooling with the air conditioner in the apartment."

"What a bar mitzvah he had. My son spared no expense."

"My grandchild is going to Emory. It's the Harvard of the south."

"She should be shaving her legs already."

"She needs a nose job."

"He hasn't lost that twitch."

GRANDPARENTS TALKING ABOUT THEIR OWN CHILDREN TO NO ONE IN PARTICULAR:

"My daughter-in-law upsets me."

"My son-in-law is out of work again."

"Why is she still single? Isn't there some guy who would marry her?"

"Maybe she's a lesbian."

"Why is he still single? Isn't there some girl who would marry him?"

"Maybe he's gay."

MARRIED COUPLES TALKING ABOUT THEIR PARENTS TO OTHER MARRIED COUPLES
(or to each other):

"This is the last time we're doing this. Your father is driving me crazy."

"Your mother never liked me."

"No, she didn't."

"I can't keep eating dinner at four thirty in the afternoon."

"Next year we're getting a hotel room."

"Kids are peeing in the pool."

"I have to call my office. I'll be back in an hour."

GRANDPARENTS TALKING TO GRANDCHILDREN
OF ALL AGES:

"Merle, stop scratching yourself there."

"Britney Berger, stand up straight."

"Beryl, you're twelve. Stop picking your nose already."

"Sammy Curley, stop crying or I'll give you something to cry about."

GRANDCHILDREN AGED TWO TO TWELVE TALKING
TO GRANDPARENTS:

"Grandpa, you have hair growing out of your nose."

"Grandma, why do your thighs shake?"

"Grandma, are you and Grandpa going to die soon?"

"I did not pee in the pool, Grandpa."

"I don't care about sea lice. I want to go in the ocean, Bubba."

"The water is too hot, Papa."

"The water is too cold, Nana."

"I'm hungry, Grandma."

"Bubba, I have sea lice."

RANDOM

Grandmother: "You don't like it here . . . go home."

Daughter-in-law: "Mom, don't talk to her like that."

Grandmother: "She's disrespectful."

Daughter-in-law: "You yelled at her."

Grandmother: "She was holding her brother's head under the water."

Daughter-in-law: "Okay, that's it. We're leaving."

Grandmother (to son as daughter-in-law departs): "I told you not to marry her!"

The traffic is so dense in Boca Raton that even the weavers stop weaving. Restaurants are mobbed by crowds of starving people who haven't eaten anything for at least an hour. The scene outside Boca delis at Christmastime is similar to the frantic crowds surrounding food trucks in the Sudan . . . except the people in the Sudan are better behaved.

It was during this Christmas crush that Lou Dewey phoned to tell me he had Noah Paretsky in his sights at ground zero: Deerfield Beach on a Sunday afternoon.

"I'm watching our geek as we speak," Louie told me. "How soon can you get here?"

"January," I said, exasperated. "Who goes to Deerfield Beach during Christmas week?"

"Everyone," he said. "Look, you told me to follow him until I was satisfied he wasn't Doctor Evil. I'm satisfied. If anything he's Doctor Boring. He's alone on the beach. Pull up to the front of the Deerfield Hilton and ask for Juan. I tipped him twenty-five bucks to park us both."

"We're only making fifty bucks an hour," I reminded him.

"The nearest parking space to Deerfield Beach this week is in Key West," Lou said. "It was Juan for the money . . . or two for the show-me-the-way-to-go-home. Don't worry, the parking is on me."

"I thought you were in this for the money," I joked with my teammate.

· · ·

Juan looked at me as I parked my MINI at his valet stand in front of the Deerfield Hilton.

"Jew Louie's fren?" he asked.

"Jes. Jew Juan?" I got right into the swing of things.

"Da's me, mang," he told me. "Gonna cos' you a Jackson an' a Lin-Cohen to park here, like I tole my mang Louie Dewey."

"Lou said he already paid jew," I told him.

"Jes, he pay for hees car." Juan was a grinning fool.

"Juan, let me tell you sumtin'," I stepped closer to him. "You get twenty-five bucks for both cars or you get a visit from immigration."

"Why didn't jew say so in the first place, homes?" The smile remained frozen on Juan's lips but the rest of his face was not happy. "Okay mang, I take good care of your MINI."

I found Lou Dewey standing on the sidewalk adjacent to the beach. He was dressed in black slacks, a black T-shirt, black shoes, and white socks. His hair was parted on the side with a big wave in the front.

Skinny Elvis.

"Hey BK." He waved. "Did you just get a Juaning?"

"Jes," I jested. "He asked for another twenty-five. So where's Otis?"

"As in Otis Elevator?"

"Jes," I told him.

The beach was jammed with jelly-bellies, six-pack abs, big boobs, small boobs, hard asses, lard asses, tan lines, sandcastles, screaming kids, sandwiches, blankets, beach chairs, tans, burns, iPods, and Frisbees.

Why does anyone come here?

"There he is." Louie pointed. "The swizzle stick with the metal detector."

Noah Paretsky was tall but stooped. He had a long face

under a floppy brimmed, shapeless hat and he wore cheap, black sunglasses. He was narrow at the shoulders and broad at the hips . . . like a parsnip. He wore a pullover shirt with horizontal blue stripes, and green checkered shorts. He wore black socks with brown sandals. He was scanning the sand with a handheld metal detector, listening to earphones.

"Do you want me to back you up?" Lou Dewey asked.

"I think I can handle this," I said. "I'll shoot first and ask questions later."

"Seriously, how are you going to approach him?"

"Maybe I'll talk to him about metal detectors," I said.

"What do you know about metal detectors?"

"I know he's using a Tesoro Umax," I said.

"How do you know that?"

"The Tesero is excellent in the sand," I told him.

"You're good." Dewey pointed at me.

"Also, the name is printed on the top."

I approached Noah Paretsky casually to avoid scaring him. I didn't want a scene . . . or a chase.

"Any luck?" I asked him casually.

He looked down at me from six feet and smiled like we were old friends.

"Hello, Mr. Perlmutter," he said. "I've been expecting you." *Whoa! Spooky!*

Paretsky removed his sunglasses. His eyes were friendly and unafraid.

"My parents told me Delray Vista hired the Boca Knight," he said. "I figured it was just a matter of time before you'd get to me."

"I'm impressed," I said.

"So am I," he replied. "How did you find me so soon?"

"The Internet," I said.

"I heard you were from the old school."

"I am," I said. "See that man in black over there?"

"The skinny Elvis with the bad overbite?" Noah said.

"My computer expert," I said.

Lou saw us looking at him and I motioned him to join us.

I introduced Noah to Lou, and they stood looking at each other.

"This is awkward, isn't it?" Noah said to Lou.

"A baby giraffe is awkward," Lou said. "This is bizarre."

We found a bench in the shade where Noah and I sat down.

"I'm going to leave you two alone so you can bond," Lou said. "I'm getting a cold drink. You guys want anything?"

We declined, and Lou walked toward a refreshment stand that was under attack by red-skinned tourists with sun-block war paint.

"First of all, I want you to know I meant no harm," Noah told me.

"I believe that," I said. "You were all neighbors from the same hometown, right?"

"Chelsea, Massachusetts." Paretsky nodded. "Low middle-class families with small summer cottages on a lake in New Hampshire. It was like a Kennedy compound for Jews. We were all best friends."

"What happened?"

"Life happened," he said. "The kids grew up, and the parents grew old. Everyone changed; friends became strangers and began fighting over little things."

"Like elevators."

"That was the final straw in a big pile of hay," he said.

"What did you expect to accomplish by sabotaging the elevator?" I asked.

"I wanted to remind them how much they needed one another."

"By scaring the shit out of them?"

"No, by giving them a common cause," he explained. "I stopped the elevator when first-floor people were riding and I stopped it when second-floor people were riding. There was no pattern and no one to blame. I hoped they would come to one another's rescue, like the old days."

"I don't know anything about their old days," I reminded him.

"They were so close," he said. "Izzy Fryberg, the guy who hired you, lives on the second floor. Mo and Maxine Myerson live on the first floor. The Myersons don't talk to the Frybergs anymore. In fact, I heard Maxine gave Izzy the finger the other day."

"I saw the whole thing."

"What you didn't see was Izzy Fryberg between Maxine Myerson's legs in the backseat of his Ford station wagon during a snowstorm in nineteen forty-nine."

"What was he doing there?"

"Delivering her third child, a son they named William," Noah told me. "We called him Billy. Mo couldn't get his car out of the driveway because of the snow. So he called Izzy, who drove a big station wagon with snow chains. Izzy rushed over with his wife, Emma. They put the Myersons in the backseat and headed toward the hospital. But Maxine was too far along. Izzy had no choice. He delivered the baby. It was a legend in Chelsea."

"Where was Mo?"

"Passed out in the front seat."

"And now they don't talk to one another," I said, shaking my head.

"That's my point," Noah said. "They've forgotten who they were and don't like who they've become. I tried to jog their memories. I wanted to show them that everyone's life is hanging by a thread . . . or in this case an elevator cable. I wanted them to reestablish their common bond by saving one another."

"Did MIT make you this stupid or did it come naturally?"

"A lot of things I did in life didn't work out the way I designed them," he said.

"Like the baby-teeth doll?"

"I wanted to make children happy," he said. "I just didn't see all the potential pitfalls."

"Like the ones involved in sabotaging an elevator?"

"Exactly." He bobbed his skinny head. "I wanted to restore friendships. Those people are very important to me. Here, look at this."

Noah removed an old black-and-white photo from an equally old black wallet and handed the snapshot to me. It was a well-preserved laminated picture showing a large group of people standing by a lake.

"That's my mother and father fifty years ago . . . and that's me." He pointed to a skinny geek.

"You haven't changed a bit," I told him.

"That's Izzy Fryberg and his wife," Noah continued without comment. "That's Mo Myerson and Maxine. That's Billy . . ."

He named every person in that photo.

"How did you preserve this picture so long?" I asked, marveling at the quality.

"My father was the neighborhood photographer so I inherited the collection of photos and eight-millimeter movies. Several years ago I took all the stuff to a professional studio and had everything transferred to discs or laminated. I was going to edit them and make a DVD for future generations. Then all this fighting started and nostalgia seemed like a waste of time."

"What am I going to do with you, Noah?" I asked, blowing air through my lips and handing him back the picture.

"I suppose you'll have to report me to the police," he said sadly. "This is really going to upset my parents. They always said I wasted my talent."

"You helped put a man on the moon," I reminded him.

"They wanted me to be a doctor," he said.

We sat in silence for a few minutes until Dewey returned holding his cell phone. "Should I call the police?" he asked, nodding toward Paretsky.

"I'm thinking," I told him.

"About what?"

"How I can turn this into a happy ending."

"This isn't a movie, Eddie," he told me.

"Maybe it could be," I said.

Chapter 22

Days Gone By

Two days after meeting with Noah Paretsky I received a call from the Ministry of Justice regarding Randolph Buford.

"Mr. Perlmutter," the minister's secretary said politely. "I'm pleased to inform you that your request regarding Randolph Buford has been approved."

You're kidding.

"That's good news," I said.

"I agree," she said. "We still require approval from the district attorney's office, the state attorney general's office, and the judge. But, we are ready to proceed from our end."

I thanked her, said good-bye, and placed a call to Bobby Byrnes, the twenty-eight-year-old public defender who had been assigned the Buford case after Aryan Army deserted.

"Bobby, we got approval from the Ministry of Justice," I told him. "I assume your client still wants the deal?"

"Absolutely," Byrnes assured me.

"Good. Make an appointment to see the Assistant DA," I told him.

"The sooner the better," Byrnes said. "The death threats just keep rolling in."

"How's his mother holding up?"

"She moved into a low-rent apartment by herself," he told me.

"What about her husband and daughter?" I asked. I hadn't heard about the move.

"They went back to South Carolina," Byrnes said. "When the old man learned about the settlement his wife and son made with the government he took his daughter and ran back to the compound."

"Did Aryan Army take him back?"

"I don't know and I don't care," Byrnes said. "I'm just glad I don't have to deal with him anymore. He's a bad man."

"His wife says he was just a typical kid from South Carolina," I said.

"No, he's not," Byrnes disagreed. "I'm a typical kid from South Carolina."

"I didn't know that."

"Go Game-Cocks." He gave a half-hearted cheer. "I'm from Columbia and I know a lot of typical kids from that state. I can assure you Buford's not one of them. Buford's not typical of anything from South Carolina except Aryan Army."

"Point well taken," I said.

I met Bobby Byrnes at the West Palm Beach DA's office the following afternoon. We were escorted into Assistant DA Barry Daniels's office immediately. I had only seen Daniels once, from a distance, at the Palm Beach Courthouse on the day Randolph Buford shot himself in the foot with a policeman's pistol. That day Daniels looked as if he had just made a motion in his pants but today he looked cool and confident. He sat behind his desk wearing an Assistant DA's navy blue suit, crisp white shirt, and a striped tie. When we shook hands I noticed my proposal was on his desk.

"Have you read it?" I asked, indicating the stack of papers.

"Yes. Interesting. In fact, very clever," he said.

"What does the DA think?" I wanted to know.

"He passed the buck and left the decision to me."

"What's your decision?" I asked.

"Personally I'd rather see this guy get the gas chamber," he said, deadpan.

"There is no gas chamber in Florida," Bobby Byrnes pointed out quickly.

"I'm joking, Bobby," Daniels said.

"Oh, sorry, Barry," Byrnes turned red.

"There are a lot of people who share your opinion about Buford," I said, "but I'm hoping for a better result."

Daniels nodded and turned to Byrnes. "Bobby, are you sure your client still wants this deal?"

"Positive," Byrnes said. "He feels he'll be safer."

"He'll be anything but safe," Daniels said, with a shrug. "But that's not my concern. When can you get me a signed agreement from Buford?"

"Today," Byrnes guaranteed.

"As soon as I have a letter from the Ministry and a signed agreement from Buford I'll approve it and forward it to the attorney general in Tallahassee."

"I'll hand carry it," I volunteered.

"I'll send it by courier," Daniels said. "I'll get you a fast answer."

The meeting adjourned.

Two days later we presented Barry Daniels with the Ministry's letter and Buford's statement. We were almost there.

New Year's Eve—2005

"How many people here will live to see 2006?" Steve Coleman asked our table of six revelers at the Boca Heights Country Club. The loud band music made it difficult to hear.

"Happy New Year to you, too," Togo Amato said, rolling his eyes. "You do this every year."

Togo and Steve were brothers-in-law, married to sisters Lenore and Barbara. Togo and Lenore were visiting from Boston for a couple of weeks. Togo was my closest friend from my North End days. He had been the best man at my wedding to Patty McGee. Steve and Togo had been instrumental in getting me my first job in Boca, which I quit after a few days.

Barbara, Steve's wife, poked his shoulder and frowned.

"Be cheerful," she said. "It's my birthday."

"Happy birthday," Steve raised a glass and we all joined him in toasting his wife. "But you have to admit there are a lot of BB people here tonight."

"What are BB people?" Claudette asked him.

"Barely breathing," Steve shouted.

"I know one person who won't be breathing in a minute," Barbara said.

"I hope it's the singer. She's too loud," Steve said, laughing. He looked at his watch. "Hey, there's only twenty minutes to midnight."

I excused myself and went to the men's room. On my way back to the party I came face-to-face with the fabulous Alicia Fine.

"What a surprise," I said self-consciously. "You look beautiful, Alicia."

"So does your girlfriend," she said, sounding like she had had too much to drink. "I can see why you chose her."

"I didn't choose anyone."

"Not choosing anyone is a choice," she said. She took an unneeded drink from her champagne glass.

A tall, handsome man in an elegant tuxedo walked up behind Alicia and put his hands possessively on her bare shoulders. He had a full head of white hair, a cosmetically enhanced smile, and a serious man's eyes.

"There you are," he said, kissing her on the cheek but looking at me.

"Jared, this is an old friend of mine," she said, turning to look up at him. "Eddie Perlmutter, meet Jared Farmer."

"The Boca Knight," he said, stepping aggressively around Alicia. He held out a huge hand, fingers stiff and poised to crush.

I'd been through this macho-mating manure before and I wasn't in the mood. I shoved my hand as far into his open palm as possible and extended my right index finger onto the veins under his right wrist. I pressed down hard enough to convince him that a squeezing contest was a bad idea.

To his credit he got the hint.

He's probably not a bad guy, I thought.

"Shall we go back to the party?" he asked Alicia, taking back his hand. "It's almost the New Year."

"Give me a minute, Jared." She smiled at him.

He hesitated then said, "Of course."

When he was gone, she turned to me. "Jared has asked me to marry him."

"Congratulations," I said, feeling a sense of loss but also one of relief.

"He's a very nice man but I don't think I love him." She slurred the words a little. "Sometimes I wish the Boca Knight would come to my rescue."

"In the end we all have to rescue ourselves," I said, and kissed her cheek. "Happy New Year, Alicia."

"Happy New Year, Eddie," she said, and went after Jared Farmer.

I rejoined my group on the dance floor just in time for the countdown to 2005. At midnight colorful balloons cascaded from a ceiling net and floated around us in slow motion. People kissed and embraced and wished one another good luck for another three hundred and sixty-five days.

The band played "Auld Lang Syne," and everyone sang along.

"What does 'Auld Lang Syne' mean anyway?" Togo asked.

"It means *days gone by* in Scottish," Claudette said. "It's like *once upon a time* or *long, long ago.*"

The six of us stood arm in arm, swaying to the music, thinking of days gone by.

Claudette watched me and sensed my melancholy.

"Enjoy the moment, Eddie," she said. "Before you know it, tonight will be *once upon a time* and *long, long ago.*"

"I know," I said, hugging her closer, "so let's dance."

Chapter 23

Death by Bagel

I spent the first couple of weeks in January working with Noah Paretsky on a presentation for the residents of Delray Vista. Late January I returned to Boston for a week to attend an event honoring Togo Amato's lifetime contributions to the North End. The cold weather was worse than I remembered. A former police chief who I had been friends with for many years was at the celebration and we spent the night reminiscing. We both agreed we were lucky to still be alive after all our near-death experiences on the force. We embellished on the events we could remember and made each other feel like heroic immortals.

The next week I almost choked to death on a bagel.

I was at a Delray deli named the Bagel Bush, exhausted after a night of coaching boxers at the PAL gym and falling asleep in my clothes at one A.M. while reading Lou Dewey's data on Delray Vista. I had arranged a ten A.M. meeting through Izzy with all the residents of Building 550 to discuss the haunted elevator. I was wearing the same clothes from the night before and still had the trainer's whistle in my pocket.

After reviewing my notes I turned to the Local section of the newspaper to read about new variations on old crimes.

I scanned the lead stories:

BOCA RIVER OFFICIALS STEAL ASSOCIATION FUNDS

TRIVIAL CASES CLOG UP COURTS AND JAIL SYSTEM

BOCA STEROID RING BUSTED

CLASSIC CAR BROKER STEALS CLIENT'S CLASSIC CAR

BOCA DOCTOR ACCUSED OF BACKING AL-QAEDA

WOMEN STEAL FIVE HUNDRED THOUSAND FROM NURSING HOME

ROAD RAGE MURDERER HAS LONG RECORD

MAN CRUSHED TO DEATH IN GARBAGE TRUCK

WOMAN KIDNAPPED BY MIAMI NEIGHBORS A YEAR AGO
    RETURNED SAFELY FROM EUROPE

Wait a minute.

I took a big bite from my bagel and leaned forward to read the kidnap story.

A seventy-nine-year-old couple from Miami, Sheppard and Seema Plotkin, kidnapped eighty-three-year-old Mia Kozlowski from her luxury apartment a year ago and took her to Poland. The kidnappers kept the woman drugged in a Polish nursing home for over a year while they slowly drained her funds, cashed her Social Security checks, and settled estate matters. Somehow Mrs. Kozlowski escaped and was found wandering in woods near the nursing home. She was recently returned to America and is recovering nicely. The Plotkins are being held without bail in Miami.

I was so fascinated by the article I forgot to chew. A large hunk of bagel slid into my throat, lodging near my vocal cords and upper airway. I couldn't talk or breathe.

Not good, I thought, knowing my brain would turn to puppy shit shortly. *Don't panic. You're a professional.*

I remembered from my first-aid training that a blockage of the upper airway was caused by food entering the trachea instead of the esophagus.

Simple enough.

All I had to do was oust the obstruction and breathe.

A piece of cake, I said to myself, knowing it was actually a piece of bagel.

I coughed loudly, trying to force the bagel out of my trachea. I only managed to move it slightly, creating a small opening that might give me an extra minute before I became a garden variety vegetable. I coughed louder, which got me a lot of attention but no breathing room.

Don't panic, I told myself again.

"He's choking," a fat woman sitting next to me said, pointing. "He's turning blue."

Okay, panic!

I stood up and pounded the table with the palm of my hand. I coughed and pointed frantically at my throat. I looked around for help and assessed my chances clinically.

I'm gonna die, I decided.

I coughed and gagged, trying desperately to dislodge the dough. I dislodged a cream cheese fart instead.

"I think he messed his pants," the fat lady said. "People do that before they die."

I did not mess my pants and I am not going die, I insisted, but I was wasting what little breath I had. No one could hear me.

"We have to help him," I heard someone shout, and people began shuffling toward me as fast as they could . . . which wasn't fast at all.

Someone was suddenly at my back, and I felt boney hands on my belly.

"Hang on, dear," I heard an old lady's voice encouraging me. Feeble fingers applied puny pressure to my lower abdomen but only succeeded in forcing another fart out of me.

"He did mess his pants," she said, letting me go. When I turned to face her she was backing away, holding her nose.

"We have to keep trying," a big, elderly guy said, and banged my back with the flat of his hand. Nothing.

"Let me try," the fat lady volunteered and tried the Heimlich maneuver on me. She only succeeded in making Mr. Johnson vaguely aware of her large breasts pressing against my back. Even at death's door the little jerk wouldn't leave me alone.

I stumbled forward and put my hands on a tabletop to steady myself. I stared at the old man sitting at the table. He had a spoon poised at his lips and I realized that he had continued eating while I was dying. He looked up at me, seemingly annoyed by my intrusion.

Self-centered son of a bitch.

I banged my forehead on the old man's table in frustration and smelled something so foul it startled me like smelling salts. My head snapped back, and I pointed at the bowl in front of him.

"Pacha," he said defensively. "It's the special."

I had heard of pacha (pronounced pah-char). In the deep recesses of my oxygen-deprived brain, I recalled an old Semitic recipe for skinless lamb's feet (hooves removed), with garlic and water. Someone once told me that finely ground lamb's balls were also used, but I never verified that.

A wave of nausea swept up from my stomach, passed through my larynx then blew the lid off my epiglottis. Bagel and bile blasted from my mouth, covering the old man and his table.

I breathed a sigh of relief and slumped into the chair across from him.

"Sorry," I said, gasping for breath

He looked at me, then at himself. He was a mess. He smiled incongruously as if he had just received a pleasant surprise. He stood up.

"I'm not paying for this," he announced, raising an index finger to the sky for emphasis. Without bothering to clean himself the old man shuffled twenty steps to the front door that was less than ten steps away.

"Tanenbaum, you come back here" a man wearing an AL name tag shouted. "At least pay half, you cheap bastard."

Tanenbaum gave Al the finger and was gone.

Al looked down at me. "Are you going to sue?" he asked.

"No," I said in a raspy voice. "It was my own fault."

"Damn right it was," Al said irritably. "And who's gonna pay for this mess?"

"Mendel, stop it," the nice fat lady who tried the Heimlich on me said. "The poor man almost died."

"It's okay." I smiled at the woman then looked at Al. "I'll take care of the mess."

"I want cash," Meyer insisted impatiently. "No charge cards."

A red spot appeared in front of my eyes, then another.

My brain must have sent a warning signal to my face because Al backed away from me.

"Never mind," he shrugged and turned his head. "Hay-zoos, bring your mop, Hay-zooooooos."

A small, dark man in an apron appeared from the kitchen holding a mop. "Oh mang," he moaned. "Pah-cha puke."

"Sorry," I said. I reached into my pocket, pulled out a ten-dollar bill, and handed it to Hay-zoos.

The little guy smiled at me, putting the bill in his shirt pocket. "Thank you, my mang. Don' feel bad. Pah-cha could make a goat puke."

I patted his shoulder and weaved unsteadily to another table. I sat down and inhaled several times before I became aware of being watched. I looked up and saw a group of Bagel Bush patrons watching me.

"You alright, mister?" a take-charge little man asked me with genuine concern.

I nodded gratefully and looked at the patrons of the Bagel Bush for the first time. I had been so preoccupied with my papers and nearly choking to death that I really hadn't checked out the place. It was enlightening.

I had previously categorized the rich people living in South Florida's more affluent communities as "The Chosen." The people in the Bagel Bush were "The Others."

If The Chosen lived in a land of plenty . . . The Others lived in a world of paltry. If The Chosen asked, "Why not?" The Others most probably asked, "Why me?" The Chosen dressed well. The Others . . . just dressed. The Chosen had more money than they needed and The Others did not.

The difference between being one of The Chosen or one of The Others can be a matter of merit or simply the luck of the genetic draw: lucky sperm or scrambled eggs. But this group was special. They had chosen to help a stranger.

"You're beautiful," I said sincerely.

"Who me?" the fat Heimlich lady asked, pointing to herself.

"All of you," I said.

After washing my face and hands I got in my MINI and drove to Delray Vista thinking how lucky I was to have chosen to eat with The Others.

Chapter 24

The Way We Weren't

I looked around the card room filled with the malcontents of Delray Vista, Building 550. According to Lou's research, not one person in the building was less than seventy-eight years old and most of them were over eighty. Remarkably all the original couples were intact; no divorces and no deaths. Unfortunately, they seemed to have outlived their friendships, forgotten their beginnings, and become fixated on the end. They had developed collective Alzheimer's . . . forgetting everything but the most recent grudge.

They sat on uncomfortable folding chairs, looking dubiously at me and ignoring one another. On one side of the room were the twelve residents of the six apartments on the first floor, and on the other side sat the dozen from the second floor. A ten-foot-wide aisle and a brick wall of resentment separated them.

I walked to a portable podium at the front of the room and

put down my notes. Lou Dewey was standing in the center aisle with his computer set on a small table, aimed at a screen next to me. He gave me a thumbs-up and I nodded. There was no turning back now.

"Can I have your attention, please," I said authoritatively. "I'm Eddie Perlmutter, a private investigator. I was hired by Izzy Fryberg to investigate your faulty elevator. I've called this meeting to give you the results."

"Did you find the problem?" an impatient male voice demanded.

"Yes I did," I said. "The elevator malfunctioned due to a stress fracture between the first and second floor."

The cross talk that followed was loud and incomprehensible.

"There's something wrong with the building?" a single male voice boomed above the babble.

"No, there's something wrong with the residents," I answered.

"Is that supposed to be a joke?" an angry woman shouted at me.

"No, it's no joke," I said. "There is so much stress between the people on the first and second floor that this whole place is falling apart."

I was surprised by the silence that followed. I walked to the wall and dimmed the lights. "I have a presentation I want you to see."

"What's the presentation about?" a woman asked civilly.

"It's about all of you," I said, and if I dropped a pin at that moment, you could have heard it hit the floor. I nodded to Lou Dewey who punched some buttons on his computer.

A blurred group picture appeared on the screen and the hauntingly beautiful melody of Pachelbel's *Canon in D* embraced the room. When the photo came into focus I heard a collective gasp as everyone in the audience saw themselves on the screen, the way they were . . . fifty years ago.

In the photo, twelve wives sat on beach blankets and twelve husbands stood behind them by the shoreline of a lake.

"Look at you in that bathing suit," Izzy Fryberg said to his wife, Emma. "You were a babe."

"Frankie, you were so thin," Zoe Mendlebaum said to her husband.

"Lucky, what a head of hair you had," Alice Freedlander said to her bald husband.

Bennett and Bertha Paretsky sat in silence, recognizing the photograph.

The canon gave way to a bouncy tune with lyrics that assured the listeners that everything old was new again.

"That's Mo and Maxine," Bunny Shpielman said when the new picture on the screen came into focus.

"That's us," Biggie Small said to his wife Ida when their images replaced Mo and Maxine's.

The photos included every resident of Building 550 in different venues at different times. They were in the snow of winter, the lakes of summer, the arcades of youth, the nightclubs of maturity, and the twilight of long lives.

"Wow," I heard from one corner of the card room.

"Ahhh," was heard from another direction.

"Oh my God, look at that."

"Look at me."

"Look at him."

"Look at her."

"I can't believe you let me wear that dress."

"I can't believe you made me buy that suit."

The bouncy music faded to a romantic ballad sung by a man with a gravely voice who kept telling some lucky person, over and over again, "You are so beautiful." It was the perfect song to accompany photos and old movies of the descendants of Delray Vista, Building 550. Noah had done a great job matching the music to the mood, and the audience was mesmerized.

When that song ended a new one began, explaining what friends are for . . . in good times or bad.

The last picture remained on screen the longest. It was a photo of twenty-four dear friends standing in front of a construction site next to a sign that read:

DELRAY VISTA—BUILDING 550—AVAILABLE SOON

When the music and the picture faded the lights came on.

"This completes our presentation," I announced.

No one said a word. No one moved.

First-floor Mo Myerson stood up, walked across the room, and embraced Izzy Fryberg.

"Izzy, I apologize," Mo said. "I forgot how much we all meant to each other."

A hugfest followed. Everyone apologized to everyone else. It was beautiful. Lou Dewey approached me smiling broadly.

"Great job, Lou," I congratulated him.

"I can't believe no one even asked who screwed up the elevator," he commented.

"That's not important now," I said. "I just hope it lasts."

"Why wouldn't it?"

I shrugged and watched the happy exchanges in the room.

"Izzy," Mo Myerson's voice boomed louder than all the others, "I'm going downstairs to write you a check for my share of the elevator."

"No no, Mo," Izzy waved away his offer. "I want you to be my guest."

"Hear, hear," said another second-floor resident. "The money isn't important."

"We should have participated in the first place," Lucky Freedlander, of the first-floor Freedlanders, said. "I'm going to pay my fair share, too."

"It's not necessary," second-floor Frankie Mendlebaum said good-naturedly. "Our friendships are more important."

"We insist," Bunny Shpielman said.

"Forget about it," Biggie Small said.

"I don't want to forget about it," Walter Hopfenberg, of the first-floor Hopfenbergs, declared. "I want to pay."

"We don't want your money," second-floor Helen Cohen said, hoping to end the conversation.

"Oh excuse me, Ms. Money Bags," Alice Freedlander said. "So now you're too good to take our money."

"That's no way to talk," Ira Cohen said sharply to Mrs. Freedlander, defending his wife.

"Don't talk to my wife in that tone of voice," Lucky Freedlander said to Ira Cohen.

"Stop arguing," Izzy Fryberg said plaintively.

"Mind your own business," Lucky told Izzy.

"You sons of bitches should have paid your own way in the first place," said second-floor man Jimmy Boorstein. "Then we wouldn't have had any of this bullshit."

"Don't use that fuckin' language in front of my wife," an offended husband shouted.

"Oh yeah!"

"Yeah!"

A shoving match ensued as the residents of Delray Vista Building 550 lost that loving feeling.

"I don't believe it," Lou said.

"I know," I said stuffing my hands dejectedly into my pants pockets where I felt my PAL referee's whistle. Impulsively I removed the plastic whistle, took a deep breath, and blew it as loud as I could. It sounded like a police raid. Everyone froze in place.

Izzy Fryberg had Mo Myerson by the collar and looked as if he was about to punch him.

Biggie Small had Arnie Litwack in a headlock.

Willa Hopfenberg was pulling Zoe Mendlebaum's hair.

It was comical but it wasn't funny.

All eyes turned to me but I had nothing to say. I started walking for the door.

"Wait, Eddie," Izzy Fryberg called. "Where are you going?"

"To the elevator," I told him. "It's the safest place in this building."

Chapter 25

WAKING WILTON MANORS—FEBRUARY 2005

When I told Claudette I was going to take Valentine's Day off and spend it with her she got unbelievably romantic and took me to bed at nine o'clock the night of the thirteenth. It was Valentine's Day by the time I fell asleep.

VALENTINE'S DAY DREAM:

I dreamed I was seated across the bar from Edik at Tropics. We were alone.

Okay, Meester Eddie, Edik said in a high-pitched voice, What can I get you?

Why are you wearing a woman's wig? I asked him.

What wig? He shrugged.

Why are you talking like a woman?

Don't be silly, he said in a woman's voice, and I watched his boobs in- flate and deflate like silicon accordions.

What's with your boobs? I asked.

You tell me. It's your fahking dream.

There it was again. That fahking word, that voice, that accent; where had I heard it before? Suddenly I remembered it all. I knew everything about the missing Dietrichs, Edik's changing voice, his wig, his inflatable boobs, and why Irene Kostanski was stranger than a bar mitzvah in Hitler's bunker. I tried to get up but I felt like I was up to my neck in quicksand. I thrashed my arms, kicked my feet, and screamed for help.

Then I heard someone else scream, "Eddie, stop it."

I knew that voice, too.

Suddenly my whole body was shaking and I felt myself falling backward until I landed hard on my back. The impact knocked the wind out of me and popped open my eyes. I saw my bedroom ceiling, and then Claudette's beautiful face looking down at me.

"Hi, Halle," I said with a stupid smile.

"Idiot," she replied as she knelt down next to me and pressed her lips to my cheek. "You were having a nightmare and I couldn't wake you. Are you alright?"

"I'm fantastic," I said, sitting up then scrambling to my feet. "See."

"Sit down." She reached for me. "You'll hurt yourself."

"No, I gotta go," I told her.

"Where are you going at one thirty in the morning on Valentine's Day? You were supposed to spend the day with me."

"I'm going to visit my two favorite homosexuals in Wilton Manors."

I got dressed and called Lou Dewey.

"What time is it?" he groaned into the phone.

"It's very late or very early depending how you look at it," I said. "I'm sorry to wake you Lou but I need some information right away," I explained.

"Who is that, Louie?" I heard Joy Feely ask, sounding annoyed.

"It's Eddie," he told her. "He needs me to do some research for him right away."

"You do whatever that man says," she replied.

"What do you need?" he asked wearily.

I told him.

"When do you need it?"

"Before the sun comes up."

"Why?"

"I'm conducting a predawn raid in Wilton Manors," I explained.

"Of course you are," Lou Dewey said, and hung up the phone.

An hour and a half later, I met Lou in the parking lot of a Dunkin' Donuts on Yamato, near I-95. He handed me a pile of computer printouts. I scanned a few pages.

"How did you get all this so fast?" I asked appreciatively.

"Dishonestly," he told me honestly.

We reviewed the notes by the map lights in his dented Cadillac.

"So, Edik *is* Natasha's brother," I said, referring to the counterfeiter I had arrested last year. "I should have noticed the resemblance sooner."

"Don't be so hard on yourself," Lou said. "You busted her a year ago then she escaped. You probably didn't get a good look at her."

"Are you kidding me?" I moaned. "I knocked her out at close range. I'm just getting old."

I resumed reading. "The guy I set on fire and the guy I shot in the knee that day were Boris and Yuri Kuznetsov, brothers from the Russian Mafia. It says here they're from Ekaterinburg. Where's that?"

Lou checked his notes. "Eight hundred and thirty miles northwest of Moscow."

"The middle of nowhere," I said.

"Actually, it's one of the top five largest cities in Russia and the crime capital of the country," Lou told me. "Tsar Nicholas was killed there and the Mafia has been big there since 1992."

"Is their Mafia powerful?"

"From what I read, the Russian Mafia is not one big happy family. There are thousands of loosely affiliated gangs," Lou said. "Ekaterinburg has at least fifteen. The Kuznetsov Kremlin Klan is one of them."

"The KKK?"

"Yes, and from what I read they're a lot like our own KKK," Lou said. "They hate the government and exclude Jews and gays. Then right across town is the Gulag Gang, made up mostly of Jews and gays. They're descendants of former Soviet prison-camp inmates."

"My kind of guys," I said.

We continued reading. Natasha's last name was Davidavitch, not Dubov, the name I remembered from her arrest. Her father was dead and her mother was living in a nursing home in Russia. Her brother Edik was mentioned but not identified as a gang member.

I looked at my watch. It was a little after four in the morning. I stuffed the papers into a leather satchel I brought.

"You want me to come with you?" Lou asked.

"No. I want you to go home to Joy," I said.

"I'm in love with her, Eddie," Lou blurted out.

"Hey, that's great. Have you told her?"

"I'm afraid to," he said. "What if she doesn't love me?"

"How could she not love you?"

I patted Lou on the shoulder and headed for my MINI.

Chapter 26

Cossack Closet Cases

Early-morning surprise raids were never a favorite activity of mine, and I was particularly apprehensive about this one. I didn't have the security of a legal search warrant or police authority. If I was wrong, my reputation would change from Boca Knight to Boca Nightmare in a New York–snowbird minute. My head was spinning.

I had phoned the boys in the gayborhood while driving to my meeting with Lou.

"Howard, it's Eddie," I told him while roaring through the deserted streets of Boca. "I need your help. I'm picking you up in about an hour."

"Your brain damage is worse than I thought," Howard had said, and hung up.

I hit *redial*.

"Have I won a contest?" he asked this time.

"You could say that," I told him.

"I never win contests," he said, making dry noises with his mouth, "except once I was selected queen of the New Jersey Turnpike Gay Pageant."

"Who is that on the phone at this hour?" I heard Derek ask. "Did someone die?"

"It's the man who was shot in the head the other night," Howard told Derek. "And no one died. Or did they?"

"I don't think so," I confirmed.

"He doesn't think anyone died," Howard said, yawning.

"Why is he calling at this hour?"

"I don't know. Why are you calling at this hour?"

"I think I know what happened to the Dietrichs," I told him. "And they didn't go on any vacation."

"I knew it," Howard said, suddenly fully awake. "Hold on a sec."

I heard him moving.

"Put the light out," I heard Derek protest.

"The Boca Knight thinks he knows what happened to the Dietrichs."

"Can't you listen in the dark?" Derek whined.

"So what happened to them?" Howard asked, ignoring Derek.

"I'll tell you when I see you," I said.

"If you're going on a stakeout, I'm not going with you," he said emphatically. "I hate stakeouts."

"When were you on a stakeout?"

"In the early seventies," he said. "A cross-country truck driver bound me hand and foot to pegs in the ground and left me there."

"That's being staked out," I told him.

"What's the difference?"

"A stakeout is when you watch people who don't know you're watching them—"

"That's voyeurism," Howard interjected.

"I like that. Can I go?" Derek asked in the background.

"I'm talking about breaking into someone's house," I told him.

"That sounds so bizarre," Howard said.

"Can I go?" Derek persisted.

"Not so fast, sweetheart," Howard told Derek. "The Boca Knight wants to break into someone's house."

"Forget I asked," Derek decided.

"We're not interested," Howard said. "We wouldn't do well in prison."

"It might be fun for a short sentence," Derek suggested.

"You're a hopeless jailhouse romantic," Howard scolded him. "Can I ask you, why you're planning to break into someone's house?"

"To help your friends," I told him.

"Derek, the Knight says we can help the Dietrichs by breaking and entering."

"What does one wear to break and enter?" Derek asked.

"I think black is an appropriate color," Howard suggested.

"Perfect," I said.

When I got to their house after my briefing with Lou, Howard insisted we travel in his Cadillac rather than my "tacky" MINI. He was in the driver's seat, I was in the passenger seat, and Derek was content to sit in the backseat.

"Where to, boss?" Howard asked.

"Edik the bartender's house," I said. "Here's the address I got from the Tropic's pay records."

"I know where they live," Howard said. "But how did you get into the Tropic's pay records."

"Don't ask."

"Okay, Double-oh-seven," Howard said, not pleased with my secretive answer. "Are you sure about this?"

"Positive."

We drove across town to the Davidavitch house. We parked a block away and scurried stealthily to a hiding place behind a clump of bushes. I was carrying the small leather satchel with Lou's notes and my equipment.

"What an adorable bag," Derek said. "Where did you get it?"

"Can we talk about that later?"

I removed a pair of ATN Viper goggles from the bag and put them over my eyes.

"Those are fabulous," Derek said. "Can you really see in the dark?"

"Yes, I can see perfectly. Now stay here."

I crept to the side of the house about twenty yards away.

"This is so exciting," I heard Howard say from his hiding place.

"I'd rather be the Peeping Tom with the night goggles," Derek said.

I crawled around the perimeter of the house looking for an alarm system. I found nothing. I returned to our hiding place.

"You have schmutz all over your shirt and pants," Howard told me.

"I've been crawling in the dirt," I explained.

"That's no excuse." He fussed and busied himself brushing me off.

As we bumbled behind the bushes, I couldn't help thinking of other early-morning raids when I was on the Boston Police Force. I was always the first to kick down a door and rush the bad guys. I had no problem with risking my life but on a few occasions my impulsive behavior put the lives of other cops in danger. I wasn't about to do that tonight.

"You guys stay here," I ordered. "I'll pick the front door lock—"

"You can do that?" Derek interrupted.

I nodded. "When you see a light go on in the house, that's your signal to come in. Got it?"

They nodded solemnly.

I removed my Glock from the back of my waistband and checked it out. I took a pencil-sized flashlight out of my shirt pocket and tested it with a quick flash.

"Why don't we have guns and flashlights?" Howard wanted to know.

"Do you know how to use a gun?" I asked.

"Heavens no, but we know how to use a flashlight," Derek said.

"You can have the flashlight," I said. "But not right now. Stay here."

I moved silently toward the totally darkened house.

The front-door lock was an old Schlage deadbolt and I opened it easily with my equally ancient lock pick set, which I always carried in my wallet. I went into the house and moved quickly through the small front room. The night goggles were effective, and I avoided the obstacle course of suitcases placed randomly on the living-room floor. I hefted one of the bags and it was heavy. Someone was planning on going somewhere soon.

The door to the bedroom was open, and I looked inside. There were two people asleep in the bed. I moved closer and was able to see Davidavitch and Irene. I put the nose of my Glock between Edik's eyes, pushed my goggles to my forehead, and switched on the lamp next to the bed.

"Happy Valentine's Day," I said loud enough to get a reaction.

Edik squinted and blinked at the bright lights.

"What the *fahk*?" he exclaimed, his eyes slowly crossing, trying to look at the gun barrel pressed against his forehead.

Irene pulled the covers up to her neck, looking extremely frightened and ugly.

I heard the front door bang open . . . followed by a loud crash and the splintering of wood.

"Son of a bitch," Howard cursed.

"Put on a light," I told them.

"Thanks for the tip, Mr. Night Goggles," Howard shouted.

I saw the light go on in the living room.

"Howard tripped on a suitcase and fell through the coffee table," Derek shouted.

I heard the shattering sound of ceramic on plaster.

"That was Hercules throwing a tacky lamp against a seedy wall."

I heard a thud.

"That was my hero kicking the suitcase he tripped over."

"Who the fuck leaves suitcases by the front door?" Howard complained.

"People planning to go on a trip," I called back. "Get in here."

Howard and Derek both tried to fit through the bedroom door at the same time.

"After you, Goliath," Derek said, backing off.

"What the *fahk* are you doing here?" Edik said, recognizing them.

"Tripping over your *fahking* suitcases, you asshole," Howard answered.

"What are you doing in my house?" Edik demanded.

"Get out of bed," I ordered them. Edik complied; Irene didn't. "Get out of bed, Irene," I said, still pressing the gun against Edik's forehead.

"I'm not dressed," Irene protested.

"Thanks for the warning," I said. "Now get out of bed."

"No," Irene refused.

"Howard." I motioned for him to move her.

"Make it easy on yourself, Irene," Howard said as he approached her.

Irene pulled the covers over her head. "Don't you dare," she screamed.

Howard looked at me, hoping I'd call him off.

"Howard, get her out of bed," I ordered.

Howard grabbed the blanket with both hands and tugged. The covers and the covered hit the floor. As threatened, Irene was naked.

Howard and Derek stared in amazement.

"She has a penis," Derek said, pointing.

I wasn't surprised.

CHAPTER 27

ONE BIG UNHAPPY FAMILY

The five of us gathered in the living room of the Davidavitch dump. The décor was cracked ceramic, wrecked wood, and funky floral. Four large suitcases sat in the middle of the room, one tipped on its side. I sat on a musty, overstuffed armchair splattered with unidentifiable, thought-provoking stains.

Edik and Irene sat on a scary sofa obviously from the same collection.

I casually pointed my Glock at the two suspects. The only danger they seemed to pose was airborne disease. Edik's Underoos were grungy and his black Rolling Stones T-shirt was gamey. Irene, now wrapped from head to toe in the bedsheet, looked like a poorly preserved mummy.

Derek and Howard hovered in the background. Derek looked confused. Howard was angry.

Howard pointed at Edik. "You communist closet case."

"*Fahk* you," Edik said predictably.

"You wish, pal," Howard said.

"Stop it," I said. "We're not here for that."

"What are you here for?" Edik asked uncertainly.

"We're here for the Dietrichs," I told him.

"No Dietrichs here," Edik insisted.

"I know," I said, waving the Glock at him. "They're with your sister in Russia."

"I don't have seester." Edik was a lousy liar.

"Sure you do," I said. "I met her last year when I raided her ecstasy lab."

"You make mistake," Edik said, his voice shaking.

"No mistake," I said. "You and your sister look exactly alike. Are you twins?"

"No, she is five years older," he blurted out, then slapped his forehead. "Idiot."

Edik looked like his sister but he obviously couldn't think like her.

"I also met Uncle Boris and Yuri in the same raid," I said. "We hit it off great. I hit your sister with a right cross and Uncle Boris with three shots to the knee."

"What happened to Uncle Yuri?" Derek asked.

"I set him on fire," I told them.

"Of course you did," Howard said. "Did they go to jail?"

"They were arrested," I said. "But they escaped."

"How?" Derek asked.

"They passed counterfeit bank checks for bail," I said.

"Clever communists," Howard said. "Where are they now?"

"In Russia," I said. "Derek, hand me that satchel, please."

He passed it to me.

"If she's in Russia why is Edik here?" Howard asked.

"Based on the information I received from my research

department," I said, removing stacks of paper from the leather bag, "I think she was trying to keep him away from her gang of antigay, anti-Semitic psychos."

"Why would a gay man want to belong to an antigay gang?"

"Edik didn't belong to the gang," I explained, referring to my notes. "His sister did. Natasha and Edik were born and raised in Ekaterinburg in the neighborhood where the Russian version of our KKK originated . . ."

"You know Ekaterinburg?" Edik was surprised.

"I know everything," I told him. "Natasha wanted to be a KKK girl since she was a kid. Unfortunately, her kid brother wanted to be a KKK girl, too. My information tells me that Natasha had to keep her gay brother's secret all these years to keep him alive."

"That's why Irene was posing as the world's homeliest woman," Derek said.

"Correct," I said. "The mob considered Edik an inconsequential noncombatant and tolerated him because of his sister's status. Had they known Edik was gay they would have circumcised him with a hammer and sickle, and cut her throat for lying."

"Russian necktie." Edik moaned, touching his neck. "They cut your throat and pull your tongue through the incision."

"Sounds very stylish," Howard interrupted. "But, what about the Dietrichs?"

"See if you can follow this. Edik's sister and the Kuznetsovs left the USA last spring to avoid prosecution. Natasha had moved Edik from Russia to New York City a few years earlier to keep him away from the KKK. When Edik met Irene in New York, his sister came up with the female impersonator idea for their protection. Then when Natasha and her boys had to leave the country she told Edik to move to Florida where he'd be safest. She figured the Kuznetsovs would never return there. Edik and Irene moved to Wilton Manors for the ambience and met the Dietrichs strictly by chance. How am I doing, Edik?"

His sullen expression told me I was doing great.

"Edik and Irene somehow learned about the entire Elliot-to-Eileen cross-country, cross-dressing saga."

"Yes, they told us everything. We told them almost nothing except the cross dressing," Irene said proudly.

I continued unraveling the story. "My guess is that Edik told his sister about the Dietrichs and the KKK contrived the kidnapping. They gave the Dietrichs two choices: your money or your life. They had the Dietrichs withdraw a large sum of money from their bank account and take a trip to Europe under the guise of a vacation. They probably drugged the Dietrichs, which would explain the wheelchair on the plane. The traveling companion the flight attendant saw was probably a hired stooge, who may or may not still be breathing."

"Why not just kill the Dietrichs after they had the money?" Derek asked.

"They didn't take all the money at once," I conjectured. "That would have aroused suspicion. Plus, Edik certainly wasn't qualified to commit a murder and cover his tracks professionally. My bet is that the Dietrichs are alive in Ekaterinburg and the KKK is slowly draining their funds and collecting their Social Security checks."

"You really think they're still alive?" Howard asked.

"Yes, I do," I said. "I think they're being kept alive until all their money is gone. I think Edik's sister told him to let her know if anyone started asking about the Dietrichs. When Howard and Derek began poking around Edik told his sister and all of a sudden postcards started arriving in Eileen and John's handwriting."

"How the hell did you come up with this theory?" Derek wondered.

"I read it in the newspaper one morning," I told them. "A Polish couple from Miami drugged and kidnapped a neighbor, stuck her in a Polish nursing home, and slowly drained her assets in the States."

"Why didn't you tell us before?" Howard asked.

"I didn't put it all together until tonight," I explained. "In a dream."

"Should we tell his sister we're on to them?" Howard pressed.

"Edik already told her," I said. "She was ordered by the Kuznetsovs to tell Edik to shoot me."

"They are not really my uncles and I am not killer," Edik said. "I told Natasha to hire professional."

"And after you missed me she told you to try again. So, you decided to run away instead." I pointed with the Glock at the suitcases.

"I go hide somewhere with Jonah."

"Who is Jonah?" Derek asked.

"I'm Jonah," Irene said. "Jonah Kaplansky."

"A Jewish, gay transvestite." Howard smirked. "Three of the KKK's favorite food groups."

"Can we make deal?" Edik pleaded.

"Of course we can make a deal," I said.

All eyes turned to me.

"Must my seester be involved?" Edik whined.

"Yes. She has to help us get the Dietrichs back without giving you up," I told him.

"Impossible," he whined.

"Call her. I'll talk to her."

"She hates you."

"She'll talk to me," I said confidently.

I checked my watch. It was five fifteen in the morning.

"It's early afternoon in Ekaterinburg," I estimated.

"I will not call her," Edik tried.

"Edik, either you call or I'm going to call the U.S. Consulate in Ekaterinburg and start extraditing your sister and your uncles."

"You cannot extradite them," he told me.

"The U.S.-Russian Mutual Legal Assistance Treaty says I can."

"No such treaty," Edik insisted.

"Bill Clinton and Igor Ivanov would disagree," I said reading from a printout.

Thank you, Lou Dewey.

"Fahk," Edik uttered.

"There's also the little matter of you and Jonah," I said, adding the frosting.

"Cell phone is in top drawer of nightstand," Edik said dejectedly.

"I'll get it." Howard moved quickly from the room.

"We're gonna die," Jonah decided.

Howard returned holding a cell phone and a handgun. "They were side by side in the nightstand."

"Would that be the gun that creased my forehead?" I asked redundantly.

Edik looked miserable as he pushed a button on his cell, waited, and began speaking in Russian.

I nudged him with the Glock.

"Speak English," I told him.

He stammered through a reasonable English explanation of the entire situation. He stopped talking and listened for a moment. He nodded his head and held the phone out to me.

"She wants to talk to you."

"Natasha, your brother looks just like you," I said cheerfully.

"Fahk you," she said.

"He sounds like you, too."

"I will have you keeled, you stupid bastard," she hissed. "One call to Florida and . . . bang, bang you're dead."

"Let's not bullshit each other," I said calmly. "If you could make one call, you would have made it already. You're protecting your brother."

"What do you want?" she said through teeth I knew were clenched.

"I want the Dietrichs returned to America safe and sound," I said.

"Impossible," she said quickly. "The Dietrichs are dead."

"Then so are you," I told her. "Say good-bye to your brother."

I handed Edik the phone.

"Natasha, he weel tell Kuznetsovs about me. They weel keel me and Jonah with Russian necktie." There was genuine panic in his voice.

He listened for a moment then looked at me.

"She wants to talk to you," he said again, and handed me the phone.

"Dietrichs are not dead," she said.

"I told you not to bullshit me."

"What do you want?"

"I want you to tell Boris and Yuri I've been tracking the three of you since you skipped bail in Palm Beach last year," I instructed her. "Tell them I know who they are and where they are."

"They don't care what you know," she said. "They will not cooperate."

"I'll make them an offer they can't refuse," I said.

"From *Godfather*, right?"

"Very good, Natasha," I said sarcastically. "Here's the offer. I'll exchange my silence and the money they already stole from the Dietrichs, for the Dietrichs' safe return."

There was a long pause.

"Keeping the money is good idea," Natasha said.

No shit.

"You have twenty-four hours to make the deal," I told her. "After that, I'm sending in the Feds. By the way, I'm sorry about your brother's broken nose."

"Fahk you," she said, and we disconnected.

"Why did you tell my seester you broke my nose?" Edik laughed nervously.

"I was making a prediction," I told him.

Edik was confused until I hit him with a short, straight right fist to the bridge of his nose, breaking the bone like a twig. He covered his face with both hands.

"Son of a bitch," he cursed, moaning in pain.

"That's for shooting me."

CHAPTER 28

FINDING SYLVIA

Later that day Sylvia Goldman's lawyer, Sanford Kreiger, called to tell me Sylvia had broken her hip while attempting to steal the coffee urn at the breakfast buffet. The urn was still plugged into the wall at the time and when she tried to walk away with it the cord went taut and Sylvia went down. I immediately went to the hospital.

Resident Dr. Marc Eisenstock, looked young enough to be a resident of Sesame Street. He gave me a brief description of Sylvia's injury.

"The ball on top of Mrs. Goldman's femur is broken completely off," he said. "It's bad."

We were in the corridor outside Sylvia's room. She was unconscious, lying motionless in her bed, looking very frail and impossibly old.

"What happens now?" I asked.

"Rehabilitation is out of the question," he began. "She's too weak. We can surgically give her an artificial hip but the operation could be very traumatic in her condition," he said unemotionally. "Or we can put her in a long-term care center and make her as comfortable as possible. Statistically speaking, I think a care center is our best option."

"Sylvia is not a statistic," I protested.

"We're all statistics in some category," he told me. "Sylvia is one of two hundred and seventy thousand people over sixty-five who fracture a hip every year in this country. She could also become part of the thirty percent who die within the first twelve months of the injury. She's a very frail eighty-year-old."

"She's not eighty yet," I said, defending my girl.

"Her actual age isn't the only problem," the doctor said. "She's elderly and brittle. Ninety percent of hip fractures are in women like her."

"Why?"

"After menopause a woman's bones lose density," he explained. "It's called osteoporosis and one out of every two women over fifty will suffer an osteoporosis-related fracture at one time or another. I'm sorry to keep citing statistics but this is the reality we're dealing with."

"So we operate or relocate," I summarized. "Who decides?"

"Her family," the doctor said.

"She has no family," I explained. "She has a lawyer who takes care of her financial affairs through her late husband's will. That's it."

"If the lawyer is her legal guardian he can make decisions for her," Dr. Eisenstock speculated.

"I don't know his status," I said. "I'll check it out."

"Good luck," the doctor said, shaking my hand, and continuing on his rounds.

I went into Sylvia's room and stood by her bed. Her skin was pathetically pasty and deep wrinkles cut into her shallow face. I never cry . . . but if I did, that would have been a good time.

I had only known Sylvia Goldman for about a year and she had only known herself for fifty-six of her seventy-six years. The end of her life was drawing near but the beginning remained a mystery. Without a beginning there could be no meaningful end, and I believed Sylvia Goldman's life deserved meaning.

I called Sanford Kreiger when I got home and told him about my hospital visit. I gave him Dr. Eisenstock's opinion about a nursing home.

"He's probably right but there's no legal guardian to make that decision," he said.

"What about you?"

"I have the power of attorney," he explained. "But I am not her legal guardian."

"Who is?"

"No one." Kreiger sighed. "She always said she didn't need one."

"She needs one now," I said.

"A court would have to provide her with protective services," he told me.

"How does that work?"

"First we'd have to get a written opinion from a doctor, preferably a psychiatrist, stipulating that Sylvia can no longer take care of herself. Then a petition has to be filed with the Circuit Court of Palm Beach County saying that a diligent search for relatives had been made and none were found. The petition recommends a suitable guardian, and then we post the entire document in the legal notices section of the local newspaper to formerly inform the public of the intended action."

"You could handle all that," I said.

"I could do the legal work," Kreiger said. "But her husband's instructions prohibit me from looking into Sylvia's past."

"If we can't prove there's no family, we can't appoint you as her guardian," I observed.

"I'm not going to be her guardian," Kreiger replied, rejecting the idea immediately.

"Why not?"

"I have a conflict of interest legally and I'm Sylvia's age," he said firmly. "She needs someone younger, with no conflict of interest . . . someone like you, Mr. Perlmutter."

"I'm not qualified to be anyone's guardian," I said. "I have enough trouble taking care of myself. I'll have to do some more investigating."

"I wish you would just leave it alone," Kreiger said.

"Sorry, I can't do that," I told him, and hung up the phone.

I went directly to Joy Feely's office and met with Lou Dewey.

"Remember you told me you could find anyone with your computer?" I asked.

He was sitting with his feet on his desk.

"If they're in cyberspace I can find them," Lou said, nodding.

"Could you find a baby born in New York City in 1929?"

"I think so," he said confidently. "New York started recording births in 1915. But we're talking about thousands of babies. Can you narrow it down a little?"

"I'm looking for a girl," I said.

"That's a start. Do you have a name?"

"Sylvia, maybe," I said.

"Sylvia Maybe is her name or maybe her name is Sylvia?"

"Maybe her name is Sylvia," I clarified.

"Last name?"

"I have no idea," I told him. "Her married name is Goldman."

"Do you have any idea of the hospital she was born?"

"No."

"County?"

"No."

"Planet?"

"Be nice," I said.

"Okay. So all we know is that we're looking for a baby girl born in 1929—"

"I'm not even sure it was 1929," I interrupted him.

"Great. We have a baby girl, born maybe in 1929, maybe her name was Sylvia, and maybe she was born in New York. Right?"

"Right."

"Is she a missing person?"

"No, she has a missing memory," I said. "She's seventy-six years old but only has fifty-six years of memories. And now she's got Alzheimer's, schizophrenia, plus she's delusional."

"Anything else?"

"She steals bagels."

"That could be the clue we're looking for," Lou said sarcastically, and laughed. "Why at seventy-six does she suddenly want to find all those missing years?"

"Actually, she doesn't," I confessed. "I do."

"Why?"

"She's my friend," I said. "Like you're my friend, and I have to find her a legal guardian. If she has family I need to know."

"Enough said. What else can you think of that might help me find her?"

"Well, if she's really seventy-six, she was born during the Depression," I said. "Her family probably had financial problems like everyone else. Maybe they gave her up for adoption."

"Wouldn't she remember her adopted family?" Lou asked.

"I don't know. Maybe she wasn't adopted," I tried. "Maybe she got stuck in an orphanage and became a ward of the state."

"Lost in the system?"

"Possibly," I said. "She has mental problems now. Maybe she

had them then and was tranferred to an institution. Check it out."

"I'll look into mental facilities," he said. "Anything else you can think of?"

I thought for a moment. "Yeah, she has a recurring dream," I remembered. "She dreams she's being tormented by a two-headed boy and a wicked witch. The witch is screaming at her, and the two-headed boy is laughing."

"What the hell is that all about?"

"She has no idea," I said.

"What do you know about her husband?"

"I know he was a doctor."

"What kind of doctor?"

"Some sort of shrink." I shrugged.

"That might explain the craziness," Lou said, shaking his head. "I knew a kid in Atlantic City whose father and mother were shrinks. He was the most screwed-up kid in town."

He was already tapping his computer keys when I let myself out.

CHAPTER 29

JUDGMENT DAY

Hate hums like an overloaded power line and fear smells like old sweat. Judge Jacobs and Randolph Buford were vibrating and giving off a fearful odor as they stared at each other from across the judge's desk. Buford's hands were clenched in his lap like a boxer waiting for the opening bell. He was flanked by the same two black officers who had wrestled him to the floor in the courtroom the day he shot himself in the foot. Both guards held Tasers by their sides. There would be no outbursts today.

Assistant District Attorney Barry Daniels sat to Buford's left, looking very much like the professional man he was. He smelled of cologne and hummed a happy tune.

No hate. No fear. Cool.

Bobby Byrnes smelled uncertain and a little fearful.

Simon Kane, the Minister for Internal Agreements Litigation and Human Rights, sat to Daniels's left, not looking as

important as I knew he was. His hooded eyes and serious de-
meanor gave him a vaguely sinister appearance. He was dressed
in a nondescript gray suit and a tie too pooped to pop. Kane
looked like he had been carved from granite with a broken chisel.
He was rough around the edges, wide, square, dense, and impla-
cable. His hair was cropped close, like a soldier's, but he was too
old for soldiering. I guessed he was in his early fifties. He didn't
smell or hum. He vibrated.

Judge Avery Jacobs glanced at the documents on his desk
then scanned the room.

"Everything seems to be in order," the judge said, shuffling
the papers needlessly.

The papers were perfect. We had approvals from the Ministry of Justice, the State Attorney General, Assistant DA Daniels,
Bobby Byrnes, and Randolph Buford himself. The junior Nazi
had even signed a document that held the Ministry harmless if
he should die during his time in custody.

Signed, sealed, and delivered, I thought.

"This is highly unusual." Jacobs sighed. "Pretrial diversions
are rare in Florida, and this particular request is unprecedented."

No one responded.

"Mr. Kane," the judge said, turning to the minister. "Are
you sure?"

"We believe we can rehabilitate this man," Kane said. "If
anyone can."

Buford hummed with hatred.

"Your anger doesn't frighten me," Kane said to Buford, lean-
ing forward and returning Buford's baleful stare. "I have killed
better men than you."

"I'm not afraid of you," Buford replied, unconvincingly.

"You should be," Kane told him. Buford blinked.

Judge Jacobs reached for a pen, poised it over the document,
then quickly signed.

"It's official," he said, looking up. "When do you want the prisoner?"

"We would like him to arrive May fifth," Kane said.

"Why that particular date?" Jacobs asked.

"It's important to our program," Kane assured the judge.

"Do any of you object to May fifth?" The judge surveyed the room.

"That's nearly two months, Your Honor," Bobby Byrnes said. "My client is being held in jail during all that time. It's unreasonable."

"Shut up," Buford interrupted rudely. "It's not safe for me on the streets anymore. I want to be held in protective custody until I leave."

"Done," the judge agreed.

"We want him delivered to us," Kane announced.

"I'll deliver him," I said without hesitation. "I've transported prisoners before."

"Do you have any problem with Mr. Perlmutter?" The judge turned to Daniels.

"He's the perfect man for the job," the assistant DA said, smiling.

"Mr. Kane?"

"I have no problem with Mr. Perlmutter." He nodded.

"Mr. Byrnes?" The judge looked at the defense attorney.

"I have no problem, Your Honor," Byrnes said.

"I have a problem," Buford told the judge.

"You'll just have to get over it," Jacobs said.

Huuuummmmmm.

The next day Edik phoned to tell me the Kuznetsovs had decided that the two hundred thousand dollars they had already stolen from the Dietrichs, combined with my silence, was a good trade. I told him we should meet in person.

I drove to Wilton Manors to meet with Edik. He was stand-ing behind the bar polishing glasses when I arrived.

"Your nose doesn't look so bad," I told him as I sat on a bar stool.

"Fahk you," he said. "Kuznetsovs ready to return Dietrichs in six weeks."

"Why so long?" I protested.

"Much red tape to get Dietrichs out of country. Many people to pay off."

"That shouldn't take more than a month," I insisted.

"There is other problem," Edik added.

"Let me guess," I said, analyzing the situation. "The Die-trichs have become drug dependent and the Kuznetsovs want to detox them before sending them back. It's probably very difficult to get withdrawing drug addicts through airport se-curity."

"You catch on fast." Edik nodded and pointed his index finger at his temple.

"What drugs have you been giving them?"

"GHB," Edik said. "We give them shot in the ass every day."

"Brilliant. The rape drug right into the bloodstream." I shook my head. "You're lucky you didn't kill them. GHB is a degreasing solvent, you idiot."

"I'm not idiot," Edik defended himself.

"Of course you are," I insisted. "How did you know what dose to give them?"

"My seester told me," he said.

"Is your sister a doctor?"

"No, she is criminal."

Moron.

"They are fine," Edik said, reading my mind. "They are in nursing home. Many doctors watching them."

"Okay, so what's the plan for their return?" I asked.

"In about six weeks Dietrichs can be picked up at Frankfurt Airport."

"Is there anything wrong with them besides the drugs?" I asked.

"They don't eat much and are a little dopey," he said, unconcerned. "But they'll be fine. Dietrichs get better. Kuznetsovs get money and everyone lives happily ever after."

Dumb shit.

I figured the Dietrichs were being given varying doses of GHB and nutrition by injection to raise and lower their level of consciousness as needed. Lower the dose for *"Sign this . . ."* and raise the dose for *"Go to sleep."* When their financial assets were totally exhausted, I felt certain the original plan had called for the nursing home to become a hospice. Eventually the nourishment would be lowered, the drug dose increased, until the Dietrichs died.

I reached across the bar and grabbed Edik by his shirt collar.

"Everyone lives happily ever after in a fairy tale," I growled. "This is no fahkin' fairy tale. The Dietrichs would have died if their friends hadn't suspected something. If anything happens to the Dietrichs, you're going down."

I released his neck.

I was walking to my car on Wilton Drive when my cell phone rang. I checked the caller ID.

"Lou," I answered the phone. "What's up?"

"It's March fifteenth," he said. "Happy birthday, Eddie. How does it feel to be sixty-one?"

"I can't feel a thing," I said. "How are you doing with Sylvia's search?"

"I found three baby girls named Sylvia but one was black and two are dead."

"What about the orphanages?" I asked.

"There were so many orphans during the Depression that

it's tough to narrow it down. Plus you're not even sure her original name was Sylvia or if she was really born in New York. How's she doing, by the way?"

"She's awake one minute, asleep the next," I said. "No communication. Did you check out the two-headed boy dream?"

"I did," Lou replied. "I didn't find any two-headed boys but I did locate a six-hundred-pound woman with a beard and a three-balled monkey."

"Now we're getting somewhere," I said, and hung up.

Chapter 30

Bad Things—Good People

I started my own personal search for Sylvia Goldman by calling "Uno" Unitas, a former partner of mine in the homicide division of the Boston Police Department. His real first name was Lazlo but he was born with one testicle and his older sister nicknamed him Uno.

"It's the Boca fuckin' Knight," Uno shouted into the phone. "How's retirement?"

"I've been too busy to notice," I said.

"I know all about it," he said sincerely. "We're all proud of you."

"Thanks, Uno," I said. "I'm calling for an information update."

"Okay, here it is," he said. "I'm still single, haven't gotten laid in a month, still like to head butt drunk drivers and insist they stumbled, haven't grown a second ball, and I'm five years from retirement."

"I had a different update in mind," I said, laughing. "Do you remember Dr. Kessler?"

"Sure, Sigmund Kessler," Lazlo said. "The department shrink."

"His name was Glenn," I corrected him.

"You call me Uno," Uno reminded me. "I call him Sigmund. Anyway, Kessler retired a while ago."

"Do you have any idea where he is now?"

"Why? Are you still crazy?"

"Yes, but this has nothing to do with me," I told him.

"He has a private practice in Cambridge," Uno told me.

"He's still working? How old is he?"

"Early seventies, maybe," Uno said. "He's famous now."

"What did he do?"

"He wrote a book called *Why Bad Golf Happens to Good People*."

"Who gives a shit why bad golf happens to good people?" I asked.

"Based on sales I'd say close to a million people care," Uno told me.

"Where can I find him?" I asked.

"He's listed in the phone book," Uno said. "But hold on, I'll get it for you." He gave me the number and asked, "Why not use a shrink in Boca?"

"I always liked Kessler," I said. "He had good judgment."

"Didn't he try to have you committed to a mental institution?" Uno laughed.

"Yeah, as your roommate."

We talked about some old times and said good-bye.

I left a message on Kessler's answering machine and he called back in minutes.

"Explosive compulsive Eddie Perlmutter," Kessler said, laughing. "How are you?"

"I have a longer fuse now."

"I doubt it," he joked. "You probably just have slower reflexes."

"I have an important psychological question I need answered," I said.

"I'm flattered," he said. "Fire away."

"Why does bad golf happen to good people?"

"You heard about my book?" he said, laughing.

"Lazlo Unitas told me."

"He hasn't taken up golf, I hope," Kessler said. "He's too volatile."

"No, but he did know where to find you," I said.

"I'm delighted," Kessler said. "Talk to me."

Without using names, I gave Kessler a quick summary of Sylvia's history plus my theories on orphanages, adoption, and mental institutions.

"A seventy-six-year-old woman has fifty-six years of memory, and you're trying to reconstruct her first twenty years," he summarized. "May I ask why?"

"I want to know if she has any living family for personal and professional reasons."

"Understood," Dr. Kessler said. "It sounds to me like she's in a fugue state or has RAD."

"And what the fugue is RAD?"

"A fugue state is when someone abandons their personal identity and memories because of a trauma," he said. "RAD is Reactive Attachment Disorder, which is the result of an infant failing to develop a normal attachment to its primary caregiver."

"Are these permanent conditions?"

"Not necessarily. But based on your friend's age, if she was in the mental health system it was during a very controversial time," Kessler said. "There was a lot of questionable experimentation in those days."

"What type of experimentation?" I asked.

"Mind control," he said. "Drugs, shock treatments, you name it. We studied it in medical school. It was called the Eliza Program."

"Never heard of it."

"Did you ever hear of the movie *My Fair Lady*?"

"Sure. Rex Harrison and Audrey Hepburn. He tries to totally change her personality?"

"That's it. Best picture of the year in sixty-four," Kessler confirmed.

"I liked *Kitten with a Whip* with Ann-Margret better."

"Excellent choice," Kessler humored me. "Anyway, in the late forties our government started some pretty bizarre experiments on mind control using wards of the State as guinea pigs. It was a Cold War thing and the CIA got involved. They were big advocates of behaviorism and pharmacology."

"Pharmacology I can understand," I said. "That's drugs. But you're going to have to explain behaviorism."

"Of course, I'm sorry," Kessler said. "Let me call you back in a few minutes. I have some books on the subject I want to review."

Fifteen minutes later we were on the phone again.

I heard him rummaging and turning pages.

"I found what I was looking for," he said. "Behaviorists believe that personalities are the result of nurturing, not genetics. John B. Watson was one of the original behaviorists. I'm going to read you a direct quote of his that should help you understand the philosophy."

"Please don't. Just give me the basics," I interrupted.

"Okay," Kessler said. "Watson believed he could mold people into whatever he wanted them to be . . . regardless of their talents or tendencies."

"It sounds like brainwashing."

"It *is* brainwashing."

"Did Watson ever prove his theory?"

"He tried," Kessler said. "But his methods were primitive and would never be allowed today. His 'Little Albert' study was the worst. In 1920, Watson experimented with an eleven-month infant named Albert. He basically made the kid a guinea pig to support his theories. Listen to this: Watson put a tiny lab rat, very harmless, into the crib with the baby along with colorful stuffed animals and toys. Little Albert responded positively to the rat. But when Watson put the rat in the crib and annoyed Little Albert with noise and distractions the infant feared the rat. Psychiatrists call it a response analysis."

"I call it horseshit," I said. "Did Little Albert grow up to be an exterminator?"

Kessler laughed halfheartedly. "Like I said, it was a long time ago," he said. "But all this experimentation was happening right about the time your friend was in the system. She could be one of those unfortunate victims."

"How many Elizas were there?" I asked.

"Who knows?" Kessler sighed. "Hundreds, I'm sure. The CIA wanted to create drug-induced, compliant personalities and that would have required a lot of subjects. They tried addictive stuff like morphine to make the patients drug dependent. They tried Thorazine, Ritalin, marijuana, heroin, Temazepam, Mescaline, Sodium Pentothal, Ketamine, and my personal favorite, LSD. The CIA did brain-electrode implants and unproven radiation techniques. They induced amnesia. Everything they did was intended to disrupt normal brain function and to create a compliant subject. It was quite a scandal in the seventies."

"How did they get away with it?"

"For a long time no one outside the CIA knew," Kessler explained.

"So you think this could have happened to my friend?" I asked warily.

"In those days anything could have happened in a mental

institution: drugs; abuse; misdiagnosis; experimentation. Do I think it happened to your friend? Statistically speaking, it's not likely. But, who knows?"

We're all statistics in some category.

"How does your friend act now?" Kessler asked.

"She's very inconsistent," I answered. "Sometimes she's charming and delightful. The next moment she goes into a trance. She steals things and can't remember she stole them. She has terrible episodes of fear. I never know what to expect."

"Her behavior is consistent with Alzheimer's and schizophrenia," Kessler said. "But it's also consistent with the after effects of drugs and a mind-altered state. A person programmed to believe they don't have enough to eat will steal food."

Bagels!

"A person programmed to believe in things that never happened will swear they happened."

I married my high-school sweetheart.

"What happened to the Eliza Program?"

"Some very determined doctors fought the system for years and exposed it," he said. "It was dismantled in the seventies."

"Those doctors deserve a lot of credit," I said. "They were heroes."

"I agree but, unfortunately, it didn't work out that way," Kessler said. "It took twenty years to change the system and the original whistle-blowers were no match for the CIA. Some of the older doctors died or retired during the process. Some were discredited by the government and a few lost their licenses fighting city hall. There was a lot of intimidation involved."

"That's terrible," I said. *I hate bullies!*

"Yes it was. I remember a young intern at Willis Psychiatric who spearheaded the original Eliza investigation in 1948. He was a real fighter. One day, in 1951, he just dropped out of the conflict without explanation."

"Do you think the CIA scared him off?"

"They must have done something to him," Kessler said. "He went from a big name one day to a no name the next."

"What was his name?" I asked.

"Harold Goldman."

Chapter 31

A Note from the Doctor

I didn't tell Dr. Kessler that my client was an Eliza but I certainly intended to tell Lou Dewey. I punched his speed-dial number on my cell phone.

"Lou, did you ever hear of *My Fair Lady*?" I asked when he answered.

"Best picture . . . 1964," he said proudly. "Though I personally preferred *Kitten with a Whip* with Ann-Margret."

"I agree," I said, then proceeded to tell him everything I had learned from Dr. Kessler.

"You're saying that Sylvia *did* get lost in the system and Harold Goldman found her at Willis in the Eliza Program. Then he goes after the CIA for their illegal programs and eventually the CIA goes after him. You figure they made a deal in the end?"

"I'm saying it's possible," I told him. "Maybe Goldman falls in love with Sylvia and trades his silence for her safety. Then he spends the rest of his life protecting her from her past while being her present and future. He's still taking care of her after his death."

"The ultimate love story," Lou said.

"You and Joy are the ultimate love story," I told him.

"Thanks, boss. I'll get right on it." Lou was excited. "But if our government is behind this . . . all the records will be destroyed. It won't be easy."

"If it was easy I wouldn't need Lou Dewey," I told him.

Betsy Blackstone called a short time later and asked that we meet as soon as possible at Bagel Kingdom again.

"Well it's the happy, horny couple," the same hefty waitress greeted us.

"I'm pregnant," Betsy blurted, smiling broadly at both of us. "I did a home test this morning."

"I'm not surprised," the waitress said tiredly, and turned to me in disgust. "And at your age."

I checked her name tag.

"Look, Bertha, I had nothing to do with this," I defended my honor.

"That's what they all say," Bertha said, shaking her head.

"I'm serious," I said. "She's married."

"That's even worse." Bertha was appalled. "Have you told your husband?"

"Of course." Betsy beamed.

"What did he say?" Bertha asked.

"He's delighted," Betsy said.

"He's delighted you're having this man's baby?" Bertha bellowed.

"I'm not having a baby with him," Betsy said, and giggled.

I wasn't sure if I was flattered by Bertha or insulted by Betsy.

"I gotta pee," Betsy said, and dashed to the ladies' room, still giggling. I chuckled.

"Okay, wise guy, what's so funny?" Bertha demanded.

I introduced myself and explained my relationship with Betsy.

"I told everyone you were a dirty old man," Bertha said, feeling guilty.

"Normally you'd be right."

When Betsy returned to the booth, Bertha gave her a big hug.

"Congratulations, honey," she said, and walked away.

"What did you tell her?" Betsy asked, sitting down.

"I told her you were crazy about me," I said.

"I am." She touched my arm, which was resting on the table.

"Okay," I said. "Now let's talk business. Are you confident in this test you gave yourself?"

"They're accurate ninety nine point nine percent of the time," she told me. "Plus, I have a pregnant feeling."

"Getting pregnant was never your problem," I reminded her.

"I know, but this time is different," she said, touching my hand.

"Okay, this time is different," I said, squeezing her hand reassuringly. "When will you see Dr. Dunn?"

"As soon as we're finished here," she said.

"Thank you for telling me in person," I said.

"I have to be honest about that, Eddie," she said, with a guilty look. "I wanted to see you for another reason. I'm sorry."

She handed me a piece of paper.

"I received this letter in the mail today. I'm afraid to show it to Bradley."

I scanned the letter and immediately saw a red spot. It was a collection letter from an agency representing Dr. Ronald Cohen.

"When we switched to Dr. Dunn, my husband refused to pay Dr. Cohen's final bill," Betsy explained. "He said Cohen was lucky we weren't suing him for malpractice."

"Bradley's right," I agreed. "But did he tell Dr. Cohen's office?"

"Yes. He told a receptionist," she said. "Dr. Cohen wasn't available.

"I'm afraid if I show Bradley this letter he'll do something stupid."

"If anyone is going to do something stupid it'll be me," I assured her.

"I don't want you to do anything," she told me. "I just want your advice."

"My advice is to let me handle this."

"This is not part of your job," she said.

"I'm the Boca Knight," I reminded her. "My job is to save ladies in distress."

"You already saved me once," she said.

"I wasn't talking about you," I told her. "I was talking about all the other pregnant ladies who go to Dr. Cohen."

Dr. Cohen's office was on the fifth floor of a five-story medical building on Glades Road. I pushed open the office door and burst into the waiting room like a raging bull. The room was filled with pregnant women, and not one of them seemed glad to see a man.

"Can I help you?" a cute dark-haired receptionist asked pleasantly.

"I'm here to see Dr. Cohen," I told her.

"I assume this is a business matter."

"I'm not pregnant if that's what you mean," I answered.

"Dr. Cohen doesn't see business people during office hours," she said politely.

"I'm sure he'll see me," I said in a tone that got her attention.

"Can you tell me the nature of your business?"

I reached into my shirt pocket and handed her the collection letter.

She looked at it and frowned.

"You'll have to talk to the agency," she said softly, trying unsuccessfully to return the letter to me.

"No," I whispered. "I think I'll talk to a lawyer and all the women in this room about Dr. Cohen's malpractice."

The receptionist's face went pale.

"I'll be right back." She got up and scurried away . . . returning in less than five minutes. "Dr. Cohen will see you right away," she told me.

No shit!

Dr. Ronald Cohen didn't look dangerous. He wore a comforting white doctor's coat and a trustworthy smile. He was an ample man and I guessed he was in his early to mid sixties. I calculated quickly that he had been practicing medicine for around forty years. If I didn't know better I'd probably be comfortable with him between my wife's legs.

"I understand you're here concerning one of my patients," Dr. Cohen said

"Ex-patient," I said.

"Mr. . . . Mr.—" He held out his hands palms up, asking for my name.

"Perlmutter," I told him. "Eddie Perlmutter."

He recognizes my name, I said to myself.

"Mr. Perlmutter, I'm a very busy man," he said nervously. "Please get to the point."

"The point is, Dr. Cohen, I think Mrs. Betsy Blackstone suffered two miscarriages as a result of your incompetence—"

"You're not qualified to make a medical judgment," Cohen said, raising his voice.

"Apparently, neither are you," I snapped back, and watched his eyes blink rapidly.

"This is ridiculous," Cohen huffed. "I've delivered thousands of healthy babies."

"So have cabdrivers and cops," I told him. "That doesn't make them doctors. It makes them lucky. You told Betsy Blackstone after her second miscarriage that she was fine and should try again."

"That was sound medical advice," he defended himself.

"Mrs. Blackstone has a septate, redacted uterus according to Dr. Albert Dunn," I told him.

A shocked look crossed Ronald Cohen's face.

"Albert Dunn said that?"

I watched Cohen's eyes glaze over. His blank stare reminded me of the old man who shot himself in the parking lot of the medical building on Clint Moore Road.

"Yes, Dr. Dunn said that and then he operated on Mrs. Blackstone to resolve the problem," I told him. "She's pregnant again and I'm betting she has a healthy baby this time. If she followed your advice she never could have carried a baby full-term."

"You can't say that for sure," the doctor defended himself.

"How could you not know she had a septate uterus?" I challenged him.

He opened his mouth but said nothing.

"I think you're guilty of malpractice, Dr. Cohen."

"That's a serious accusation," he said, with the look of a condemned man.

"Yes it is," I said, flipping the collection letter at him.

He scanned it briefly. "I'll withdraw the collection action as a courtesy."

"You're not a courteous person," I told Cohen. "You're a self-centered prick."

"While it is possible I may have misdiagnosed Mrs. Blackstone"—Dr. Cohen cleared his throat—"you can't draw a conclusion on all my work or my character based on one misdiagnosis out of the thousands of cases I've handled successfully."

"You didn't misdiagnose a case," I said. "You were criminally negligent."

"You can't prove that," he protested, but there was no fight in his voice.

"We can try. We'll start by checking your records for similar situations," I said.

"I doubt you'll find anything. But does Mr. Blackstone intend to take me to court," he asked.

"Mrs. Blackstone doesn't want to take you to court," I told him. "I do."

"I don't understand," Dr. Cohen said.

"Mrs. Blackstone wants to go on with her life," I explained. "She wants to have healthy, happy babies and put this whole mess behind her. But, I'm concerned about your current and future patients. I can't allow you to continue practicing at the risk of all these people."

"I am a very good doctor, Mr. Perlmutter," he insisted.

"Maybe you were once," I said.

"I still am," he said, and it sounded like he was trying to convince himself.

"It doesn't look that way to me," I said.

His eyes filled with tears and he turned away.

"Look again," he said, his voice cracking.

I left his office, less sure of myself than when I arrived.

Chapter 32

Leaving the Stone Age

Lou Dewey came to my office, lugging large boxes.

"I bought you a computer, a printer, and some paper," he said. "Now I can e-mail you instead of running over here all the time."

"I'm too old to learn how to use a computer," I told him.

Within forty-five minutes Lou had the equipment connected and functioning. Two hours later I could send e-mails, receive them, print in color, and access the Internet.

"Let's see you log on," Lou challenged me.

"A piece of cake," I said, pushing the wrong button and shutting off the computer.

Lou showed me how to reboot.

"Check your e-mail," he said when we were connected again.

"I don't have any e-mail," I said. "I've only been online for thirty seconds."

"I sent you one about Dr. Cohen before I came here," he told me.

"Where's it been since then?"

"Cyberspace."

"I've never been in cyberspace," I protested. "Will I be weightless?"

"Clueless," he told me. "Now log on."

I followed the instruction sheet. When the printer clattered to life, I jumped up, and knocked my chair over.

"What was that?" I shouted.

"Welcome to the computer age." Lou patted me on the shoulder.

"What did you learn about Dr. Cohen?" I said, taking the sheets off the printer.

"Read it," he said, walking to the door.

"What about Willis Psychiatric and my two-headed boy?"

"I'm still working on it," he said, and closed the door behind him.

I sat down and started to read.

Ronald Cohen was born in 1939 in Polk County, an hour north of Orlando, Florida. He was the youngest of three boys. His parents were orange growers, and his two brothers worked in the family groves. Richard was the only son to go to college. He graduated the University of Florida, College of Medicine in 1965, and entered the field of obstetrics. He married a nurse he met at the Florida Hospital in Orlando. They had a son in 1968 and named him Michael Aaron.*

Ronald Cohen's career was meteoric. In the early '70s he became famous for innovations with ultrasound equipment for obstetrics. He was considered one of the most knowledgeable doctors in the field. His notoriety paved the way for the private practice he opened in Fort Lauderdale in the early '80s and the second office in Boca Raton a few years later. Dr.

Ronald Cohen, LLC, was recognized as having the biggest and best obstetrics practice in South Florida.

I read a long list of awards Dr. Cohen won, organizations he joined, and charities he supported. The final paragraph of the final document dated March 1999 referenced Mrs. Celia Cohen's long commitment to neonatal care. The article made the two of them sound like Dr. and Mrs. Mother Teresa.

I put down the papers and rubbed my eyes. Where was the monster I expected? Where was the hubris? Where was the incompetence? And, lastly, where was the publicity after 1999? Not one article was written about him in the new millennium. Where had he been for the past six years? I reached for the last article again and reread it slowly. This time I noticed the asterisk next to Michael Aaron Cohen's name. I went to the bottom of the page.

*Michael Aaron Cohen died of heart failure in 1999. He was thirty-one.

And there it was. Dr. Ronald Cohen had lost a child and when his only son died part of the father died with him; the part that cared.

Claudette had sympathy for Cohen when I told her the story.

"He brings children into the world but loses his own," she said sadly.

"Don't feel sorry for him," I said. "He's done a lot of damage."

"You don't know that for sure," she argued. "And maybe you put him back on track."

"I'm trying to derail him," I said.

"But maybe he can still do some good?" Claudette tried.

"It's too late for that," I said.

"It wasn't too late for Lou," she reminded me. "Look what you did for him."

"Lou Dewey saved my life."

"And you saved his," she said. "Now save Dr. Cohen. The world needs doctors."

"I'm not responsible for the world."

"Okay, then how about being responsible for Osceola Park," she challenged me. "My little corner of the world. We need good doctors there."

"Dr. Cohen is not a good doctor anymore," I told her.

"You said he just stopped caring. Make him care again."

"I'm not a magician, Claudette," I said.

"You're better than a magician," she said. "You're the Boca Knight."

How could I argue with that kind of logic?

I called Ronald Cohen and set up a meeting with him the next morning at Patch Reef Park on the south side of Yamato. The park was adjacent to an area I had named The University of God. No marker identifies the U of G campus but the signs on the five holy buildings in a row, stretching from St. Andrews east to Military Trail told the story: Spanish River Christian Church, First Baptist Church, St. David's Armenian Church, Temple B'Nai Israel, and St. Mark's Greek Orthodox Church.

Patch Reef Park, a beautiful complex of softball, baseball, and soccer fields complemented by a batting cage, two basketball courts, and a shaded playground, was right after the Greek Orthodox church, west of Military. It was a Saturday morning, and every playing surface was alive with children of all ages.

I sat in the metal stands adjacent to one of the soccer fields and watched a girls' team wearing red-and-blue East Boca All Stars shirts play against a group wearing black-and-gold West Boca All Stars shirts.

Nine to ten year olds, I guessed.

I don't know much about soccer so I watched the dynamics of the event instead of the details of the game. I found myself trying to match the girls on the field with the parents on the sidelines. I was really getting into it when a loud whistle blew and the Boca Raton–East-West All Stars Girls' soccer game became history in a heartbeat. Who won? Who cares?

Suddenly Dr. Ronald Cohen was standing in front of me.

"You look tired," I said, noticing his red-rimmed eyes.

"I couldn't sleep after you called last night," he said. "I was up all night thinking about this meeting."

"What were you thinking?"

"I was thinking if I should kill myself or you."

"Have you decided yet?" I said calmly.

"I just did," he said, removing a nine-millimeter handgun from his pants pocket and pointing it at me. I checked it out. It was an M9 Beretta.

"What are you doing with an old army handgun?" I asked calmly.

My question surprised him. "Aren't you afraid I'm going to shoot you?"

"No," I said.

He pointed the gun at his right temple. "Then maybe I'll shoot myself so you can have my blood on your hands," he said.

"Be my guest," I told him.

He pulled the trigger. *CLICK! Empty gun!*

"Do you feel better now?" I asked him.

"You didn't care if I killed myself or you," he said incredulously.

"Actually, I saw there was no clip in the gun."

He slumped down on the metal bench and handed me the empty gun.

"My uncle was a marine," he explained. "The gun was a present."

"You haven't used it much, I guess."

"I never had it out of the box before."

"Are you suicidal?" I asked.

"I think so," he said, nodding his head.

"What's stopping you?" I asked.

"I keep hoping I'll wake up one morning and be the man I used to be," he said.

"That's not going to happen," I told him. "There's only the present and the future."

"I don't have a future." Dr. Cohen sighed. "You'll see to that."

"I have to stop you from hurting people," I said without apology.

"I understand and I'm sorry about Mrs. Blackstone," he said.

I saw a red spot but it faded quickly. "Saying you're sorry is not going to do it," I said. "What happened to you? You were a brilliant doctor once."

He stared off into space, probably remembering a better time. "Did you ever lose a child, Mr. Perlmutter?" he asked.

"I never had a child," I told him.

"My son died from congenital heart failure when he was thirty-one years old," Cohen said sadly. "He was born with a hole between the chambers of his heart so small it took an autopsy to find it." He shook his head slowly. "Ironic, isn't it? I dedicate most of my life to delivering healthy babies but my own son is born with an undetectable heart defect."

"Actually, I think it's tragic," I said. "But it's not an excuse for malpractice."

"I'm not making excuses," he said. "I'm just trying to explain why . . . I stopped being a good doctor. I stopped caring."

"You should have stopped practicing," I said.

"I needed to keep busy," he explained. "My wife and I were

having a terrible time dealing with our son's death. I thought I could keep practicing without doing any harm." He sighed. "Obviously I couldn't."

"Do you think you could be a good doctor again?" I asked.

"I didn't lose my skills," he answered. "I lost my sense of purpose."

"And if you had a sense of purpose again?" I prodded him.

"Why do you ask?"

"I have a girlfriend who looks like Halle Berry," I told him.

"Congratulations," he said. "But what does that have to do with me?"

"She wants me to help you be a good doctor again," I explained.

"Why?"

"Do you know anything about Osceola Park, Dr. Cohen?" I asked him.

"I know it's somewhere in Delray but that's about it," he said.

"Well, you're about to learn a whole lot more."

We sat in the stands and talked while three more soccer games were played. When we were done we had a goal.

CHAPTER 33

SILLY PUTTY AND THE TWO-HEADED BOY

I sat up and turned on the light next to my bed.

"I can't sleep," I said.

Claudette sat up, rubbing her eyes. "What's wrong?" she asked.

"I'm not the man I used to be," I said.

"I like the man you are."

"I've lost my edge," I complained.

"You're as sharp as a Cossack kinjal," she said, referring to a Russian dagger.

"I'm like Silly Putty," I said. "I'm getting pushed and pulled all over the place."

She poked my stomach. "You're hard as a rock."

"Not anymore," I complained. "I never should have given Cohen a deal. The man deserved to be punished."

"Maybe he's been punished enough."

Maybe, maybe not.

"And the guy who shot himself in the head outside the medical building . . ."

"That was terrible."

"I should have saved him," I said, mourning my diminishing ability more than the man's life.

"You're being ridiculous," Claudette told me.

"And Noah Paretsky?" I raved.

Ranting is next, I promised myself.

"What about him?" she asked.

"Instead of turning that geek over to the police I made a home movie with him."

"You said he meant well," she recalled correctly.

"I'm supposed to arrest criminals not analyze them," I said. "And Edik the Bolshevik bartender? I should have made him play Russian roulette by himself with a fully loaded gun. But I arranged a deal with him and the Ekaterinburg Mafia instead."

"You negotiated the release of hostages," she defended me against myself.

"And I should have arrested Lou Dewey, too," I ignored her.

"He saved your life."

She's making sense. Change the subject.

"I was wrong with the deal I made with that Nazi bastard, Randolph Buford."

"What you did with Buford was brilliant," Claudette said.

"It's just not me," I complained.

"It's the new and improved you," she said. "The old you was a young slugger. Now you're a veteran counterpuncher," she told me. "You win by decisions instead of knockouts." She kissed my cheek. "You said when an old champion slows down he has to change his style."

I said that?

"Have I slowed down at everything?" I asked, rubbing her stomach.

Hey, what's up? Mr. Johnson stirred.

"Right now I'd say your timing is perfect."

I had a lot of things going on that were beyond my control so I took a few days off and drove to the Keys with Claudette. We went fishing off the coast of Islamorada on a charter boat. We spent a few hours bobbing in the ocean with two fat ladies from Minnesota and a father and teenage son from Tennessee. Claudette caught three bonefish. I caught the father and son looking down her blouse. The fat ladies got one grouper apiece and bad sunburns. I reeled in a Michelin tire and an Alabama license plate.

Claudette and I had a romantic dinner at an oceanside restaurant where we drank wine and watched the sun go down. When the moon and Mr. Johnson came up, we hurried off to our room at the Surf Motel, which had a great view we didn't see until dawn.

I was enjoying the predawn stillness on the hotel balcony the next morning when my cell phone rang. The caller ID told me it was Lou Dewey. I glanced at my watch. It was five thirty.

"You're up early this morning," I said softly, not wanting to wake Claudette.

"I couldn't sleep," he said. "I had an epiphany."

"Probably something you ate," I told him.

"Eddie, I'm serious," Lou said. "I had a dream last night that I was screaming at my father the morning after he encouraged my brother to enlist in the Marines. My father kept apologizing to me and saying he couldn't remember a thing and I just kept screaming."

"It was just a bad dream, Lou," I comforted him.

"No it wasn't," Lou raised his voice. "I *did* scream at my father that day after he got my brother to enlist in the Marines and my father *did* say he couldn't remember anything from the night before. It actually happened . . . exactly like in my dream."

"Meaning what?"

"Meaning maybe Sylvia's vision of the two-headed boy isn't a dream. Maybe it's a memory."

"Lou, Sylvia doesn't remember anything," I reminded him. "She thinks Harold was her high-school sweetheart. She didn't even go to high school. She can't remember the first twenty years of her life . . . she can't remember lunch sometimes . . ."

"She remembers a two-headed boy?"

"It's just a dream," I insisted.

"What if I'm right?" Lou asked. "What if it is a memory?" he asked defensively.

"I'll kiss your ass."

"Don't make promises you can't keep," Claudette said as she stepped out on the balcony. "Who are you romancing so early in the morning?"

"Lou Dewey," I told her. "He had an epiphany last night."

"Probably something he ate," she said, sitting on my lap.

Look who's here, Mr. Johnson stirred.

"Lou, I gotta go," I said.

"Will you think about what I said?" he asked.

"Later," I told him.

Later I was standing in the bathroom after showering. I noticed there were two mirrors in the room positioned so that I could see two of me. I admired my reflection from both angles.

You two are looking good, I joked with my reflections and then I had my own epiphany. *Holy shit! That's it.*

I dashed from the bathroom with a towel wrapped around my waist, grabbed the phone, and raced to the balcony.

"What's up?" Claudette asked.

"Lou Dewey is a genius," I said to her as I punched in his number.

"Does this mean you have to kiss his ass?" she asked.

"Possibly."

"Ask him if he'll trade positions with me," she suggested.

Lou answered on the first ring.

"Twins," I shouted into the phone. "Sylvia was remembering twins."

"What?"

"Sylvia said she dreamed repeatedly of looking up at a two-headed boy and a wicked witch. I'm betting she had older twin brothers and a crazy mother. You were right, Lou. It wasn't a dream. It's a memory."

"I can find her now," he promised, and disconnected.

Lou called me later that day while Claudette and I were driving back to Boca.

"I found her," he shouted into my ear.

"You're the best," I told him. "Tell me."

"I searched for twin boys born between 1923 and 1927 because you said they would be older than her. I found plenty," he said. "Then I narrowed it down to twin boys with younger sisters."

"Good thinking."

"I still had too many possibilities so I went deeper searching for twin boys with a younger sister and no father."

"Why no father?"

"She had no memory of a man," Lou explained.

"That's a bit of a reach," I said.

"I thought so, too," he admitted. "But I started digging anyway. I hacked around every city system I could think of until I found twin boys and a younger baby sister whose father died October 29, 1929, on Wall Street."

"That was Black Tuesday," I said. "The day the stock market crashed. Was this guy a jumper?"

"No, a jumper landed on his head," Lou said.

"Is this a joke?"

"No. Listen to me," Lou pleaded. "The guy who jumped was a financier named Abraham Bengloff who had just lost all his money. Instead of landing on Wall Street he landed on his son-in-law, Jacob Dubin, who had just lost all his money, too. Jacob Dubin had twin boys and a three-month old girl named Sylvia."

"That's got to be her," I said, amazed by Lou Dewey.

"Wait, there's more," Lou said.

"How much more do we need?" I asked.

"I want you to hear this, Eddie," he insisted. "It's important to me."

"I'm listening."

"Do you believe there's someone looking over us?" Lou asked.

"Everyone looks over us, Lou," I replied. "We're short."

"No, I mean do you believe in fate?" he said, trying a new tack.

"No," I said. "I believe life is totally random."

"Then, Mr. Random, see if you can explain this," Louie challenged me. "Do you remember I told you the story about my grandfather, Ferris Dewey?"

"Didn't he shovel shit against the tide in Atlantic City . . . or something like that?"

"That's him," Lou said. "And I told you he died jumping off a forty-foot high tower on the Steel Pier in Atlantic City."

"Dixie the Diving Horse," I recalled.

"Exactly." Lou was thrilled I remembered. "Well, he jumped the same day Abraham Bengloff jumped, October 29, 1929."

"Amazing," I said. "Is all this information on the Internet?"

"Not all of it," Lou said. "Bengloff and Dubin's death were in the newspaper back then but Ferris Dewey died in obscurity. I only know about the connection because my grandfather's jump became a family legend. Do you believe in fate now?"

"It sounds fateful to me," I conceded. "Sylvia Dubin is Sylvia Goldman."

"There's one problem," Lou added.

"What would that be?"

"According to the records, Sylvia Dubin drowned in 1932," he told me.

CHAPTER 34

SYLVIA'S PIECES

Lou and I pieced together the computer puzzle of Sylvia's past by creating an imperfect but plausible picture.

After Jacob Dubin and Abraham Bengloff banged heads in 1929, our research showed that their survivors moved to Long Beach, Long Island, where the family owned a large old house on the island's south shore. Bengloff had invested in the house and three waterfront empty lots in 1922, seven years before the crash. The "summer home" was rarely used when the Bengloffs were wealthy but it became their only home during the Depression. They sold the three empty lots for cash.

Rachael Bengloff, Sylvia's grandiose grandmother, was miserable without her millions, minions, and mansions. She became a recluse in the old house and protected the remaining family funds with fierce determination. She put money in trusts for her three grandchildren and kept the remainder away from her drunken daughter, Ethel.

Sylvia's mother, Ethel Dubin, had changed her surname back to Bengloff after her father landed on her husband's head. She was an alcoholic and a wanton woman at the time of the accident and things only got worse when she became a widow. She went from flapper to floozy, earning her liquor on her back if necessary. Prohibition was still the law, but there was no shortage of booze in Long Beach, thanks to the city's perfect bootlegger's bay and raucous speakeasies. When Prohibition ended in 1933, so did the life of Rachael Bengloff who suffered a massive heart attack while reading her most recent bank statement.

The three children were left with their irrevocable trust funds under the supervision of their constantly intoxicated mother who had outlived her era and her money. Three months after Rachael Bengloff died . . . three-year-old Sylvia was missing.

The police inspected Sylvia's empty bedroom the morning Ethel Bengloff reported her daughter's disappearance. They found an unmade bed and an open window facing the ocean. On the blustery beach they discovered a trail of toys leading to the water. At the shoreline was a Raggedy Ann doll soaked by the sea. There were no footprints to follow but the wind and waves could have swept them away . . . along with the little girl. Sylvia was officially declared missing and presumed dead.

Ethel Bengloff was appointed trustee of her late daughter's estate and used most of the money to destroy what was left of her health. Five years after her daughter's disappearance, Ethel was found floating lifeless at the water's edge.

"Maybe she wandered into the water in a drunken stupor," I said to Lou as we compared notes during a telephone conversation.

"Filled with remorse?"

"Rum probably," I decided.

Lou stated the obvious. "Sylvia didn't disappear in the ocean, Eddie. She disappeared on dry land. Her mother took her to New York City and dumped her at an orphanage. The whole beach scene was staged."

"That's what it sounds like," I said. "But how did the orphanage know Sylvia's real name?"

"Maybe her mother left a note," Lou guessed.

"Why would she leave a clue for the police?" I pointed out.

"Maybe she had the subconscious desire to get caught and punished," Lou tried.

"Maybe her subconscious was so pickled she couldn't think straight," I said.

"She was able to think clearly enough to fake a crime scene," he countered.

"Yes, and she was aware enough to keep her two sons while abandoning her daughter. Why would a mother do that?" I wondered. "I wish I could ask her."

"Ask the twins," Lou suggested.

"Very funny," I said.

"I'm serious," Lou insisted. "They're eighty-three years old, alive and well, and still living in the same house in Long Beach."

"How is that possible?" I stammered. "When their mother died they became orphans, too."

"A spinster aunt from their father's side, Bertha Bengloff, became their guardian. As soon as the twins were of legal age, they put the old lady in a nursing home where she died, penniless. The boys were filthy rich by then from real estate. They're heartless bastards."

"They're still Sylvia's family," I said. "We have to contact them."

"Even though they haven't seen her since she was three?" Lou asked.

"In the eyes of the law they're still family," I said. "Besides, they were kids when this happened. Their mother told them their sister drowned. They believed her."

"Maybe," Lou said reluctantly. "But, from what I learned about these two sons of bitches, they're terrible landlords, make no charitable donations, never married, and have no families."

"It doesn't matter. We still have to tell Sylvia's lawyer they exist," I said.

"I wouldn't tell anyone anything just yet."

"We still have a legal obligation," I told him.

"We have a moral one, too," Lou insisted. "Sylvia's very vulnerable. That's why you have to pay the twins a visit."

"What makes you think they'll meet with me?"

"They already agreed," he told me.

"When?"

"Yesterday. I called and told them a representative of the state of New York wanted to meet with them about an unclaimed seven-figure trust."

"They believed you?"

"Not at first," Lou said. "They demanded a confirmation by e-mail on New York State stationery so I sent it to them, one with a State House return e-mail address. They wrote back agreeing to meet and I intercepted the message."

I didn't bother to ask him how.

The next day I flew to JFK from West Palm Beach International Airport on Blue Sky Airlines. On the three-hour flight I read the file Lou Dewey had e-mailed me regarding the terrible twins. It read like a rap sheet of legal crimes. Evictions and foreclosures were among their nicer activities. They were sued for building violations, fraudulent marketing, and a myriad of moral malfeasance.

I rented a car and drove to Long Beach in a depressing

drizzle. I learned from the road map that Long Beach is an island connected to the rest of Long Island by three bridges. I only had to cross the Atlantic Beach Bridge from JFK. Also, Long Beach was not named Long Beach because the beach is long. Long Beach was named Long Beach because it's longer than it is wide. But that's like naming me "Tall Eddie" for the same reason. It just isn't so.

The entire city is maybe five miles long and less than a mile wide, with the maximum amount of housing squeezed onto a minimum amount of land. The city's claim to fame is the ocean, but on this rainy day, the Atlantic only made things darker, damper, and drearier.

An annoying film of moisture hindered my view and reappeared immediately after the wipers streaked the windshield. I tried leaving the wipers on, but the glass wasn't wet enough and the wiper blades snarled in protest. I was in windshield-wiper hell.

There wasn't much traffic in Long Beach that morning, making my meandering manageable. I alternated between looking at the road and reading the directions given to me by the rent-a-car attendant who wanted to know if I was friends with Billy Crystal who came from Long Beach. I assured the kid that Billy and I were close, and he said, "Cool."

Armed with computerized, state-of-the-art directions, I got lost within a half hour and infuriated five minutes after that.

"Either rain or don't . . . you son of a bitch," I shouted, losing my patience with Mother Nature. I pounded the steering wheel with my palm but Mother Nature continued to ignore me and I felt totally out of control. I hate driving lost.

Magically, a sign for Ocean Drive appeared through the windshield.

"It's a miracle," I decided.

Eighty-five Ocean Drive was a neat, old, two-story, white stucco house with a red roof. The Atlantic Ocean was the back-yard.

Not bad.

Taking my folder, I went to the front door and rang the doorbell.

David and Solomon opened the door together and despite their names, they didn't look biblical. They didn't look likable, either. They had sullen faces, suspicious eyes, and an air of supe-riority. I don't know what they felt superior about. They were homely little guys, shaped like twin pears and their large, droopy white mustaches made me think of a Beatles song: "I Am the Walrus" *(koo koo ka chu).*

"I'm David Bengloff," one of them said, not offering to shake my hand.

I noticed he had a mole to the left of his left eye.

"And you must be Solomon," I said.

He didn't have a mole. I could tell them apart.

They didn't ask my name.

They sat on the sofa and I sat in a chair, a coffee table be-tween us.

"What a great view," I pointed at the ocean.

"Yes, we know," David Bengloff said smugly.

It was going to be easy to hate these guys.

"Let's talk about the trust that may belong to us," David got down to business.

"There is no trust." I smiled.

"We received an e-mail from the state of New York about a large, unclaimed trust," David snapped at me.

"It's a fake. A friend of mine sent it to you."

"How dare you?" David fumed.

"We're daring guys," I said.

The twins stood simultaneously.

"This meeting is over," David announced.

"This meeting hasn't started," I replied, calmly.

"Get out," David shouted.

"Sit down and shut up." I aimed my right index finger at them.

"W-w-who are you?" Solomon stammered, warily.

"Eddie Perlmutter," I said, tossing a Boca Knight card across the table.

Solomon read the card. "You're that crazy cop from Boston we read about."

"The one who hunts Nazis in Florida," David added to my résumé.

Solomon pointed at me with a shaky finger. "You've killed people," he said.

"I've never killed twins," I assured them.

They sat down.

"We're not Nazis," David said.

"Are you working for one of our competitors?" Solomon asked.

"I'm here regarding your sister, Sylvia."

They exchanged confused glances.

"Our sister drowned seventy-three years ago," Solomon said. "She was three."

"Wrong. Your sister is seventy-six years old now," I said. "And she's a friend of mine."

Neither of them responded.

"You knew she didn't drown, didn't you?" I stared at them.

They exchanged glances but didn't answer.

"We don't have to tell you anything," Solomon said, asserting himself.

"It might be financially advisable for you to talk to me." I chose my words carefully to get their attention.

"Is this about money?" Solomon asked. "Does our supposed sister want money?"

"She wants nothing," I said. "She doesn't even know you exist."

They both looked surprised. "Then what *do* you want?" Solomon asked.

"Your sister's life is ending," I said. "I want to give it a beginning and a meaning."

CHAPTER 35

Two Heads Are Better than One

"I want my lawyer present," David decided.

"You don't need a lawyer," I told them. "I'm not accusing you of anything."

"He's right, we have nothing to hide," Solomon said. "Okay you want to know what happened? One afternoon we saw our mother put Sylvia in a car and drive away."

"Did your mother leave you at home alone often?"

"All the time," David said. "Our mother had problems."

"I know all about your mother's problems," I said.

"You and everyone else," David said. "We tried to wait for them but fell asleep. The next morning we were told that our sister had wandered into the ocean and drowned. We never really knew what happened and we didn't care. We hated her."

"How could you hate your three-year-old sister?"

They looked at each other as if they had twin telepathy.

"There's something you should see," Solomon said solemnly. "Wait here."

Tweedledee and Tweedledum left the room in lockstep.

They returned in minutes with Solomon carrying a letter-sized envelope. They sat down across from me again. He handed me the envelope.

"It took the two of you to get this for me?" I questioned them.

"Neither of us wanted to be in the room alone with you," Solomon admitted.

"Our father wrote this letter to our mother minutes before his accidental death."

"I know how your father and grandfather died," I told them.

"You seem to know a lot about us," David worried.

"I know all about you," I said cryptically, hoping to scare the shit out of them.

"The stains on the letter are dried blood," Solomon said. "It was found in my father's shirt pocket by the funeral home and given to our mother. Read it."

I removed the brittle paper from the envelope.

October 29, 1929
Ethel,

I've left you and taken our daughter with me. We will not return.

This is my only chance to save Sylvia from becoming infected with the Bengloff virus that kills the soul with greed, avarice, and indifference. Regrettably, I cannot save our sons who are already infected.

Your virus didn't kill me, but it weakened me to the point where I was useless. I will never fully recover but I believe I can get better than I am now.

I want my daughter to lead a meaningful life and be remembered as someone who made the world a better place.

Don't try to find us. We don't want you in our lives.

Jacob

I looked up from the letter.

"Obviously your sister never saw this letter," I said.

"No, but our mother did." Solomon rolled his eyes. "She became insanely angry and took it out on Sylvia every day. We call it the *screaming years.*"

"Meaning?"

David took a turn. "Sylvia was a colicky baby and cried a lot. After my mother read this letter she couldn't stand the sight of Sylvia anymore. She would pick her up from her crib, shake her like a rag doll, and scream things like, 'I hate you,' or 'You're weak like your father,' then she would drop Sylvia back in her crib and ignore her for hours."

"What did the two of you do?" I wanted to know.

"We didn't do anything," Solomon said. "Our mother had read us our father's letter over and over again to prove he loved Sylvia and hated us. So, of course, we hated her."

"Did you scream at her, too?" I asked.

"No," David said. "We laughed at her when she would cry."

"Sylvia still dreams of a screaming witch and a laughing, two-headed boy," I said.

I didn't bother telling them she remembered nothing else.

"I suppose we could have looked like a two-headed boy to an infant," David said.

"Did the *screaming years* ever end?" I asked them.

"Yes. One day, after one of our mother's screaming and shaking fits Sylvia stopped crying and never cried again. In fact, she never spoke again." David sighed. "It was strange. She just stared at us with her big, bloodred eyes all the time and never made a sound. I'll never forget it."

What was that all about? I asked myself.

"Then one day she was gone and we never saw her again," David finished.

"Would you like to see her now?" I asked.

"What's in it for us?" Solomon asked, and David nodded.

"Financially, nothing," I told them. "She needs help."

"Why don't you help her?" Solomon asked sarcastically.

"I'd be honored," I told him.

"But, you want money, right?" Solomon raised his eyes, suspiciously.

"I don't want your money," I said. "I want your permission to be your sister's legal guardian and your guarantee that you will make no future claims against her."

I produced a document and slid it across the table.

"Just sign this paper and you'll never see me again."

"I'm not signing anything," Solomon said. "We'll have our lawyers look into this. It's always about money, Mr. Perlmutter."

"Don't confuse your motives with mine," I said. "If you read the document you'll see that I volunteered to be Sylvia's guardian free of charge and that upon her death all money remaining in her estate will be donated to charity."

They both turned their attention to the document and read it thoroughly.

"Why are you willing to do this?" Solomon asked, confused.

"I love your sister like she was my sister and I want to take care of her," I said. "She needs a legal guardian and you two are her only family. Either you assume responsibility or sign this document."

They processed the facts.

"What if we refuse to sign?" Solomon asked.

"You can become her guardian and be responsible for her," I said.

"Maybe that's what we'll do then," Solomon challenged me.

"That's fine." I shrugged. "That's your right. And it's my right to protect my friend's interests by watching every move you two make."

"Is that a threat?" David asked.

"It's a promise," I told them.

"I see." Solomon looked at me. "Well, there's no point in arguing, is there? If you've deceived us you'll be hearing from our lawyers."

Solomon stood up and walked to a desk. He returned with a pen and signed the document without saying another word. He handed the pen to David, who also signed. They were emotionless. I found it hard to believe that these people came from the same parents as Sylvia.

I returned the signed documents to the folder and stood up. The twins stood and walked toward the front door. I followed them.

I walked toward my rental car. When I didn't hear the front door close behind me, I turned to face them. They stood like twin statues at the door.

"That paper is worthless," Solomon announced. "It requires a notary."

"No problem," I assured them as I opened the car door.

"You may be hearing from us," Solomon said.

"That would be your mistake," I said. "And by the way, your father was right. You are infected."

Chapter 36

Howard and Derek's Great Adventure

"It sounds like Shaken Baby Syndrome," Dr. Ronald Cohen said.

I phoned him from JFK airport, while waiting for my flight back to West Palm Beach.

"Where have I heard that before?" I wondered aloud.

"It's been in the news," Cohen told me. "A baby boy died a few months ago from SBS. If your friend's mother shook her repeatedly there's a very good chance the child suffered brain damage. The red eyes indicate a rupture to the retina."

"Is the damage permanent?" I asked.

"It can be permanent," Dr. Cohen confirmed. "It can be temporary, and it can be fatal. It's hard to predict."

"So my friend could have suffered brain damage as a child."

"Especially during the 1930s. SBS wasn't really understood until the seventies."

"Can SBS be reversed?" I asked.

"The injuries can heal, if that's what you mean," Dr. Cohen said. "The time lost from the injury is often irretrievable."

"Permanent memory loss?"

"Technically, no. With SBS there would literally be no memories to lose," he said. "You can't forget what you never experienced."

I heard my flight being called. "Thanks, Doc," I said. "I gotta go."

"Mr. Perlmutter," Dr. Cohen said quickly before I hung up. "I know I'm not your favorite doctor. Why did you call me with this question?"

"I'm offering a special on second chances this month," I told him.

After a good night's sleep, I left Claudette asleep in my apartment and drove to my nine A.M. appointment with Sylvia's lawyer, Sanford Kreiger, at the St. Andrews Country Club.

"Hey, it's da Boca Knight," Tito the gate guard said in his singsong voice while he flashed a big smile. "You're becomin' a regular at St. Andrews, munh."

"I have a lot of people here bidding on my car," I told him.

"I'll give you five bucks for it." He laughed, raising the gate.

"That's the highest bid so far," I told him.

I saw Santos take a break from trimming the hedges.

"Hey, Santos, you missed a spot," I shouted to him.

"Mr. Boca Knight." Santos waved. "Come here and I'll trim your MINI."

"It's already been done," I told him. "A long time ago."

I left them laughing.

Sanford Kreiger read the brief document and looked at me across the table. "This will never hold up in court, Eddie."

"You wrote it, Sanford," I reminded him.

"Yes, but I told you it had to be notarized." He refreshed my memory.

"I was lucky to find their house, never mind a notary," I said. "Plus I never expected them to sign it right then and there."

"I just want you to be aware that they can contest this document."

"They won't," I said confidently.

"You didn't threaten them, did you?"

"Not by my standards, I didn't."

"We'd be much better off if Sylvia had a will." He put the agreement in a folder.

"So write one."

"She has to be mentally competent to sign it," he told me.

"She has her moments," I said. "We have to catch her at the right time."

"I'll write something up fast," he agreed. "I also have to petition the Probate Division of the Circuit Court to have you appointed her guardian."

"Do you anticipate a problem?" I asked.

"You're like a saint around here," he told me. "The judge will probably want you as his guardian, too. We also have to make a public announcement in the newspaper, but it's all procedural."

"So we're almost done," I said.

"The only real problem I can foresee is if she dies without a will. She has a few million between her house and insurance. What do we do with that?"

"I've already worked that out," I said.

I told him about Sylvia's father's letter and the plan I had developed.

"It's a great idea, Eddie," he said when I had finished explaining. "But she has to sign the will to make it work."

"Write the damn will, and let's get this show on the road."

I went to the hospital to look in on Sylvia. I sat next to her bed for two hours, but she didn't wake up.

I was at my office checking messages when my cell phone rang. It was Edik Davidavitch.

"Kuznetsovs will release Dietrichs May sixth in Frankfurt," he said.

"Okay," I said quickly then realized I had a conflict. "Wait, I can't go on that date. I have to transport a prisoner a long distance."

"Change your plans," he told me.

"I can't," I said, thinking of all the complications.

"There is an open window first week of May and then it closes. It has to be then or delayed till August."

"Why so long?"

"It's not easy to move two kidnapped people out of Russia," Edik said. "It takes much planning and payoffs."

"I'll have to get back to you," I said, frustrated.

"Don't fahk this up," Edik advised me.

I called Howard Larkey and gave him the bad news.

"Howard, I can't change my plans," I told him. "I'm moving a prisoner on the fourth of May and need to stay with him for a while."

"The Dietrichs can't wait two more months in Ekaterinburg," Howard decided.

"There's nothing I can do about it."

"I have an idea. Let me call you back," he said.

Howard phoned me two hours later.

"Problem solved," he told me. "Derek and I will get the Dietrichs."

"No, I can't let you do that. It's too dangerous."

"Danger is my middle name," Howard announced.

"You didn't say anything about danger," I heard Derek protest in the background. "You said we were going on a cruise."

"What is he talking about?" I asked Howard.

"We already booked an excursion," he told me. "We're flying from Miami to Hong Kong via Hawaii, then to Vietnam where we board a cruise to China. We fly from Beijing to Vladivostok where we board the Trans Siberian Railroad to Ekaterinburg. We're not going to meet them in Hamburg."

"Frankfurt," I corrected him.

"Whatever."

"This is not a game, Howard," I told him. "This is the Russian Mafia, and I'm told this particular Mafia family hates gays and Jews."

"So, who's gay and Jewish?" he asked, feigning a gruff, macho voice.

"You are!"

"Oh, that's right," he reverted to his normal voice. "Well, no matter. We're going. Tell that bitchy bartender to change the rendezvous to Ekaterinburg."

"I can't let you do this," I protested.

"I'm touched by your concern, but you can't stop us. Someone has to rescue our friends," Howard said. "Just call that Cossack closet case and tell him we'll be there on the fifth to pick up our friends on the sixth. We have tickets from Ekaterinburg to Moscow and for our return flight to the States. They have to arrange the paperwork for the Dietrichs."

"I'll have to make some arrangements," I told him. "Don't go anywhere yet."

"Derek," Howard said to his partner, "Eddie is so sweet. He's concerned about us."

I phoned Edik and told him the new developments.

"This is bad." He sighed. "I call my seester."

Within an hour Natasha called my cell phone.

"Kuznetsovs say no problem with your friends coming," she said. "Will arrange meeting in Ekaterinburg."

"Do the Kuznetsovs know these two guys are gay?"

"Yes. No problem," she said.

"I thought the KKK hates gays and Jews," I said.

"You misunderstand me," she said. "Kuznetsovs don't hate gays and Jews. They just don't allow them in gang."

"Why not?"

"Boris doesn't trust them," she clarified.

"I thought Boris was anti-Semitic and homophobic?"

"No, Boris is psychotic and bisexual," she announced. "He doesn't believe in any religion and he would fahk anyone. He would fahk a cheeken I think."

"I don't understand," I told her. "If Boris doesn't hate gays, why did you lie to him about your brother? I thought you were afraid Boris would kill him if he knew."

"No, I lied to Boris about Edik so Boris wouldn't try to fahk him," she said.

"Now I'm lost."

"Boris had a gay lover named Vasily in gang many years ago," she explained. "Vasily was nice-looking Jewish boy but he screwed Boris more ways than one. He left Boris for rival gang leader also gay and Jewish . . . and they tried to take Boris's business away. Boris never trusted Jews and gays after that. Issued an order, no Jews and gays ever in KKK. Fahking is okay but no business."

"What happened to Vasily?" I asked.

"He lost his balls," she said.

"Boris scared him away?"

"No, Boris cut his balls off and threw them in meat grinder," she said. "The other guy's balls, too. So, when Boris tells me he wants to fahk my little brother I don't want Edik to go near him. Too dangerous. I tell Boris that Edik hates homos and Boris should fahk me instead."

"Did he?"

"Of course," she said. "I told you, Boris fahk anyone."

"So, you lied to your boss and told him your brother was straight to protect him," I said.

"Is that so bad?"

"In a sick way it makes perfect sense. And now if Boris ever finds out you lied to him he'll kill both of you," I summarized.

"Now you know everything," she said. "You take care of my brother; I take care of your friends."

"Deal."

Two days later, "Howard and Derek's Great Adventure" began.

Chapter 37

Plans and Planes

The night Howard and Derek departed I took Claudette for dinner at the Cheesecake Factory in Boca. There was a waiting line for a table and the hostess estimated it would be forty-five-minutes. We found enough space to stand at the bar.

Before we could order drinks I heard someone call my name and felt a hand on my shoulder. I turned to see the smiling faces of Mo Myerson and Izzy Fryberg. We shook hands and I introduced them to Claudette.

"I've heard so much about you," she said. "I'm Claudette, Eddie's friend."

"Any friend of Eddie's is a friend of ours," Mo said enthusiastically. "He saved our community."

"You could have fooled me," I said. "The last time I saw you two together you were trying to give each other tonsillectomies."

"That's in the past," Izzy smiled. "We're all friends again because of you, Eddie."

"What happened after I left the meeting?"

"That little assistant of yours who looks like Elvis with buck teeth—"

"Lou Dewey," I said.

"Yeah, Lou," Izzy confirmed. "He left us a DVD copy of your presentation on the front table. Old man Paretsky and his wife . . . did you meet them?"

Noah's father and mother, I thought to myself. "No," I said to protect the not so innocent.

"Well, they took the disc to their apartment to replay it. We all stopped arguing long enough to follow them to their apartment and watch the thing again. The second time was a charm. The room melted like an iceberg in the Everglades. There wasn't a dry eye in the place."

"That's great." Claudette clapped her hands. "And you thought you failed."

"I'm as surprised as anyone," I admitted.

"We were going to call you," Izzy said, "but we wanted to be sure the peace would last. It's been great."

Claudette looked so proud of me, and I felt like a world-class schmuck for all the whining I had done about my changing personality.

"We made copies of the DVD," Mo enthused, "and everyone got one. We had some of the pictures framed and hung them in common areas like the card room—"

"And the elevator," Izzy chimed in.

"As reminders of what you all mean to one another," Claudette gushed.

"It's too bad we had to be reminded," Izzy said.

"It's human nature," I said. "Where are your wives tonight?"

"In the card room at Delray Vista," Mo said. "It's canasta night."

A buzzer vibrated in Izzy's hand. "Our table's ready," he said. "We've been waiting fifty minutes."

Mo paused before leaving. "I've been trying to think of who you remind me of," he said to Claudette.

"Halle Berry," I said confidently.

"No, not her." Mo put his index finger to his lips and closed his eyes. "I got it," Mo exclaimed. "Eartha Kitt."

Claudette thanked him politely and giggled when they were gone.

"It must be a generational thing." I apologized for Mo's comparison.

"Eartha Kitt is beautiful," Claudette said. "I'm flattered."

My cell phone rang. There was no caller ID on the screen when I answered.

"Wait a minute," I said when I couldn't hear the caller and went outside. "Hello, this is Eddie," I said with the phone pressed to one ear and my finger plugged into the other ear.

"Hello, Mr. Perlmutter. This is Minister Kane," I heard. "Is this a bad time?"

"No no, Minister," I said. "I'm having dinner in a noisy place. I couldn't hear you so I went outside."

"Sorry to interrupt your dinner," he said. "I'll be brief."

"That's alright, take your time."

"Your travel arrangements have been confirmed," he told me. "You depart the fourth of May at two thirty in the afternoon."

I had a little more than two weeks to get ready.

CHAPTER 38

THE GUARDIAN

On Monday of the following week I appeared before the Probate Court with Sanford Kreiger and, by Friday, I had been verbally approved as Sylvia Goldman's guardian. The probate judge was a big fan of mine.

Sanford Kreiger had given me the will he'd prepared for Sylvia and I took it to the hospital, hoping she would be alert enough to sign the document. She was asleep when I got there.

I sat in the chair next to her bed and looked at her tiny face. Her skin was pasty, and her mouth was shrunken. She looked ancient. I stared at her features and tried to picture the younger Sylvia, the one I had seen in the old photos at her house.

What could you have been if you had the chance? I wondered.

I touched Sylvia's forehead with my fingers.

"I visited your past, Sylvia," I told her. "Your father and your husband loved you very much."

Her eyes fluttered and opened. This had happened before

and occasionally she would visit for a while. But not this time. She sighed and her eyes closed again.

"I love you, too, Sylvia," I said.

I never cry but if I did, that would have been a good time.

I took her hand in mine and held it for a while but I felt the need to be closer to her. There was barely enough space on the bed but I managed to lie next to her on her right side and put my arm under her head. Unexpectedly, Sylvia turned on her side and put her left arm across my chest. She never spoke and I don't think her movement was a deliberate action. It seemed more like an instinct to be closer and to be held.

I thought about telling her more about her past but I decided I had already told her all she needed to know.

We fell asleep holding each other.

I woke up an hour later but Sylvia didn't.

When I realized she was gone I placed her head on the pillow and called for a nurse.

I called Sanford Kreiger after Sylvia's body had been removed from the room. I told him she had died in her sleep.

"It's probably for the best," he said. "Did you get her to sign the papers before she died?"

The papers!

I had totally forgotten about the will and guardianship documents. They were in my pocket, and I had forgotten.

Idiot!

"Of course she signed the papers," I told him. "It's just a scribble but it's signed."

"Was someone there as a witness?"

"Yes," I said.

"Who?"

"You."

"Eddie, I can't do that," Sanford protested. "I'm a lawyer."

"Lawyers lie all the time."

"I won't," he said.

"Sanford, you know the will is a good thing. I'm going to bring you these signed documents," I said, "And then I have to go away for a while. You do what you have to do."

I scrawled an illegible signature on the two documents by Sylvia's typed name and went to meet Sanford at TooJay's Deli on Champion Boulevard by the Polo Club. I handed him the documents. He glanced at them quickly.

"This could be anyone's signature," he said.

"Which means it could be Sylvia's," I told him. "I say it's her signature. You can believe me, and carry out her instructions, or you can refuse and let her estate go into probate."

"You ask a lot from people," he told me.

"I never ask anyone to do anything I wouldn't do," I said.

"Yeah, but you're the Boca Knight."

"We're all Boca Knights if we want to be," I told him. "It's up to you."

I walked away, leaving the man alone with his conscience.

CHAPTER 39

A Nazi in Business Class

Frustrating points and counterpoints ricocheted off the stone walls of my mind.

I'm sure. I'm not sure. This is good. This is bad. I'm right. I'm wrong. This will help. This will hurt. What was I thinking? Was I thinking?

I was standing near the security area at Miami International Airport watching Randolph Buford approach. He was being escorted by two humongous uniformed policemen who looked capable of guarding the entire Aryan Army. They flanked little Buford like boulder-sized bookends and the Nazi looked frightened. He saw me and grimaced.

"Eddie Perlmutter," the block of granite to Buford's right said formally as the three of them stopped in front of me.

I checked out his name tag. Officer Jeffrey Stone.

"We are delivering prisoner Randolph Buford into your custody," he said formally.

"I'm a lucky guy," I said with a nod. "Why is he handcuffed and shackled?"

"The State considers him a flight risk and a dangerous man," the giant to Buford's left said. His name tag identified him as Officer Kevin Troy.

"Is he officially in my custody?" I asked.

"In a second," Troy said, extending a piece of paper to me, which I read and signed.

When I handed the paper back to Troy, Stone said, "He's all yours."

"Good. Please take off the restraints," I said politely.

"Are you sure?" Stone asked.

"He's got a bull's-eye on his back. Where's he gonna run?"

"I really don't care. He's your problem now," Stone said after removing Buford's shackles.

The little Nazi rubbed his wrists and shook his legs for circulation.

"Good luck," they both said, and departed immediately.

"Do you expect a thank you for having the cuffs removed?" Buford grumbled.

"I expect you to be a complete asshole and you haven't disappointed me," I said.

We cleared security quickly because of my ID papers but after we completed the standard scan we were escorted to a private room. Buford was taken to what must have been a maximum security room where he was subjected to a strip search. He came out rattled.

"Sons of bitches," he muttered, flustered.

"You wouldn't have lasted long in jail," I told him.

We were ushered into a large waiting area bustling with people. There were uniformed guards armed with machine guns standing on opposite walls carefully sweeping the room with their eyes.

"Are those guards here because of me?" Buford asked.

"Don't flatter yourself," I said.

We stood apart from the crowd and didn't talk. I glanced at our tickets. We were on a 747-400 and our seats were in the upper deck. We were in the last row, far away from everything vital on board except the toilets.

A voice over the loudspeaker announced preboarding for those needing special assistance and ended with, "Mr. Edward Perlmutter and traveling companion, please board now."

We negotiated the narrow stairs to the upper deck and found our seats in the last row. It was the end of the line. I told Buford to take the window seat so he would have to step over me to go anywhere. We sat in silence while over four hundred passengers boarded the plane. Randolph Buford watched the other passengers warily: men in black hats, black beards, black suits, women in wigs.

"This is a freak show," he muttered.

"And you're the star," I said, removing some papers from my carry-on bag.

I unfolded an e-mail from Howard Larkey that I had received that morning. He was in the second week of his excellent adventure and was scheduled to arrive in Ekaterinburg shortly. I had printed his message without reading it and stuffed it in my bag before leaving for the airport.

"You got anything for me to read?" Buford asked.

"Sorry. I left my copy of *Mein Kampf* in the oven," I said.

"Very funny," Buford responded sullenly, and looked out the window.

I began reading Howard's e-mail.

Dearest Eddie,

The trip is fabulous. We saw Prince at the LA airport. What a sexy thing he is. Next stop was Hawaii with lava fields and eleven climate zones. What to wear? Hong Kong was very gay, which was interesting but I found Vietnam depressing. China? What's with that wall? We're in Moscow. Fabulous architecture, Lenin's Tomb, the Kremlin. Every sign looks like an eye chart.

Ekaterinburg is our next stop.

We are very excited about bringing our friends home.

Good luck with your secret mission, wherever you're going.

Hugs,

Howard and Derek

I looked at Randolph sitting next to me and thought of my last phone conversation with his mother. Contrary to my advice she had contacted her husband and told him about Randolph's deal.

"I wanted to hear his reaction," she explained to me.

"What did he say?"

"Forrest told me to tell Randolph that he was no longer his son and he didn't want anything to do with him anymore," she said sadly. "He said Aryan Army would probably kill him if he ever comes back."

"What did you say?"

"I asked him to talk to them for our son's sake but he refused," she told me. "He told me he was on probation with the Aryan Army himself and they wouldn't listen to anything he had to say. He blames Randolph for everything bad that's happened to him."

"That's what your husband does," I reminded her. "Do you want me to tell Randolph?"

"Yes, he has to know," Mrs. Buford said.

I turned to the little Nazi sitting next to me and decided

now was as good a time as any to relate his father's words. "I have a message for you from your father," I told him.

"Bullshit," he said. "My father would never talk to you."

"Your mother called him," I clarified the situation. "She told him where you were going and he gave her a message for you. She asked me to relay it."

The kid turned a strange shade of gray when I repeated his father's words.

Sometimes tigers eat their young, I remembered.

"Ladies and gentlemen," a female voice with an accent announced over the loudspeaker, "at this time please turn off all electronic devices, make sure your seatbacks and tray tables are in an upright position and fasten your seat belts."

I felt the plane move backward as we taxied away from the departure gate. I got a cold chill and folded my arms across my chest. What was I nervous about?

I saw Buford look anxiously out the window.

Scared?

Suddenly we were jetting down the runway. Buford closed his eyes and gritted his teeth. He *was* afraid. I was afraid. Our reasons were different.

The plane lifted smoothly and gradually began gaining altitude. The cabin was quiet except for the roaring of the engines. The 747 slowly banked toward the east.

"Ladies and gentlemen," the pleasant voice of the flight attendant came through the intercom after we had leveled off. "You may now use electronic devices and you are free to move about the cabin."

She told us about the movies available during the flight and the dining service offered on board. She said the trip would be smooth with no expected turbulence in the forecast.

The young man sitting across the aisle chuckled softly and turned to me.

"The turbulence starts after we land," he said with a smile.

"So sit back, relax, and enjoy the flight," the comforting inter-com voice told us. "Estimated flight time is thirteen hours and twenty minutes. At nine A.M. tomorrow morning, Thursday, May fifth, you will be in Israel."

Chapter 40

What Do Nazis Dream?

I glanced at Buford who had fallen asleep minutes after takeoff.

What do Nazis dream? I wondered. *Is he dreaming of bombing Poland, invading Stalingrad, goose-stepping around the Eiffel Tower or firing up the ovens? Or is he just having a wet dream like any other nineteen-year-old jerk-off?*

I jabbed him with my elbow.

He sat up, dazed. "What?" he sputtered.

"Nothing," I said. "Go to sleep."

"I was asleep," he grumbled. "Something hit me."

"You're dreaming," I said.

I closed my eyes, satisfied.

"I gotta go to the can," he said moments later.

I unsnapped my seat belt and stood up. Buford slid past me. The young man in the seat across the aisle from us looked up at Buford and made eye contact.

"What are you looking at?" Buford growled.

"You tell me," the young man said politely.

"Shithead," Buford muttered as he walked toward the lavatories.

"It's right in front of you," the young man said.

I laughed. He smiled. Buford slammed the lavatory door.

"Danny Baker," the young man introduced himself, and held out his hand.

"Hi, Danny," I said, shaking his hand. "Eddie Perlmutter."

"I know who you are," he said. "Everyone in this section does. We know who your friend is, too."

"How's that?"

"The airline thought we had a right to know who we're traveling with," he told me.

"And you still took the flight?"

"The odds are four hundred to one in our favor," Danny Baker smiled.

He was a good-looking young man in his early twenties. He had a hint of a beard that offset thinning hair at the top of his head. His body looked hard, but his eyes looked mellow. I wondered if he was someone special.

"Where are you from?"

"Worcester, Massachusetts," he told me.

"I'm from Boston," I said.

"I know," Danny said. "I'm a big fan of yours. That rally last year in Palm Beach made me a Boca Knight, too."

"Glad to hear it," I said. "Why are you flying from Miami if you're from Worcester?"

"I was visiting my grandparents before this trip," he said.

Buford returned, and I stood up to let him take his seat again.

Danny Baker leaned forward and looked at Buford across the aisle.

"Can I ask you something?" he spoke softly to the Nazi.

"What?"

"Why do you hate me?"

"I don't even know who the hell you are," Buford grumbled.

"Yes, but I know who you are," Baker said. "You're a neo-Nazi and you hate Jews. I'm a Jew. Why do you hate me?"

"None of your fuckin' business." Buford turned toward the window, folding his arms across his chest.

"He's not very articulate," I explained.

"Most neo-Nazis aren't," Danny said. "They're good at repeating . . . like anti-Semitic parrots. You know: 'You Jews are all alike,' or 'There was no Holocaust,' or 'Hitler didn't kill enough of you Jews.'"

Buford glared at Baker. "You're pretty brave in a plane full of Jews. I'd kick your ass in the street."

"I don't think so." Baker smiled.

"Why? Are you such a tough guy?" Buford challenged.

"I'm a trained combat soldier," Baker said. "Are you?"

"No, he's not," I interjected. "My girlfriend kicked his ass at the Boca Mall."

"Fuck both of you," Buford turned away again.

"He has a way with words, doesn't he?" I said with a sad smile. "So, were you in the Marines?"

"No, I was in the Israeli Defense Force," he told me.

"I thought you were American."

"I am. But I was in the IDF for sixteen months," he said. "I was what they call a *chail boded*; a lonely soldier."

"I didn't know foreigners could be in the Israeli Army," I said.

"Sure. Foreign Jews have been fighting in the IDF for over fifty years," Baker told me. "During the 1948 War, thirty-five hundred volunteers from forty-three different countries went to Israel to defend the new state. David Ben-Gurion, the prime minister at the time, created a special fighting force called

MAHAL, an acronym for *Mitnadvei Hutz La'aretz*; overseas volunteers. Some Israelis joke that MAHAL stands for *Mishuga'im
Mi'hutz La'aretz*, or crazy guys from outside of Israel. We're also
known as *Mahalniks*."

"Are there many *Mahalniks* in Israel now?"

"Over five thousand."

"Do they receive the same training as regulars?" I asked.

"Absolutely," Danny said. "It's a lot like Marine boot camp."

Buford glanced at Baker but said nothing. I got the strange
feeling that the stupid son of a bitch might actually be listening.

"Are you going back into the Army?" I asked.

"No, I'm visiting family," Danny told me. "I have aunts,
uncles, and cousins in Israel. This is my ninth trip not counting
my service time. I just finished my freshman year at the University of Hartford. I think I'm the world's oldest freshman."

"How old are you?" I asked.

"Twenty-one," he told me. "What about him?"

"He's nineteen going on five," I said.

"Fuck you," Buford said.

"See? He's got a steel-trap mind. Nothing gets in and nothing gets out." I laughed. Danny Baker laughed with me.

Several bearded men gathered in the aisle in front of us. They
were dressed in black, including wide-brimmed black hats. A
few of them looked disdainfully in Buford's direction then turned
toward the front of the plane. I was confused. Buford was concerned.

"What are they doing?" he whispered.

"I don't know," I admitted.

Danny Baker leaned toward me. "It's just *Mincha*," he said.

"Who's he?" I asked.

Baker chuckled into his hand. "*Mincha* is the Hebrew word
for afternoon prayers."

"Why did they turn their backs to us?" Buford asked.

"They're facing east, toward Jerusalem," Baker told him.

When the group began chanting, Buford shrank back in his seat.

"What the fuck is that?" he asked in a hushed tone.

"Relax. That's the *nigun*, the melody of a chant," Baker explained.

"They don't sacrifice anyone, do they?" Buford looked worried.

"Only one first-born Christian son per service," Baker said seriously.

"I *am* the first-born son in my family." Buford's eyes widened.

"Sorry about that," Danny said, and laughed.

One man praying in the aisle turned toward Baker and gave him a disapproving glance.

"Sorry," Danny whispered, holding up his hand in apology to them.

Buford was looking out the window, muttering.

I never thought I'd have fun flying with a Nazi to Israel, but so far, so good.

Danny Baker got out of his seat and joined the men in the aisle. He put on a *yarmulke*, winked at me then started chanting.

The entire scene was bizarre to me and I could only imagine Buford's impression. I closed my eyes and let the chanting lull me to sleep.

I woke for food. Buford was still sleeping. The flight attendant gave me choices, and I ordered the chicken for both of us.

"I assume all the food is kosher," I said to Danny Baker as he tried a piece of fish.

"Everything on El Al is kosher except for the guy sitting next to you," Baker said. "Do you really think Israel can change him?"

"He's been programmed to hate," I said. "I was hoping the IDF could deprogram him."

"That's been tried," he said. "It hasn't worked. They've been programmed from birth. I think the only solution might be to kill their programmers."

"Isn't there another way?" I asked.

Chapter 41

Inspiration, Meditation, Perspiration, Education

While Danny thought about the answer I thought about the question.

How do you to stop someone from wanting to kill you?

If your face is in your enemy's crosshairs and the infrared dot of death is between your eyes, how do you convince the man with the gun not to pull the trigger?

Do you smile to show your soul? Do you wave, one human being to another? Do you hold up two fingers in peace? Do you display one finger in defiance?

"If you can get a kid like Buford to listen," Danny finally said, "I would try to deprogram him by getting him to understand Israel and Israelis."

"How would you do that?" I asked.

"I'd teach him what a teacher in Tel Aviv taught me years ago," Baker said. "The teacher explained that Israel is a country born from inspiration, meditation, perspiration, and education.

He used Masada for inspiration; *Ya'd Vasham* for meditation, kibbutz farming for perspiration, and Hadassah Hospital for education.

"I need an explanation myself," I admitted.

"Okay, let's start with inspiration. Masada is a little mountain near the Dead Sea," Danny took a deep breath. "It's about thirteen hundred feet at its highest point, a large, flat plateau."

"How large?" I asked.

"Large enough for nearly a thousand Jews to build a small fortress after the Romans invaded and conquered Israel in 70 CE," Danny explained.

"Why did the Romans invade Israel?"

"Why does anyone invade anywhere?" Danny grumbled. "For the land, the money, the power . . . and for the hell of it."

"Bad question," I said.

"Actually, it's a good question," he said. "I just don't have a good answer."

"So, why is Masada inspirational?" I asked, changing direction.

"Sigari Jews—religious fanatics—occupied Masada after the Roman invasion and refused to surrender. It took the Roman army over a year to defeat this small group."

"Why so long?" I asked.

I noticed that Buford was listening.

"It was a thirteen-hundred-foot uphill battle for the Romans," Danny explained. "Eventually the Romans built a ramp up the mountain using Jewish slaves as human shields. It was only a matter of time."

"Did the Romans kill the Jews when they reached the top?" I asked.

"No. The Jews had killed themselves rather than become slaves," Danny said.

"Bullshit," Buford interrupted. "I don't believe it."

"I don't care what you believe." Danny looked at him. "That little mound in the desert is meant to be a symbol for Israel. It reminds them that Masada will never fall again."

"It'll fall. All you gotta do is drop a bomb on it," Buford said.

"Israel has bombs, too," Baker said patiently. "Very big bombs. If Masada should fall, the entire world would fall with it." Buford said nothing.

"Let's talk about meditation," I said, clearing my throat and trying to clear the air.

"For meditation I'd take an enemy to *Ya'd Vasham*," Danny continued.

"What's that?" Buford asked.

"*Ya'd* means 'a place,'" Danny explained. "*Vasham* means 'and a name.'"

"A place and a name for what?" Buford asked Baker.

"A place and a name for victims of the Holocaust," Danny answered.

"There was no Holocaust," Buford said confidently.

"At *Ya'd Vasham* there are sixty-eight million pages of documentation, three million names of victims, five thousand names of communities destroyed, and living testimony."

"The testimony of Jews means nothing," Buford challenged Baker.

Danny gritted his teeth. "It's not just the testimony of Jews. In the Avenue of the Righteous at *Ya'd Vasham* there are over twenty thousand names of gentiles who helped Jews during the Holocaust. Were they lying, too?"

"I don't care what you say," Buford said stubbornly. "It never happened."

They had a staring contest, which I interrupted.

"You said something about perspiration." I shifted gears.

"I was referring to all the hard work and technology Israel dedicated to turning the desert into a garden," Danny said, moving on with me.

"Yeah, on stolen land," Buford snapped.

"We took back our own land," Baker said. "Besides, the Arab territory is six hundred and fifty times greater than Israel and their population is only fifty times larger. That hardly seems unfair."

"Bullshit," was all the Nazi could come up with.

Baker's face darkened and I thought he might be seeing red spots.

"What about Hadassah Hospital?" I segued into another subject.

"It is one of the finest medical facilities in the world," Baker said, checking his temper. "It's a monument to education and civilization. At Hadassah Hospital, Arabs and Israelis are treated side by side."

"You expect me to believe that?" Buford smirked.

"Seeing is believing," Baker said. "That's why you're going to Israel. And now if you'll excuse me, I need to rest. Your ignorance is tiring."

We slept for a while, ate again, and finally felt the tires hit the runway accompanied by the sound of soulful music. I glanced at Buford. He was just waking up. When the plane came to a complete stop all the passengers began clapping.

"Why the applause?" I asked Danny Baker, who was stretching and yawning.

"It's for safe arrival in our homeland," Danny says. "It happens every flight."

I heard singing from the main cabin and then singing began in our compartment. The voices blended with the music from the plane's loudspeakers.

"What are they singing?" I asked Baker.

Buford looked nervous again.

"'*Hatikvah*,'" Danny said. "It means 'The Hope.' It's the Israeli National Anthem."

"I can't understand a damn word," Buford complained.

"They're singing in Hebrew," Danny explained.

"What does it mean?" I asked, a little embarrassed that I didn't already know.

Danny translated:

"As long as within our hearts
The Jewish soul sings,
As long as forward to the East
To Zion, looks the eye—
Our hope is not yet lost,
It is two thousand years old,
To be a free people in our land
The land of Zion and Jerusalem."

"I know about Zion," Buford blurted. "Zionists are bad."

"More wisdom from the village idiot." Danny sighed.

We could hear the bustling of passengers in the main cabin preparing to disembark. A male flight attendant came up the stairs.

"Mr. Perlmutter," he said to me. "Please remain seated until all the other passengers have deplaned. Someone will come for you."

Danny Baker stood and retrieved a backpack from the overhead bin. He reached down to shake my hand.

"It was nice talking to you, Mr. Perlmutter," the young man said.

"Thanks for the education," I said, looking up and smiling.

Baker turned to Buford.

"I have advice for you," Baker said.

"I don't need your advice."

"In this country you do," Baker told him. "You should not express the same hateful sentiments to your Israeli supervisors as you did to me. I'm an American. Many Israelis have zero tolerance for your ignorance."

"Yeah, so what are they gonna do, kill me?" Buford said with disdain.

"Yes," Danny Baker said, and he disappeared down the stairs.

I turned to Buford. "I want you to listen to me carefully," I said quietly. "When we get off this plane you're going to be surrounded by people you hate and people who hate you. Some are peaceful and some are violent. The trouble is we won't know who's who. So keep your eyes open and your mouth shut. I didn't bring you here to get killed by some fanatic who doesn't like your attitude."

"Why *did* you bring me here?" he asked.

"To teach you how to coexist with people different from you," I said.

"You're wasting your time," Buford said. "I am who I am."

"That's too bad," was all I could think of to say.

"Mr. Perlmutter." An IDF soldier approached. "It's time to go."

Together we went into the land of Israel.

CHAPTER 42

THE SOUND OF SIRENS AND SILENCE

We followed the soldier into the busy airport.

A siren sounded.

"Stop," the soldier said, and held up his hand.

"Shit," Buford said, surprised.

"*Sheket*," the soldier snapped.

Sheket sounded like "shut it" so Buford and I stopped speaking, and everyone stopped moving. I surveyed our silent surroundings. Ben-Gurion International Airport looked like a display at Madame Tussaud's Wax Museum. All the figures were lifelike, but they were as motionless and mute as mannequins.

Two full minutes passed before the sound and movement returned.

Our soldier began walking again, and we followed.

At the end of the long airport corridor I saw a familiar face. Simon Kane, the Israeli Minister for International Agreements, was dressed casually in slacks and an open-necked shirt. He didn't look any less formidable than the day I met him in the Palm Beach chambers of Judge Jacobs. Kane was flanked by two armed soldiers. The soldier closest to Kane's right was a woman. As we approached, Kane stepped forward to greet me with his hand extended. Buford was detained by our guard.

"Mr. Perlmutter, it's nice to see you again." He smiled and shook my hand with both of his own. "Did you have a pleasant flight?"

"Yes, and an informative one," I told him. "I sat next to a former IDF soldier from Massachusetts."

"A *Mahalnik*." Kane's smile grew wider. "We're very proud of them."

The soldiers flanking Kane nodded their agreement. I noticed the young woman was remarkably attractive and appeared to be in her early twenties. She had black hair and smooth brown skin offset by bright, beautiful green eyes. She had a sturdy athlete's body with perfect posture. I must have been staring because Kane cleared his throat to regain my attention.

"Were you alarmed by the siren?" he asked.

"Yes," I said immediately. "I thought it was an air raid. What was it?"

The soldier guarding Buford moved him forward toward the minister so the Nazi could hear.

"Today is Yom Hashoah, Holocaust Remembrance Day," Minister Kane explained. "It is the reason I asked that Mr. Buford be delivered today. We thought it would be a perfect date and time for a Holocaust denier to visit us. Remembrance Day always falls on the twenty-sixth day of Nissan, according to the Jewish calendar."

I nodded my understanding. "Why did everyone in the airport stop walking and talking?"

"Everything everywhere in Israel stops for two minutes in

memory of the six million victims of the Holocaust," Minister Kane told us.

I glanced at Buford. He was staring at the floor.

"National radio and television stops. Buses stop. Cars stop. People get out of their vehicles and stand still in the middle of the road," the minister said. "There are remembrance ceremonies all over the country. The national observance started last night in Jerusalem at *Ya'd Vasham*. It's the sixtieth anniversary of the Holocaust this year. Time is passing. We don't want people to forget."

"I know I'll never forget," I said honestly.

"And you, Mr. Buford?" Kane asked.

I hoped Buford would not forget my advice to keep his opinions to himself. To his credit he just shrugged in response.

"That's the most intelligent answer he's given since we left Miami," I said. "What's the plan from here?"

"Buford will be sent to a receiving center," Kane explained. "We are taking you to a hotel in Jerusalem where you will stay for a few days. Your short itinerary is well planned, and you will be kept busy."

"Will I be seeing Buford again while I'm here?"

"Probably not," Minister Kane said. "Mr. Buford will be going through intensive training from this point on. You have another agenda."

I looked at Buford. He looked scared, and although we certainly weren't friends, I think I was the closest thing to a friend he had in Israel. I wondered if I would ever see him alive again.

"Sergeant Oz will take charge of Mr. Buford," Kane announced.

I was surprised to see the young woman step forward and stand next to Buford. They were about the same height.

"Buford is violent," I said. "No offense intended here, but is Sergeant Oz the best person for this job?"

"She is a *krav maga* instructor," Kane said. "She's an expert in close combat, capable of inflicting the maximum amount of damage in the minimum amount of time. She is a lethal weapon. Mr. Buford would be well advised to mind his manners with Sergeant Oz."

I looked at Oz. She was the most beautiful professional killer I had ever seen.

"I understand your concern," Kane continued. "Sergeant Oz does not look the part of a weapon, but I assure you she is deadly and motivated. Her grandparents are Holocaust survivors who immigrated here in 1947. She is a Sabra, a native-born Israeli. Very beautiful and very dangerous."

"I'll take your word for it," I said, and held out my hand to Sergeant Oz.

She gripped it firmly and looked me in the eye. She exuded strength and confidence.

"I'm Eddie Perlmutter," I introduced myself.

"Sergeant Zivah Oz," she said in a low, professional voice. "Are you prepared to hand over your prisoner?"

"He's all yours." I held out my arm like a head waiter. "Do you need any special instructions from me?"

"I am very familiar with Mr. Buford," she said, looking at him without emotion. "I have studied his file and totally understand who I am dealing with."

She convinced me.

"I would only like to add, Mr. Perlmutter," she continued, "that I think what you are trying to do with this man is very commendable and I promise to do everything I can to help. Unfortunately I am not confident we can change such a person but I will do my best."

She gripped the kid's arm and his knees buckled. Oz held him upright with minimal effort and physically guided him in the direction she wanted him to go. A tall, armed soldier accompanied them as they entered a room with no sign on the door.

"Where are they taking him?" I asked.

"He is no longer your concern," Kane said. "You don't need to know."

"He is under orders to e-mail me once a week with a report of his activities," I reminded the minister.

"And he will, Mr. Perlmutter, I assure you," Kane said.

Minister Kane and I were escorted outside by the two remaining soldiers. I was led to a large green IDF Hummer. I saw that my luggage was already in the vehicle. I sat in the backseat with Kane. The two soldiers were in front. The interior of the Hummer was all metal except for the seat.

"Bulletproof," Kane told me, rapping his knuckles against the window.

"Where are we going?" I asked, ignoring the inherent danger in a bulletproof car.

"We're going to check you into the King David Hotel and give you a couple of hours to relax," Kane told me. "Then we'll show you some sights."

"I don't want you to go to a lot of trouble."

"It's a pleasure," Minister Kane insisted.

The ride from Ben-Gurion Airport to Jerusalem took thirty-five minutes without traffic. The hotel's six stories of pink sandstone were in the middle of the New City. The soldiers checked me into the hotel and Kane escorted me to my room. The suite had a living room and bedroom, and was larger than my apartment in Boca. I had a magnificent view of the Old City and King David's gardens.

"Very impressive," I said.

"You are our special guest." Kane smiled. "Please join me on the terrace."

I had an unobstructed view of the old wall of Jerusalem.

"It's quite a sight, isn't it?" Kane said proudly.

"It certainly is," I agreed.

I heard a distant chant emanate through an unseen loud-speaker.

"*Allah u Akbar . . . Allah u Akbar.*"

"What's that?" I asked.

"That's the Muslim call to prayer," he explained. "It's called the *Adham*, and the man singing is a *muezzin*. It happens five times a day."

"What does it mean?"

"*Allah u Akbar . . . Allah u Akbar,*" was repeated for the fourth time.

"It means God is great," Minister Kane translated.

"*Ash-hadu al-la ill-Allah,*" was chanted.

"I bear witness that there is no divinity but Allah," Kane said, reciting the English version.

"*Ash-hadu anna Muhammadan Rasulullaah.*"

"I bear witness that Muhammad is Allah's Messenger."

"*Hayya la-se-saleah, Hayya la-se-saleah.*"

"Hasten to the prayer."

"*Haya la-l-faleah.*"

"Hasten to real success."

"*Allah u Akbar,*" three times.

"God is great. God is great. God is great."

"*La llaha ill-Allah.*"

"There is no divinity but Allah," Minister Kane said. "That's it."

"That's enough," I said.

"That was just a call to prayer. The serious praying hasn't even started yet." Minister Kane went back into the room and walked to the front door. "It's noon," he said. "Rest awhile, freshen up, and meet me in the lobby in two hours."

"Okay," I said. "Can I ask again where Buford is going?"

"I don't want to tell you too much," he said. "It's better if you don't know everything. But I will tell you that he is heading for a receiving base near Tel Aviv. They will give him a physical to determine his health. Then he will be issued a uniform and toiletries. Tomorrow he will be transferred to an education base in the north where he will begin his training."

"Will Zivah Oz be with him the whole time?" I asked.

"She will be with him every step of the way during his training," Kane told me.

"Is that good or bad?" I asked.

"We'll see," Simon Kane said, and he closed the door behind him when he left.

I returned to my balcony to behold Jerusalem.

CHAPTER 43

HOLOCAUSTS HAPPEN

How the hell do Hitlers and Holocausts happen? How does a leader convince followers that killing six million people will make the world a better place?

> **LEADER:** *Let's kill six million people.*
> **FOLLOWER:** *Why?*
> **LEADER:** *We suck because of them.*
> **FOLLOWER:** *Really? It's not our own fault we suck?*
> **LEADER:** *No . . . it's their fault . . . and if we kill them we won't suck as much.*
> **FOLLOWER:** *I don't know if this is such a good idea.*
> **LEADER:** *Did I mention we can take all their stuff if we kill them?*
> **FOLLOWER:** *Count me in.*

Six million people . . . about as many as three quarters of the New York City population, I thought as I exited the Holocaust Museum. I shielded my eyes from the bright sun and looked out at the Jerusalem valley.

"Are you alright?" Kane put a hand on my shoulder.

"No, I'm not," I said.

"I'll give you some time," he said, and left me standing alone with my thoughts.

The Holocaust Museum is cut into a mountainside. My tour began underground in a triangular walkway that gradually ascended back to the surface.

I counted ten halls each dedicated to a different aspect of the Holocaust. There was too much to absorb and comprehend.

There were twenty-five hundred personal items in the museum and forty-six thousand audio and video testimonies taken from survivors and witnesses.

The Great Hall contained over six hundred photographs of atrocities, mass graves, murdered babies, living skeletons, gas chambers, cremation ovens, the Auschwitz Album, and German soldiers shooting unarmed men, women, and children at point-blank range.

Railroad cars used to transport the victims to death camps were on display. A pile of shoes and containers of human ashes evidenced the murder of so many, including one and a half million children.

The Hall of Villages identified thousands of destroyed shtetels, and the Hall of Remembrance listed the names of millions of destroyed lives. Incredible. I breathed deeply and looked for Kane.

He came back to my side and patted my shoulder.

"It's a tough experience," he said, and sighed.

"How can Buford say the Holocaust never happened?" I wondered aloud.

"A lot of Nazis say that."

"He says Hitler didn't kill enough Jews." I shook my head.

"A lot of Nazis say that, too."

"Maybe he'll learn something here," I said.

"And maybe not," Kane responded. "Remember, all those atrocities were committed by people who would do it all over again if they had the chance."

The sun was low in the sky. I glanced at my watch. It was six P.M. We had been in the museum for three hours.

"Are you tired?" Kane asked. "I can take you to the hotel to rest."

"No, I'm alright. I want to see as much as I can," I said.

The minister patted my shoulder again.

"Good for you Mr. Perlmutter."

We went with our two armed guards to the Wailing Wall in the Old City. We stood in a well-lit public square and looked at the ancient wall of stones. Kane explained some of the Wall's history including stories of King Solomon's original tenth-century temple, Herod's massive expansion in 19 BCE, and the destruction by the Romans in 70 CE.

"After Emperor Titus destroyed the temple," Kane said, "this wall became a place of mourning . . . a place for wailing . . . or so the story goes. Nowadays some people call it the Western Wall. This section of wall was built on top of an original section of wall. It's very symbolic."

"What are all the pieces of paper between the stones?" I asked, pointing and walking around a group of praying, bearded men dressed in black. The men glared at me and I assumed I had intruded on their prayers. I smiled apologetically, but they continued glaring.

A red spot in the Holy Land? Stop it you hothead.

I turned my attention to Kane before I turned into an ugly American.

"The notes are put there by people who believe all of God's bounty emanates from this place," Kane whispered. "They write notes of prayer and place them in the wall for God to read."

"Do you believe God reads all these notes?" I asked Kane politely.

"I doubt He has time for all the faxes."

I laughed. The men in black turned and looked down their noses at me. Their stares were hateful and intolerant. I became hostile in a heartbeat and contemplated whaling someone at the Wailing Wall. Minister Kane put his hand on my shoulder and led me away.

"I don't think they like me," I said to Kane.

"They don't like me, either," he told me.

"But you're one of them."

"No I'm not." Kane shook his head. "I'm an Israeli and a Zionist. Those Jews are Neturei Karta, Guardians at the Gate. They represent a tiny percentage of Israelis but they make a lot of noise. They say Israel can't exist until the Messiah comes."

"When is that?"

"I don't know but I'm not waiting," Kane said. "I love this country and the Neturei Karta wants to give it to the Palestinians."

"Why?"

"It's their interpretation of the Bible . . . not mine," Kane said. "They believe that Jews are in exile because of divine decree."

"That's ridiculous," I decided.

"Christians disagree with Christians, don't they?" Kane asked. "Muslims disagree with Muslims. People are always interpreting the word of God differently, to suit their purposes. A hundred religious people can have four hundred opinions of what God meant when He said something."

"Maybe God should have been more specific."

Later, I stood on my balcony at the King David Hotel watching the Old City glow like gold in the setting sun and I heard the *muezzin*'s call to evening prayer. I was in the birthplace of the greatest story ever told . . . surrounded by holy books that were read constantly . . . with very few readers on the same page.

The next morning, at five A.M., I stood in the dark desert, shivering from the cold, looking up at a thirteen-hundred-foot-high flat rock.

Masada will never fall again. Remember the Alamo, I couldn't help thinking.

"We can climb using the snake trail like those people from the buses are doing," Kane said, pointing at silhouettes. "Or we can take a cable car to the top."

Men, women, and children were heading toward the snake trail.

Let's climb, Mr. Johnson prodded me . . . and like an adolescent I listened to him.

"Let's climb," I said, regretting the words as soon as I said them.

I tried to follow Kane and our two-man army closely but soon lagged behind. It didn't take me long to learn why the path was called the snake trail. About a third of the way up, the steep trail coiled like a cobra and bit me in the ass. My knees and sciatica reminded my sixty-one-year-old body that I should be on one of those little cable cars climbing halfway to the stars. I pushed myself to pick up the pace. I thought I was doing better until a group of teenage girls trotted past me.

"Isn't this wicked awesome?" one of them said to another.

I was so discouraged I stopped in my tracks. *Wicked painful*, I thought, bending at the waist and trying to stretch the burn out in my butt.

"You okay, mister?" a little boy asked me.

Bent over to half my height, I was at eye level with the kid, but I felt two inches tall.

"I'm fine," I lied. "How old are you kid, thirteen?"

"I'm eight," he said proudly, and left me in the desert dust.

I limped in silent agony until I heard loud pounding footsteps behind me. I moved to the side and pressed my back against the rock wall. A long line of young soldiers stampeded by me like I was standing still, which I was. They were shouting encouragement to one another in a mad dash to the top. They carried rifles and large packs on their backs, and some of them held stretchers on their shoulders in four-man teams. On the stretchers I saw large full bags I guessed were meant to simulate body weight. When the last of the soldiers had passed me I started climbing again and found myself reenergized . . . for about ten steps.

"You're doing great," I heard encouragement from above.

"For a dying man," I gasped.

My escorts laughed.

"Take your time," Kane advised. "You're not a kid anymore."

"Why didn't you tell me that at the bottom?" I joked and bent at the waist again. "Who were those maniacs running up the mountain?"

"They're soldiers finishing their training program," one of my armed guards said. "They'll be sworn into the army at the top of Masada."

"They didn't even look tired," I remarked.

"Oh, they're tired, Mr. Perlmutter," the other bodyguard said. "Those guys are finishing a fifty-kilometer march they started last night. They walked thirty-five kilometers carrying their own equipment and they each marched fifteen kilometers in four-man teams carrying a stretcher weighted with sandbags. They've been hiking for twelve hours."

"Did you go through the same training?" I asked, standing upright again.

"Of course," the young soldier said.

"It must be tough," I commented.

"It is, sir," he said proudly. "We have to be tough so that Masada never falls again."

Remember the Alamo.

I took a deep breath.

"Let's go," I said, and I made it to the top without another stop. Once there I was rewarded by the site of soldiers and civilians celebrating a spectacular sunrise.

CHAPTER 44

I LOVE YOU—I'M SORRY

I arrived at Miami International Airport at eight forty-five the same morning I left Tel Aviv. A coffee-colored goddess with the face of an angel was waiting for me at the baggage claim where I had no baggage to claim. I had traveled light with only a carry-on.

God she looks great, I said to myself. *I'm a lucky guy.* When she was born I was in high school dating my future wife, Patty Mc-Gee.

I smiled and waved. Claudette waved, but didn't smile. She had an anxious look on her beautiful face.

We hugged briefly. She let go first.

Something's wrong, I sensed.

"Welcome home, Eddie," she said stoically.

"Thank you, Eartha Kitt." I tried to read her mind but couldn't.

We walked to the car making uncomfortable small talk. I threw my one bag in the trunk and got in the passenger's side.

"So, how was Israel?" she asked, not looking at me as she inserted the key in the ignition.

"Too many Jews," I told her, removing the key from the ignition. "What's the matter?"

"Nothing," she said unconvincingly.

"Is Queen okay," I asked about her ninety-plus grandmother. "She's fine."

"What's wrong, then?" I asked again. "I'm a detective, remember? I know when a person is lying."

Did you finally realize I'm too old for you or something? I thought.

Tears came to her eyes.

"I have to stop seeing you," she said, her lower lip trembling.
I knew it!

"Did I do something wrong?" I asked as calmly as I could.

"It's not you . . . it's me," she said.

I think I've used that line myself.

She slept with someone else, Mr. Johnson decided. *The little tramp.*

Look who's talking, I scolded him. *You'd screw anyone.*

Of course I would. I'm a penis, he explained. *What's her excuse?*

"Is there someone else?" I blurted out before I could stop myself.

"There hasn't been anyone else since I met you," she said.

"Okay. Did you kill someone?"

"Not lately." She reminded me that she had cut off a bad man's head with a machete before she fled Haiti.

"Well, what could be so bad then?" I asked her.

"Promise not to get angry?" she asked timidly.

"No."

"Promise to *try* not to get angry?"

"Yes."

"While you were gone I missed you so much—" she said.

"That's okay," I interrupted. "I missed you, too."

"You don't understand," she went on. "I couldn't eat. I couldn't sleep. I was afraid you might not come back. Then I realized I had done something really stupid."

"What?"

"I'd fallen in love with you, Eddie." She started crying. "I didn't mean to. I know you don't want any attachments and I understand. I'm sorry."

"You're telling me you want to stop seeing me because you love me," I said slowly. "Have I got that right?"

She nodded. "I know you're going to leave me someday," she said. "It's what you do. You told me that when we started seeing each other and I thought I could handle it. But the longer we stay together the harder it will be for me when you want to leave."

I looked at her, knowing what I wanted to say but not saying anything.

"Aren't you going to say anything?" she asked.

Oh, alright.

"I love you, too," I told her.

"You do not." She shook her head. "You're just saying that to shut me up."

"That's partially true," I conceded. "But I also love you."

"Since when?" She refused to believe me.

"Since a minute ago when you said we couldn't see each other anymore," I answered. "I got very upset. I haven't been that upset about losing a woman since my wife died."

"I know I can't replace your wife," she added quickly. "But do you love me for real, Eddie?"

"I love you for real . . . for now," I said sincerely. "Is that good enough?"

"For now," she said, smiling.

We didn't consummate our spoken love that night. Mr. Johnson wasn't up for it and I blamed it on jet lag.

E-mail from Russia the next morning at my office:

Hello, dear boy,

You must be frantic worrying about us. Don't worry. Be happy. We're still in Ekaterinburg with the Kuznetsovs. Boris, the boss, literally has fallen in love with me in his own psychotic way. Boris is bisexual by the way and Yuri is bipolar. They admire our loyalty to our friends and think we're marvelously Mafioso even though we're gay Jews. Boris says he wants to fahk me but I told him I was married and monogamous. Now he wants me more. What is it with you men?

Yesterday Boris had two of his goons take us to the Ekaterinburg Cemetery, a graveyard for gulag goombahs. It was fabulous. There are life-size, color pictures of the deceased on the tombstones. It's so hard to describe I suggest you Google: Ekaterinburg Cemetery Mafia . . . and see what I mean. Of course, the Internet is not like visiting dead people in real life, but you'll get the idea.

Dasvidaniya.

Howard and Derek.

P.S. The Dietrichs are fine.

E-mail from Randolph Buford—Israel—May 12, 2005:

This is my first e-mail. I was in Bakom Army Base for a few days. I am in north Israel now in the Magen Division for problem recruits and criminals. We are expected to do seventy-five push-ups and eighty-six sit-ups and run two

kilometers in less than nine minutes. I can't do it. I hate it
here.

Sergeant Oz is at the base and she teaches self-defense.
She treats me like everyone else—bad.

Buford's message included no hello and no good-bye, but at
least he was doing as he was told, and I considered that a good
sign.

CHAPTER 45

MY SECOND SOUTHERN SUMMER

Fifteen hurricanes hit America's southland in 2005, felling a few Florida fronds before knocking the jazz out of New Orleans.

Four storms—Dennis, Emily, Katrina, and Wilma—did one hundred and twenty-eight billion dollars' worth of damage and caused over two thousand deaths nationwide. During a lull in the storms I got organized.

Dr. Cohen's project in Osceola Park would be ready to open before the New Year and Claudette was working at the facility as head nurse and as Dr. Cohen's watchdog.

Sylvia Dubin-Goldman's estate had been settled to my satisfaction, which meant Sanford Kreiger, her lawyer, had to lie. He did a great job. I had several meetings with the trustees of the Dubin-Goldman trust and I was pleased with the way it was taking shape. I thought we could finish both projects before the end of the year.

Derek and Howard e-mailed regularly. They had moved on to the Scandinavian countries and expressed no interest in returning to Florida until the temperature in Wilton Manors became "civilized." The Dietrichs were having a great time and showing no ill effects from their ordeal.

Buford also sent his mandatory weekly e-mails.

E-mail excerpt from Israel—mid June 2005:
I am being pushed very hard. I am learning nothing. I hate it here.

E-mail excerpt from Israel—late June 2005:
Today I did twenty-five sit-ups and thirty push-ups without stopping but I couldn't complete the run in nine minutes. I hate it here.

E-mail excerpt from Israel—early July 2005:
Today I did seventy-five push-ups and a hundred sit-ups without stopping. I completed the run in eight minutes and fifty seconds. Sergeant Oz told me I was doing better.

E-mail excerpt from Israel—August 2005:
Several of us were moved to a Kibbutz. I am working as a farmer. People are nicer here. Not so military. I was told there are about two hundred and seventy places like this in Israel and they produce forty percent of the agricultural products. I work hard and don't mind. I like to watch things grow. I never knew that. I have two Jews I talk to now. They are Russians. They are the closest I have to friends.

I think Sergeant Oz doesn't hate me so much anymore. She talks to me more now.

Randolph

E-mail excerpt from Israel—September 2005:
I was taken to Ya'd Vasham. After the tour Sergeant Oz re-
minded me that I had once said that Hitler didn't kill enough
Jews. I said I was sorry and told her I'm trying to learn.
    Randolph Buford

Throughout September, Buford's e-mails became increasingly insightful. He told me about the helicopter ride over Israel
with other soldiers from his unit.

E-mail excerpt from Israel—late September 2005:
It was just like that guy on the El Al plane said, Israel is this
little strip of land in a vast desert. It doesn't take up much
room.

In early October, Buford wrote:

I climbed Masada yesterday with my group after a twenty-five
kilo overnight march in the desert. When we reached the top
we celebrated.
    I don't love these Jews. I don't even like most of them. I
don't like the Arabs and Christians any better but I don't hate
any of them either. I am very confused.

I had not responded to Buford's e-mails but I responded to
this one.

Randolph,
It is not important that you like people who are different than
you. It is only important that you let them live in peace. You
can do it.
    Eddie

E-mail excerpt from Israel—October 2005:

I am an orderly at the Hadassah Hospital at Ein Karem in south-west Jerusalem. I like the work, but this place confuses me.

I thought of my own visit to Hadassah Hospital. It *was* confusing. Enemies slept side by side, swaddled in bloody bandages like immobile mummies, their lives mending or ending randomly; all in the name of God.

Gloria in excelsis Deo, Glory to God in the highest.

BING!

Baruck ata Adonai, Blessed art you our God.

BANG!!

Allah u Akbar, God is great.

BOOM!

Excerpt from the same Buford October e-mail:

I talked to a Palestinian patient the other day who lost a leg. He was a victim of a suicide bombing. He said he was not a terrorist himself but he had no anger for the bomber. He tried to explain the Palestinian cause to me and Jihad . . . Holy War. His argument seemed reasonable. An Israeli soldier two beds away told me his side of the story and he sounded reasonable too. I don't know who to believe and have decided to learn more. This is a new way of thinking for me. Is that why you sent me here?

Buford had broken through the gravitational pull of hatred.

Blastoff!

That's one small step for a man . . . , I thought.

CHAPTER 46

EARTH TO EDDIE

I plummeted back to Earth two days later.

> E-mail from Israel—October 2005:
> Dear Mr. Perlmutter,
>   I regret to inform you that Randolph Buford was killed today by a suicide bomber on a bus in Tel Aviv. The Israeli government will be contacting Randolph's mother with the official notice, but I am writing to you on a personal basis.

I felt bile rising in my stomach and fought the urge to vomit.

> Randolph Buford died saving my life and the lives of several other passengers by shielding our bodies with his own an instant before the explosion. His act of heroism saved Muslims, Jews, and Christians, all of whom believe it was fate that put Randolph between them and harm's way.

The survivors and their loved ones would like to honor Randolph with a memorial service here in Israel. We request your permission and attendance. We will make all necessary travel and financial arrangements on your behalf and we will plan the service at your convenience. We will also arrange for Randolph's body to be transported to the U.S. on your return flight.

If Mrs. Buford should decline our invitation, we will have her son's remains transported as soon as possible to the airport of her choice in the United States.

Please extend our deepest sympathy to Mrs. Buford and tell her that her son died a hero. We await your response.

Sincerely,

Sergeant Zivah Oz

Crimson spots burst in front of my eyes like popping balloons of red paint. I slammed my fist on my desk. "This is not fair," I roared as a fireworks display went off in my head. I heard tapping on my office door.

"Eddie," the receptionist's voice came through the door. "Are you alright?"

"I'm fine," I snapped, and heard her footsteps retreating down the hall.

I called Claudette and told her.

"That's terrible," she said emotionally. "Does his mother know yet?"

"I don't think so," I replied.

"Are you going to tell her?"

"I'm not good at this," I said.

"No one is," Claudette said. "I love you."

"I love you, too."

We hung up.

I reached for the phone several times but my hand kept

coming up short. Finally, I grabbed the damn thing and punched in Mrs. Buford's number. She answered.

"Mrs. Buford, this is Eddie Perlmutter," I said as calmly as I could manage.

"He's dead, isn't he?" she said before I could utter another word.

"Yes," I told her. "He died this morning in a suicide bombing."

"He was a suicide bomber?" she asked in disbelief.

"No no no," I said quickly. "Your son died a hero, Mrs. Buford."

"You don't have to lie to me, Mr. Perlmutter," she said in a shaky voice. "My son was no hero."

She started to cry.

"I'm not lying," I said. "Can I read you the e-mail I received from his Israeli supervisor this morning?"

"What difference will that make?" she said angrily.

"I think it will make a lot of difference," I said calmly.

Her silence indicated she would listen.

I read Sergeant Oz's e-mail to her slowly from beginning to end.

She sniffled. "I can't believe anyone would want to honor my son."

"He died a hero. He may not have lived like a hero, Mrs. Buford," I said, "but it appears he died like one."

She seemed stunned. "What should I do?"

"I can't tell you that, Mrs. Buford," I said. "I can tell you that I've already decided to go to Israel to honor your son's memory."

She hesitated for a moment.

"I'll go with you," she finally answered, and then she was crying again.

I expected the worst: flying fourteen hours to a foreign funeral with the mother of the deceased. Martha Buford did cry often but it was a dignified sorrow. I was very impressed.

She asked the same questions I asked Danny Baker on my first flight to Israel, and I tried to answer her. When the men in black got up to pray, I explained the chanting as best I could and why they had turned away from us.

She told me about the little apartment in Boca Raton she had rented and the job-hunting she had done. She told me she had decided to stay in the area and had no intention of following her husband to South Carolina. She was worried about her daughter, Eva, but felt powerless to battle for her custody against her husband. He was too strong for her to fight.

I held her hand when she seemed fragile and I think I helped her get through the flight.

I explained the clapping and singing when we touched down on the runway at Ben-Gurion International Airport. She thought it was a nice tradition.

Sergeant Zivah Oz was waiting for us when we got off the plane. She shook my hand. "Welcome back," she said somberly. "I'm sorry for your loss," she said, taking the grieving mother's hand.

Mrs. Buford smiled bravely. "Thank you for meeting us."

"Your son saved my life," Zivah Oz told Martha Buford.

The floodgates of emotion burst open and the grieving mother threw her arms around the young sergeant and cried. Zivah Oz held the woman firmly and patted her back. They rocked in each other's arms.

Mrs. Buford's sobbing subsided but they remained holding each other. Martha Buford let go first, leaned back, and looked at Sergeant Oz. She stroked the girl's cheek with the palm of her hand.

"You're so beautiful," the older woman said.

"All the lives Randolph saved were beautiful," Oz told us.

The sergeant drove us to the King David Hotel and accompanied us to our adjoining suites facing the Old City. Our luggage had already been delivered. We stood on the balcony of Martha Buford's room looking at Tel Aviv and the Old City walls.

"This is unreal," Mrs. Buford said.

"I assure you, Mrs. Buford, it's very real," the Israeli soldier told her.

We went to the lobby where we ordered cold drinks. The two women sat on a sofa, and I pulled over a nearby chair.

"Tell me how my son died," Mrs. Buford said, her voice cracking.

"First I would like to tell you how he lived," Oz said.

"Sergeant, I'm his mother. I know how he lived."

"Not here, not in this place," Oz reminded her.

"You're right, of course," Randolph's mother said. "Tell me."

Sergeant Oz moved closer to Martha Buford and spoke softly. "When your son arrived in Israel, he was like a caged animal: frightened and frightening," Oz said. "We sent him to *Havat Hashomer*, a training camp in the north. He was assigned to the *Mak'hal* division, for special population groups."

"What's a special population group?" Mrs. Buford asked.

"It's for problem people," Oz said diplomatically.

Boris Kuznetsov would have called them a group of "fahk-ups."

"I suppose he fit right in." Mrs. Buford looked down at her lap.

"To the contrary," Oz said, "he was a misfit in a company of misfits."

For sixty minutes Oz told a grieving mother about the last few months of her son's life.

"Randolph barely spoke during his first month here," Oz noted.

"That would be my fault," I interrupted. "I told him to keep his mouth shut."

"Well, he took your advice to heart and talked to no one," she said.

"Did something change after the first month?" Mrs. Buford asked.

"Randolph changed," the sergeant said. "He was the most unfit in a company of misfits and he blamed everyone else for his shortcomings."

"His father was like that," Mrs. Buford said, nodding.

"When he finally realized he had no one to blame but himself he started trying harder. In fact, he became the hardest-working member of the company. He went from last to first. The entire *Mak'hal* group was proud of him. He became an inspiration."

Tears welled in Martha Buford's eyes. "He died when he was just starting to live," the grieving mother said.

"Many young men here are cut down before they grow up," Oz said. "Your son saw many young people die when he worked at Hadassah Hospital."

"He e-mailed me about the hospital," I said. "It made a great impression on him."

"He told me about one Palestinian college student in particular," Sergeant Oz told us. "The boy's name was Ibrahim Elwan and he was a victim of a suicide bombing. He lost a leg. The attack took place at a Tel Aviv restaurant and the bomber was Palestinian. Despite his injuries, Elwan told Randolph that he had no animosity for the bomber and that he shared the man's beliefs."

"Randolph wrote to me about this guy," I said, remembering an e-mail.

"I wouldn't be surprised," Oz said. "Randolph was very impressed by Elwan. Then again, Randolph was equally impressed by Shlomo Lev."

"Who's Shlomo Lev?" Martha Buford asked.

"The Israeli college student in the bed next to Elwan," Oz explained. "He sustained a head injury in the same explosion."

"Did Lev and Elwan ever talk to each other?" I asked.

"All the time," Oz said.

"Did they agree on anything?" I asked.

"Randolph said they argued about everything until Lev died," Oz told us. "Randolph said Elwan cried when Lev died."

This is a strange place, I thought.

"What happened to Elwan?" Martha asked.

"He was released from the hospital, walking on a prosthesis designed by a Jewish doctor," Oz told us.

"Did my son ever see Elwan again?" Mrs. Buford asked.

"Yes," Oz said solemnly. "I was with Randolph at the time, along with some other members of our unit."

"Did Randolph get a chance to talk to Elwan again?"

"In a way, I suppose he did," Oz told her. "We were in a crowded bus in Tel Aviv, and apparently Elwan got on the bus after we did. Randolph pointed him out to me and called his name. The young Palestinian seemed startled to see Randolph and a mournful look came over his face. Suddenly your son grabbed my arm and threw me to the floor. On my way down, I heard someone scream '*Allah u Akbar.*' Then the bus exploded."

CHAPTER 47

"THE GIANTS WIN THE PENNANT"*

I wonder if Ibrahim Elwan's final thoughts on earth were about the seventy-two virgins he was going to meet in heaven . . . or about the young American orderly he was about to murder.

That night I dreamed in black and white with English subtitles.

I dreamed that the Romans marched into Israel and tossed out the Jews.

"Who burned our temple?" a Jew in my dream asked.

A Roman soldier who looked like Sylvester Stallone shouted, "Yo, Abraham, I did it."

"Finders keepers," one Arab decided when the land was mostly vacated.

"What if the Jews or Romans come back?" another Arab asked.

"Elhasi teezi."

---

*Russ Hodges—Announcer, 1951

"I don't think they will kiss your ass."

And so it went for two thousand years.

"I was here first, Yassir."

"You were not, Hymie."

"Was too."

"Was not."

"Khul khara we moot *(Eat shit and die).*"

I dreamed about the Great Arab revolts of the 1930s and 1940s, which weren't so great for the Arabs.

Then suddenly my dream shifted to a 1951 baseball game at the Polo Grounds in New York City. A guy named Bobby Thompson had just hit a home run for the New York Giants against the Brooklyn Dodgers. An announcer named Russ Hodges screamed into a microphone, "The Giants win the Pennant. The Giants win the Pennant" . . . *over and over again.*

"The Giants win the Jihad," I shouted, and woke myself up. I jumped out of bed in a daze. I was totally confused. I felt like my brain was melting and all my memories were blending together into a senseless mush.

I looked at the clock on my nightstand. It was three thirty in the morning. I flopped down on my pillow and prayed for dreamless sleep. Prayer reception apparently is good in this part of the world because I slept peacefully the rest of the night and didn't wake up until my wakeup call.

I put on my King David Hotel bathrobe, walked out on my balcony, and took a deep breath of holy air. The sun was shinning. It was a beautiful morning for a memorial service.

I met Sergeant Oz in the lobby at nine.

"Mrs. Buford will be here in a minute," she told me. "Did you sleep well?"

"I was restless. I had a dream that Sylvester Stallone burned down the Holy Temple."

"Rocky Balboa?"

"It was just a dream." I shrugged. "I also dreamed that a baseball player named Bobby Thompson hit a home run for the New York Giants and beat the Brooklyn Dodgers to win the Pennant."

"What is a Pennant?"

"It's a championship flag."

"Who are the Giants?"

"They were a baseball team from New York," I explained. "But now they're in San Francisco."

"Because they won the Pennant?"

"No."

"Who are the Dodgers?"

"They were a baseball team from Brooklyn but they moved to Los Angeles."

"Because they lost the Pennant?"

"It's complicated," I said with a shrug.

Mrs. Buford joined us. She shook my hand and hugged Sergeant Oz.

"Did you sleep well?" Oz asked Mrs. Buford.

"I had a restless night," Martha Buford told her.

"So did Mr. Perlmutter," Oz said. "He dreamed that Sylvester Stallone burned down the Holy Temple and Bobby Thompson hit a home run."

"I don't understand," Mrs. Buford said.

"I don't, either," I told them.

A four-door, black Mercedes sedan was waiting for us outside the hotel. Zivah Oz got in the front with a young man in an IDF uniform. Mrs. Buford and I got in the back.

The soldier turned to face us. "Mrs. Buford," the soldier said courteously. "I just wanted to tell you that your son did a very brave thing, and you should be very proud of him."

I glanced at Randolph's mother. She looked flustered, as if no one had ever complimented her son before.

"That's very nice of you to say, young man," she replied, misty-eyed.

"Where are we going this morning?" I asked.

"First we are going to Mount Herzl," Sergeant Oz explained. "It is the site of Israel's national and military cemetery."

"Will the memorial service be there?" Mrs. Buford asked.

"In that area," Oz said.

Mount Herzl is located on a hilltop overlooking the Jerusalem Forest.

"This memorial park was named after the father of Zionism, Theodore Herzl. He is buried over there." Sergeant Oz waved a hand in the direction of a monument. "Three prime ministers are buried here: Levi Eshkol, Golda Meir, and Yitzhak Rabin. The entire area is called *Har Hazi karon*, Mount of Memories."

She told us that thousands of IDF soldiers were buried on the north slope of Mount Herzl and *Ya'd Vasham* was not far away; two mountains alive with millions of memories of the dead.

We walked silently among the graves, reading names and ages. Most had died too young.

"These men and women were heroes, like your son," Oz said.

"Could Randolph have been buried here?" she asked.

"Legally yes, technically it would have been difficult," Oz told her. "There is an Orthodox Jewish population in this country that does not believe Jews and Gentiles should be buried in the same cemetery."

"After death why does it matter?" Mrs. Buford asked.

"Religion and traditions are sometimes beyond reason," the sergeant said.

We spent an hour among the graves and were emotionally weary when we left.

"So many sacrifices," Mrs. Buford remarked.

"There will be more today and more tomorrow," Oz said.

My inner police alarm alerted me to the presence of a small group of people walking in our direction. Suddenly we were surrounded.

"What's happening?" Mrs. Buford asked nervously.

"Mrs. Buford," Sergeant Oz said. "These are the people who have come to honor your son. He saved their lives or the lives of their loved ones. They are Randolph's legacy and they asked to be at his memorial service."

I smiled uncertainly at the grateful faces around us while Mrs. Buford fidgeted nervously. Sergeant Oz backed away, leaving us alone in the center of the circle.

What happens next? I wondered.

An elderly woman stepped forward with a younger woman and an adolescent boy behind her.

"My name is Gertrude Abramowitz," she said. "Your son saved my daughter and my grandson." She pointed to them. "They were on the bus. He shielded them. Thank you."

The grandmother embraced Randolph's stunned mother, then she approached me. "Thank you for sending him to us," the grandmother said, and she kissed my cheek. Her daughter did the same, and her grandson shook my hand.

I'm no stranger to memorial services. I've attended too many of them in my life: my wife, my parents, fellow police officers, and friends. But I have never been part of a memorial like this. No one gave a eulogy. No one offered a testimonial. Most of those in attendance didn't even know Randolph Buford. But he had given all of them the gift of life at death's door, and that was all they needed to know. No words besides "Thank you" were necessary.

An Arab woman holding a toddler approached Mrs. Buford

and spoke to her in a language we didn't understand, though her message was clear: "We were on the bus. Your son saved us. Thank you."

We were the most beloved living people in the cemetery at that moment.

We were hugged and tugged, lauded and applauded, revered and cheered.

I shook hands, smiled, and said, "You're welcome," over and over.

I hugged so many people my arms got tired. I was about to avoid the next hug but noticed it was Zivah Oz and I was not going to turn down a hug from her. I wasn't disappointed.

We were all swept up in a tsunami of feelings that flooded over us and carried us away. We rode the wave of emotions until it peaked and finally ebbed . . . leaving everything in its wake drained.

Chapter 48

Unconditional Love

The three of us stood alone after the crowd dispersed.

"Are you okay?" Sergeant Oz asked.

"I'm fine," I said, forever macho.

"I'm stunned." Mrs. Buford cleared her throat. "I never expected this."

"I didn't know what to expect," Sergeant Oz said. "We didn't discuss who would say what. It was totally spontaneous."

"It made me so proud of Randolph," Martha Buford said, fighting back tears.

"We should go," Sergeant Oz said, looking at her watch as she walked toward the car. "We have to meet Minister Kane shortly."

Mrs. Buford stopped.

"I'm not meeting with Minister Kane," she said firmly.

"He has some important matters he needs to discuss with you, Mrs. Buford," Sergeant Oz said.

"I will not meet with Minister Kane or anyone else from the Israeli government," Mrs. Buford said adamantly. "I phoned that man several times after Randolph's death and he never had the courtesy to return my call. All I ever got from his office was an official announcement and a death certificate."

"I assure you he had his reasons, Mrs. Buford. He'd like to explain them to you now that you are here. It's very important."

"I don't care about his reasons." Martha Buford was angry. "When I desperately wanted to speak to that man he didn't have the courtesy to return my calls. Now I have nothing to say to him. It's too late."

"I ask that you reconsider." Sergeant Oz tried to do her duty.

"No," Martha Buford said adamantly. "And that's final."

"Mr. Perlmutter?" Oz turned to me for help.

"This is strictly Mrs. Buford's decision," I answered.

"Then I must call Minister Kane and let him know we will not be visiting him," the sergeant said. "He is expecting us."

She punched a number on her cell phone and walked away.

"Am I being unreasonable?" Mrs. Buford asked me.

"You have reason to be unreasonable," I said.

"I hope I don't get the sergeant in trouble," she said.

"Sergeant Oz can take care of herself," I assured her. "Don't worry."

Zivah Oz returned. "Minister Kane says he understands your feelings and apologizes," the sergeant said. "He did make a request, however."

"He's got a nerve asking me for anything," Mrs. Buford said.

"I'm making the same request," the sergeant said.

"What can I do for you, Sergeant?" Mrs. Buford smiled.

"There is a survivor of the bus bombing still in the hospital who could not attend the memorial service," the sergeant explained. "Would you be willing to visit him today? I was going to take you there tomorrow, but since we have time now we could go directly there."

"Of course," Mrs. Buford agreed. "I'd be honored."

Hadassah Hospital, high on a hill in the Ein Karem suburb of southwest Jerusalem is an immense facility with twenty-two buildings, one hundred thirty departments, and seven hundred beds.

"We're here to visit Private Lukas Neumann," Sergeant Oz said to the receptionist in Intensive Care.

"Of course." The nurse smiled and pointed to a room.

"Thank you," said Sergeant Oz.

We followed her.

I saw the name Neumann on the wall outside the room as I walked quietly behind Zivah Oz.

The lighting in the room was dim. I saw the silhouette of someone in the bed and as I moved farther into the room I saw that the left side of the patient's head, including his left eye, was covered with white bandages. The contours of the blankets over the small body showed there was no left leg. His left arm was in a cast from his shoulder to his fingertips.

I heard Mrs. Buford draw a deep breath and choke back a sob.

The shallow rise and fall of Lukas Neumann's chest was the only sign he was alive. He looked like half a mummy, the left side of his body entirely wrapped in bandages.

I nudged Mrs. Buford closer to the bed and motioned her to talk to him.

"H-hello," she began haltingly. "My name is Martha Buford."

Neumann's right eye fluttered open and was surprisingly clear compared to the damage to the rest of his face.

"I'm Randolph Buford's mother," she told him.

The young man reached toward her with his right arm. She moved closer to the bed and took his hand. "Randolph died so I could live," he said in a barely audible voice.

"I know," Martha whispered, and tears came to her eyes.

"Was he always so brave?" the young man asked in his phantom's voice.

"No, not really," she responded, honestly.

"Was he a good man?"

"He could have been a good man," Martha Buford managed. "But he wasn't."

"Did you love him anyway?" Neumann whispered his question.

"Of course I loved him. I was his mother," she said. "A mother's love is unconditional."

"If your son wasn't brave and he wasn't good, why did he give his life to save us?" Neumann asked, sounding very tired.

"He must have changed," Martha Buford said. "I'd like to think he was a better man when he died."

"I was told Randolph had a younger sister," Neumann said.

"Yes, my daughter Eva," Mrs. Buford told him.

"Where is she?" the soldier asked.

"She lives with her father in South Carolina."

"Do you live with them?"

"No, I live in Florida," she said. "My husband and I recently separated. My daughter chose to live with him."

"Why?"

"My husband is a very domineering, frightening man," Mrs. Buford said. "He intimidated our children, and I didn't know how to protect them from him."

"What could you have done?" the young man asked.

She took her hand from the soldier's fingers and covered her eyes.

"I don't know. I should have done something." She wept softly.

I watched the young man reach for Martha's hand again and remove it from her face. "Don't cry, Mother," he consoled her in his raspy voice, and I saw him squeeze her hand. "Randolph is gone but I'm still here."

CHAPTER 49

The highest point I know of in Palm Beach County is a garbage dump in Deerfield, across from a porno supermarket on Powerline Road. As inclines go, think bunny slope.

The Deerfield Beach graveyard is flat like the backyards, front yards, ball yards, jail yards, and junkyards in south Florida. Monuments and tombstones provide the only elevation.

At dusk I stood with Martha Buford in the gathering gloom looking at a casket, six feet under. The marker read:

RANDOLPH BUFORD
1986–2005

Wanting total privacy, we had paid a premium for a twilight burial in the most remote plot available. We were near a grove of trees at least two hundred yards from the nearest grave site.

I looked at my watch. "We'll give your husband ten more minutes to show up and then we'll get on with it," I said.

A solitary grave digger stood a respectful distance away, waiting to refill the hole.

"I told you he wouldn't come," she said.

I shrugged. "It's his son's memorial service. I thought he might come to pay his final respects."

"I told you," she said, "as far as Forrest is concerned Randolph died the day we made our deal with the government. He wants nothing more to do with us."

"Well, you told him I was going to be here," I added. "I thought the Aryan Army might send him to bury me with Randolph."

"They obviously don't care enough about you to make the trip," she said.

"I'm a little disappointed, to tell you the truth," I admitted.

"Well, I sure wouldn't want to disappoint you," Forrest Buford said, swaggering out of the shadows of the tree line.

"Forrest?" Mrs. Buford looked surprised. "I never thought you'd come."

"You invited me, Martha," he said sarcastically. "I'm here to bury my son the traitor, and the Boca Knight with him. Then I'm taking you home."

"Hey Forrest," I interrupted. "It's not very often we can get together like this."

"I promise it will be the last time," Forrest said, turning in my direction.

"Yes it will," I said seriously.

"You remember Harland Desmond." Buford pointed to the small man on his right who only last year had been a big man with the Aryan Army.

"Sure. I thought you were dead, Desmond," I said, sounding disappointed.

"I been laying low," Desmond said, grinning.

"Like a snake," I said.

"Smart-ass," Desmond hissed.

The third member of the group was more a mound than a man. He was holding his left arm in front of him for the purpose of pointing a gun at my head.

"Remember me?" the big man asked. "Luther Lumpke."

I scanned him from head to toe. "I remember those Xelement Fearless Flame boots," I told him. "Weren't you trying to kick my teeth in with them last spring when I sliced up your friend's Achilles tendons?"

He nodded. "Now I'm gonna shoot you between the eyes and even the score."

"That would make us more than even Luther," I pointed out. "You'd be way ahead."

He cocked the hammer with his thumb.

"Stop it," Martha Buford shouted. She stepped in front of me.

"Get out of the way," her estranged, strange husband warned. "We're gonna kill this son of a bitch."

"Over my dead body," Martha Buford declared.

"That is not a good career choice on your part," I said, moving her aside. "Aryan Army will accept you . . . dead or alive."

She stared at her husband.

"Y-you would shoot me?" she stammered.

"He hasn't got a choice, do you, Forrest?" I said, doing some quick detective work.

"Keep your mouth shut," he shouted.

I ignored his order. "You, Desmond, and Haystack over there were sent here to redeem yourselves, weren't you?"

"You better shut up," Luther threatened, and cocked the hammer of his handgun.

"Aryan Army has the three of you on probation," I said, ignoring his threat, "because of last year's fiasco in Palm Beach. Right? If you dummies want to get back in the Army you have to kill me and bring Martha back for reorientation. If she refuses to go with you peacefully you were told to kill her, too. And let me guess. The two of us get buried in the same hole with Randolph."

"You're a clever guy," Desmond said.

"You would never do that, Forrest." Martha stepped in front of me again.

"Tell her, Forrest," I said, moving her out of the line of fire.

"You better shut up," Luther threatened.

"What are you gonna do, Bumpy, kill me twice?" I asked. "C'mon Forrest. Be a man. Tell her."

"You would kill me, Forrest?" she asked in disbelief.

"Don't make me," he said, pointing at her. "Just get out of the way."

"You're insane," she answered, pointing back at him.

"I don't want to say I told you so—" I tried.

"Shut up." Lumpke waved the gun in my general direction.

It was silent in the graveyard until I heard someone whistling.

"Who the hell is that?" Luther Lumpke asked, directing his gun at a silhouette staggering in our direction.

"That's the grave digger," I told him. "We're running late."

The digger was short and slight, shouldering a shovel and wearing a baseball cap, pulled low. I watched the weaving, heard the whistling, and smelled the whiskey from ten paces away.

"Well, he just dug his own grave," Lumpke said, taking aim.

Suddenly the grave digger stumbled on a tombstone and sprawled face-first in the dirt, dropping the shovel.

Lumpke laughed.

"Dumb son of a bitch," Harland Desmond cursed.

I watched the drunk struggle upright, pick up the shovel, and stagger head-first, toward Lumpke.

"Luther, shoot that silly bastard," Harland Desmond ordered.

BING!

The business end of the shovel hit Lumpke like an iron uppercut, directly on the knockout button at the tip of his chin. Luther toppled backward into the grave and we heard a loud thud when he landed on the casket.

"Get down," I ordered Mrs. Buford, forcing her to the ground from behind and blanketing her body with mine. I was on her back, the left side of my face flush with the right side of hers.

"What's happening?" she gasped.

Before I could answer we heard Harland Desmond shout, "Don't shoot," followed by another thud.

I figured Desmond had stumbled into the open grave and landed on the casket or Luther Lumpke. Loud footsteps surrounded us.

"Where the fuck did all you Jews come from?" Forrest Buford shouted, which was probably the same basic question General Custer asked the Indians at Little Big Horn.

Suddenly the air was filled with the pop . . . pop . . . pop of automatic weapons muffled by silencers. I heard another thud and assumed Forrest Buford was now four feet under . . . allowing two feet for the casket. A deadly silence followed and I got off Martha's back. We both rolled over and turned toward the grave. A dozen men were pointing smoking machine guns into the hole.

"Please . . . ," I heard Harland Desmond's voice from the grave.

Martha and I winced when a dozen machine guns set the

night on fire. She screamed in horror and made a dash for the graveside. The grave digger stood in her way.

"You killed them," Martha screamed, striking out and knocking the cap off the grave digger's head. Long black hair tumbled down to the digger's shoulders. Martha Buford stopped struggling. "Sergeant Oz?" she said.

It was then Harland Desmond talked from the grave a second time. "Buford, get your bony ass off my face," he said.

Zivah Oz took a dazed Martha Buford by the arm and escorted her to the hole in the ground. I followed. The shooters stepped aside so we could pass. We stood at the grave's edge and looked down.

"Not a pretty sight," Sergeant Oz said, and she was right.

Harland Desmond was sprawled on Luther Lumpke and Forrest Buford was on top of Harland Desmond. Buford's ass was, in fact, in Desmond's face. The three of them were covered with lumps of dirt that had been blown off the four walls of the grave by machine-gun bullets. Lumpke spat out a clod of dirt. Harland pulled something out of his ear. Desmond coughed up some grass.

"You cut that pretty close, Sergeant," I said to Oz, a little annoyed.

"Sorry," Oz said.

Martha stared at the two of us. "What s going on here?" she demanded.

"It's a Zionist plot," I said.

Martha turned to Oz and Oz pointed at me. "It was his idea," she said.

Martha turned to me again. I shrugged and took her by the arm, leading her away from the graveside.

"You scared me to death," she said, and slapped my shoulder. "You didn't tell me this part of the plan."

"I didn't know if it was going to be necessary," I told her. "I wasn't sure Forrest would even show up or what he would do if he did come. I had to get some answers."

"Well, you got your answers." She quieted down a little. "Aryan Army wants us dead."

"Actually if Aryan Army wanted to kill us they would have sent real killers," I said. "Not the three stooges down there in the hole. This was an Army maneuver they couldn't lose."

"I don't understand."

"You know your husband is not real popular with Aryan Army right now because of the mess he got them into last spring," I reminded her. "And Lumpke, down there, was one of the executioners who couldn't execute my execution. And Desmond, as you know, blew the whole rally. These guys were lucky they didn't face a firing squad when they slinked back to Army headquarters. Instead they were sent here to kill or be killed. I don't think the Army cared which way it went. It was a win-win for them. Either they get rid of enemies or idiots."

Desmond spoke to us from the grave again. "Will someone help us out of this hole?"

"Help yourself," Oz told them.

Lumpke served as a ladder for the two smaller men and then they hauled the big man up using the shovel. They looked like they had been buried in an avalanche of dirt. The twelve Israeli soldiers encircled the six of us, automatic weapons at the ready.

"What happens to us now?" Desmond asked Oz.

"You're free to go back to Aryan Army," I said.

They exchanged worried glances. "We can't go back there. They'll kill us," Desmond said, pointing at me. "He's right. This was our last chance. We're finished there."

"You're finished here, too," I said.

"What do you expect us to do." Forrest Buford laughed sarcastically. "Disappear?"

No one in our group laughed.

"Okay," Desmond said understanding his dead-end situation. "Disappear to where?"

"We found a nice wildlife preserve not too far north of Wasilla, Alaska," Oz informed them.

"W-w-where the fuck is Wasilla, Alaska?" Forrest Buford stammered in shock.

"Twenty-nine miles north of Anchorage," I told them. "Think of it as a witness protection program without witnesses."

"What's in Wasilla, Alaska?" Buford asked.

"Moose." I smiled.

"I like moose," Lumpke said. Buford told him to shut up.

"Why there?" Desmond asked.

"They don't take shit from anyone in Wasilla," I told them. "And no one will ever know you're there . . . or care. If you refuse to go, everyone will know where you are. Understand?"

We exchanged nods and Mrs. Buford and I left the Aryans with Sergeant Oz, their new travel agent.

Chapter 50

Thanksgiving Day 2005 closed with an opening . . . in Osceola Park. When the sun went down, the curtain went up on the hottest new show in town.

SYLVIA DUBIN GOLDMAN—
MICHAEL AARON COHEN
MEMORIAL MEDICAL CLINIC
NONPROFIT CARE FOR THOSE IN NEED

The electricity in the air was generated by a surge of human energy reminiscent of the highly charged atmosphere at the rally by *Boca Knights against Aryan Army* in front of the Palm Beach Courthouse months ago.

My reporter friend at the *Palm Beach Community News*, Jerry Small, had given the clinic a lot of advance publicity in his column and the turnout was enormous. He wrote:

"No patient will ever be turned away for financial reasons from the Dubin-Goldman-Cohen Clinic," Dr. Ronald Cohen, founder of the clinic said. "Hundreds of doctors in Palm Beach County have volunteered their time and money to guarantee the success of this project and the outpouring of support from the public has been fantastic."

The clinic is named in memory of Dr. Cohen's son Michael Aaron, who died of congenital heart failure in 1999, and Sylvia Dubin Goldman, former resident of Boca Raton. Mrs. Dubin Goldman's trust, under the management of well-known local resident Eddie Perlmutter (aka the Boca Knight) donated two million dollars to the clinic. Perlmutter was quoted as saying, "Sylvia Dubin Goldman was a remarkable woman who made the world a better place." Several charitable organizations have put the Dubin-Goldman-Cohen Clinic high on their donations list for next year. Apparently, when the Boca Knight talks, people listen.

I saw Dr. Cohen bobbing in the sea of humanity in the reception area of the clinic. I worked my way in his direction and patted him on the shoulder. He hugged me and said, "I can never thank you enough."

"You already have," I said. "This clinic is phenomenal."

Dr. Koblentz, my urologist grabbed my hand. "Congratulations, Eddie," he said, loud enough to be heard over the din.

"Thanks, Doc," I said. "I heard you volunteered a day a week."

He nodded.

"Don't keep anyone waiting." I wagged an index finger at him.

"He's really a sweet boy," a smiling, white-haired woman told me. The resemblance was unmistakable.

"You're only saying that because you're his mother." I smiled at Mrs. Koblentz.

"He's more thoughtful since he met you," Mrs. Koblentz said, shaking my hand.

I thought of the first time I met Dr. Koblentz at his office and of Carl Mann, who had pitched two no-hitters and invaded Normandy before blowing his brains out in a parking lot. *You can't save everyone*, I finally conceded.

Dr. Albert Dunn, Betsy Blackstone's specialist, approached with an incredibly pregnant woman next to him.

"My hero," Betsy Blackstone gushed. Then her water broke. "Oh my God, was that me?"

"We have to get her to a hospital," Bradley Blackstone said, holding her upright. "Get an ambulance," he shouted.

"You're at a medical clinic, Bradley," I said softly in his ear.

He looked at me like he was an imbecile. "Right," he said.

"Is there a doctor in the house?" I asked needlessly.

Dr. Cohen pushed his way into the inner circle. "What's the problem?" he asked.

"Her water broke," Dunn explained to him.

Bradley Blackstone looked dubiously at Cohen then to Doctor Dunn.

"Dr. Cohen can handle this situation. It's his specialty," Dr. Dunn said.

Bradley looked at Betsy. She looked at Dr. Cohen, bit her lower lip tentatively, then nodded.

I heard Claudette Permice ordering people to get out of her way. The circle parted and my personal nurse appeared with a stretcher. She was in uniform for the opening. She looked gorgeous as usual. Dr. Cohen calmly gave instructions, and Betsy was on the stretcher and into the back operating room in a minute. Bradley followed.

"Talk about a dramatic opening," Lou Dewey said, clapping me on the back.

I turned to face him. "How was your vacation?" I asked.

He smiled. "Great."

"You have a '59 Invicta chrome grille in your mouth," I remarked.

"I got braces," he told me. "Joy, too."

Joy Feely stepped forward and grinned ear to ear. I squinted.

"Let me guess," I said, "A '57 Olds Victoria."

They laughed.

"You two got more than just braces," a man about my height and Lou's age said as he stepped between Joy and Louie and put his arms around their shoulders. "In order to correct your dramatic overbites we had to pull two of your premolar teeth to allow your six front teeth to come together. Then you had conventional brackets glued to your teeth."

"With all due respect," I asked the talkative little fellow, "who the hell are you?"

"Eddie," Lou said enthusiastically, "this is Stan Starr, the guy I told you about from Atlantic City. He lives parttime in Boca now."

I thought for a minute. "The three-card monte shill?" I asked.

"I'll never live that down," Stan moaned. "It's been over thirty years."

"We met waiting in line at J. Alexander's a few weeks ago," Joy explained. "Stan recognized Lou immediately. He offered to fix our teeth so we went to Boston where he has his practice."

"That was nice of you," I said to Dr. Starr.

"My father said I would fix Lou's teeth one day so I had to keep his promise," Stan told me.

"I know the whole story," I said. "So did you marry that girl from Atlantic City?"

A woman's voice answered for Stan. "Yes, he did. I'm Suzy."

I shook her hand. "The butcher's daughter," I remembered. "Lou said you were prime and he was right."

That remark made everyone happy.

Sanford Kreiger, Sylvia's lawyer, appeared. "Great place, Eddie," he said.

"I couldn't have done it without you, Sanford," I thanked him.

Frank Burke waved to me and gave me a thumbs-up sign.

Assistant DA Barry Daniels and Judge Avery Jacobs were there and both expressed their sadness regarding Randolph's death. I nodded somberly, not bothering to tell them that Randolph was alive and well and living in Israel. Randolph's mother, Sergeant Oz, Minister Kane, and I knew the truth . . . and that was enough.

The truth was that Randolph *had* recognized the bomber on the bus in Tel Aviv and he *had* thrown himself in front of Zivah Oz. He *had* dragged several other passengers to the floor and shielded them from the brunt of the blast with his body. Shrapnel *had* torn into his left side as he went down, destroying his left leg, tearing away part of his buttocks, breaking his arm, and gouging out his left eye. Nearly thirty people had died in the bombing but Randolph Buford wasn't one of them. A young German Mahalnik named Lukas Neumann was.

Randolph was badly injured and not expected to survive the ambulance ride to the hospital. He asked Zivah Oz to tell his mother he had died doing something good. The Israeli sergeant promised the dying man she would honor his final request . . . but then he didn't die. Never losing consciousness, he survived the ride to the hospital, received the best medical care possible, and lived. It was Zivah Oz who pointed out that Randolph's survival might only be temporary if he was returned to America alive. Aryan Army would kill him for sure. So, alive, Buford was dead; dead, he might stay alive. Needing to act quickly, with Buford's consent, Oz and Minister Kane officially swapped Buford's identity with the deceased German *Mahalnik*, Lukas Neumann, who had no known family. The transfer was a carefully guarded secret revealed only on a "need to know" basis.

In the explosion Randolph did lose his left leg, a large piece of his butt, and an eye. Those were the body parts buried in the grave in Deerfield Beach. Randolph's mother had been part of the deception including the fake funeral but she had known nothing about the potential violence at the cemetery. Eventually she forgave me for the omission.

Medical experts in Israel were already building a state-of-the-art prosthetic limb for the new Lukas Neumann and his prognosis was excellent. He would definitely walk and maybe even run again. His left arm was saved but his glass eye was strictly decorative.

Izzy Fryberg interrupted my reverie by slapping me on the back, which reminded me of my near-death experience at the Bagel Bush. Del Ray Vista Building 550 was all present and accounted for. I accepted twenty-four handshakes and absorbed over a hundred slaps on the back.

The sea of familiar faces began to look strange to me so I decided I needed some fresh air and a new perspective. I struggled through the well-wishers and made it to the front door that was now blocked by Howard Larkey.

"We're baaa-aaack." He held out his arms and we hugged. I hadn't seen him since he departed on his great adventure.

"What about me?" Derek said, and the three of us joined arms.

"Okay, where are they?" I asked about the famous Dietrichs.

"They decided not to come," Howard said. "They don't like crowds, especially crowds of police and politicians."

Derek winked at me. "Eileen couldn't find a thing to wear."

"When do I get to meet them?"

"Dinner this Friday, our house?"

"You're on," I said. "And I'm off for some fresh air. See you in a few minutes."

"Anything exciting going on inside?" Derek asked.

"A woman is having a baby in the operating room," I told him.

"What a unique idea," he exclaimed. "Can we watch?"

Suddenly the door to the back room opened and Bradley Blackstone emerged, holding a bundle in his arms. He was beaming like the new father he was.

"You're too late for the delivery," I said. "But just in time to meet the baby."

"It's a boy," Bradley shouted. "And we named him Edward. We're going to call him Eddie."

I don't cry, but if I did that would have been a good time.

Everyone cheered and began searching for me in the crowd. I slipped out the door unnoticed.

Alicia Fine and her fiancé, Jared Farmer, had just arrived. I again congratulated them on their engagement; we were more comfortable with each other than New Year's Eve.

"Everybody needs somebody, sometime," I sang to myself as I walked away.

I passed a caterer carrying a case of champagne to the party and removed a bottle without breaking stride. I walked across the street and sat on the curb in the shadows. I popped the cork, held up the bottle, and toasted the building that second chances had built.

Here's to Jacob Dubin's little girl. I saluted her memory and took a long swallow of bubbly. With the second swallow, I toasted Ferris Dewey and Dixie the Diving Horse, and wondered how Danny Baker, the lonely soldier, was doing at Hartford. I thought about bad golf and toasted good people.

When the bottle was half gone I thought about all the

changes I had experienced through the year and tried to make peace with them. I drank some more.

Speaking of changes, I thought, feeling woozy, *here's to Randolph Buford trying to do the right thing in a foreign land without picking sides. Here's to Randolph's mother who had the courage to send the police into the Aryan Army compound and reclaim her mentally challenged daughter, Eva. And here's to their mysterious disappearance one day later. I knew where they were now but I wasn't telling anyone. And here's a toast to Stewart Dewey and all the other young men who died in wars they didn't start.*

I laughed at the thought of the Kuznetsov brothers, the Davidavitch siblings, the Bengloff twins, and Irene Kostanski. There was nothing funny about any of them but I laughed because by now I was drunk.

Have another drink. Thank you, I will.

I tried to get up but I fell back on my butt on the curb. I laughed at myself.

I decided, with my next swig, that Seymour Tanzer should have said "I love you" more when he was alive. *Everyone should say I love you more.* I toasted love and Claudette Permice. I wished she was here right now, but knew that I would be with her later tonight.

I finally managed to get off the curb and weave my way across the street as only a drunk can. Through the window I could see all the happy faces celebrating life. I felt good knowing I was part of the celebration.

"*It's perfect*," I said. "Moments like this should last forever."

I know nothing's perfect and nothing lasts forever, but on some Boca nights . . . for some Boca Knights . . . there's no Boca mourning.

About the Author

Steven M. Forman was born and raised in the Boston area. After graduating from the University of Massachusetts, Amherst, in 1963 he founded a one-man business and built it into a multimillion-dollar, highly successful worldwide enterprise.

Boca Mournings is his second novel. *Boca Knights*, his debut novel, was published in February 2009.

He divides his time between the Boston area and Boca Raton, Florida, with his wife, Barbara, and their family . . . with special attention given to their grandchildren, Taylor and Bradley Cooper and Tyler Forman.